I Do?

Karen King

Published by Accent Press Ltd 2016

ISBN 9781910939345

Copyright © Karen King 2016

Dedication

To Beth Jones, who discovered **'I Do – Or Do I?'** in the slush pile and loved it enough to champion it. Thank you, Beth.

Acknowledgements

To my friend and fellow author, Ann Evans, for drawing on her years as a feature writer on the *Coventry Telegraph* to answer my many questions on journalism, to Rob Tysall of Tysall's Photography for answering my questions on photography, to my four daughters Julie, Michelle, Lucie and Naomi for being a constant source of inspiration and who might just find snippets of themselves in here somewhere, my editors Rebecca Lloyd and Alex Davies for their invaluable advice and expertise, all the team at Accent for believing in me and publishing this book, and to my husband Dave for his unfailing love and support and to who I'm very glad I finally said 'I Do!'

One

'June! That's only two months away!' Sam squealed down the phone. 'You can't plan a wedding in two months.'

Which is exactly what Cassie had told Timothy when his mother, Sylvia, had suggested it. She could hardly believe she'd let them both talk her in to it.

'The thing is, Sylvia heard there was a cancellation at Hollington Castle and she booked it for us. It's a really sought after venue and we'd be mad to turn it down,' she told Sam.

'Are those Sylvia's words or yours?'

'Sylvia's,' Cassie admitted. 'She's right, though. We got a good price, too, because of the cancellation. Timothy and I went to look around yesterday and it's an amazing place. It dates back from the eighteenth century, you know.'

'You only got engaged on Valentine's Day,' Sam pointed out. 'I thought you weren't planning on getting married until next year?'

'We weren't, but it seemed too good an opportunity to miss. It's normally booked up at least eighteen months ahead. Especially in the summer.' She was repeating Timothy's words to her yesterday when she'd expressed some doubt about arranging the wedding so quickly. 'You do want to marry me, don't you, darling?' he'd said, and when she'd assured him she did he'd pooh-poohed her protest that two months wasn't long enough to plan a wedding, saying his mother would help, and she'd found herself agreeing. Now it was all arranged, the venue was booked, they were getting married on 26th June – and she was starting to panic. How the hell was she supposed to organise everything in that time? There was her dress, the bridesmaids' dresses, invitations, flowers, food, reception, favours, wedding cake ... she was hyperventilating just thinking about it.

'Look I know it's short notice but you will be my maid of honour, won't you?'

'Yes, yes, yes!' She could just see Sam, jumping up and down with excitement. 'Oh, I was hoping you'd ask me.'

'Of course I'd ask you, you're my best friend. Who else would I want?' Cassie told her. 'Can you meet me for lunch and I'll fill you in on all the details? Twelve thirty at Benjo's? We've got an appointment with the photographer this morning so I can tell you all about that, too.'

'What, already? I'm guessing that's Sylvia's doing, too?'

'Yes, the people who cancelled the wedding had booked I.D. Images so of course they have a cancellation too, and Sylvia knows Daniel, the "D" in I.D., so he's agreed to hold the slot for us. If we want it.'

Sam whistled. 'As if you'd turn that down!' She paused. 'I thought you were going to the Discover France show today.'

'I was, but Sylvia booked the appointment and Timothy can't make it. He's got to work.'

'Whereas you just mess around... '

Cassie sighed. Sylvia never took Cassie's job as a features writer for the local newspaper seriously. Timothy was a partner in a law firm, whereas Cassie filled in time until she became Timothy's wife as far as Sylvia was concerned. Sylvia had given up her secretarial job when she married Timothy's father and devoted her whole life to looking after him, then Amanda and Timothy when they came along. She made it obvious that she expected Cassie to do the same when she married Timothy, even though Cassie had clearly stated that she had no intention of giving up work. 'Luckily, Owen's cool about it. He said I can swap my day off.'

'Well, it seems you've got a lot to fill me in on. Can't wait.' She could hear the grin in Sam's voice. 'Catch you later.'

2

Cassie had just finished the call when Timothy came into the room. 'Spreading the good news?' He smiled. He opened the wardrobe, pulled out the sliding tie rack, and selected a navy pin-striped tie.

'I was just telling Sam about the cancellation and I've asked her to be my maid of honour,' Cassie told him.

'Really?' He sounded surprised. 'I think Amanda was hoping you'd ask her.'

The thought of asking Timothy's sister had never occurred to her. She'd only met her a few times and Amanda had been rather cool towards her. 'Is she? Oh, but Sam's my best friend. We've always promised we'd be maid of honour at each other's wedding.' This was not strictly true, as they had never actually discussed it, but it was taken as a given. She couldn't imagine getting married without Sam by her side, and would be gutted if Sam didn't ask her to be maid of honour when she and Paul eventually got married.

'Of course, if that's what you want. Now you have remembered that you're meeting Mother at the wedding photographer's today, haven't you?' Timothy asked, expertly tying a knot in his tie. 'Don't be late, will you? You know how she hates to be kept waiting.'

'Don't worry, I'll be there in plenty of time,' she promised.

'Good. I wish I could make it too but I've got an important meeting.' He picked up his briefcase. 'I know you and Mother are quite capable of handling it and you can fill me in on all the details later.' He gave her a quick peck on the cheek and was gone.

Cassie took the sugar out of the cupboard, put a spoonful into her coffee, and began sipping slowly. She was dreading spending the morning with Timothy's mother. She was so ... controlling. They'd only been engaged two months and already Sylvia seemed to be taking over everything, suggesting that Cassie watch her weight ('There's nothing worse than a fat bride, dear'), booking the venue (although she had to admit that Hollington Castle was gorgeous), and now choosing the photographer.

I shouldn't be so hard on her, Cassie reprimanded herself. It's only natural that Sylvia wants her only son to have the best wedding possible. Cassie's mother would love to be involved more but it was the holiday season in Cyprus and she was too busy running the guest house with Cassie's stepfather, Steve. They were coming over for the wedding, of course. Her father would be there too, to give her away – thank goodness her parents' split had been quite amicable, with both parents feeling they'd outgrown each other.

She reached for her mobile as it started to ring. That was probably Sylvia now, checking what outfit she was wearing. But when she glanced at the screen she was surprised to see it was Owen. Surely he wasn't going to tell her he needed her in work today after all?

'Hi, Owen,' she said. 'I'm guessing you're not phoning for a friendly chat.'

'I've had a brilliant idea,' he boomed. She flinched and moved the phone away from her ear. 'I want you to write a weekly column for me in the Saturday Femail section.'

Blimey, another feature. How many did he think she could write? They were all so stretched thinly at the moment; he seriously ought to think about employing more staff to cope with all his *brilliant* ideas. She didn't dare say that, though. Owen was a good boss but he had a short fuse. 'Er ... OK. Anything in particular you want me to cover?'

'Yes, which is why I'm ringing. You know we're doing a summer wedding feature – well, I'm going to expand on that. I want you to write a weekly sort of bride-to-be diary. You know, telling our readers about your efforts to get the perfect wedding dress, choosing a photographer, the wedding cake, and how you've only got two months to do it all. I reckon it'll be really popular. What d'you think?'

She frowned: writing wedding features didn't really float her boat. Mind you, a regular feature in the glossy weekend supplement would be nice although she wasn't sure Timothy would approve. He was a very private person and would hate his personal life being put out there for everyone to read. And Sylvia would definitely consider it tacky.

4

'You can use a pseudonym and I wouldn't expect you to name the photographer, venue, or anything like that,' Owen continued. 'Just write a humorous, helpful account that our readers can relate to. As you're about to go to the photographer's I thought you might like to make some notes for the column. Obviously keep it light-hearted. No heavy promo, but we could offer some advertising space to photographers, wedding dress retailers, etc. It could be just the boost we need for our circulation figures.'

She could see Owen's point; a regular feature like that would have mega-reader interest. At least it would mean any time off she needed to organise the wedding would be research for the article. And if she was writing under a pseudonym, then Timothy and Sylvia wouldn't know it was her. Not that either of them ever read anything she'd written.

'OK, no problem.'

'Fab. Get me the first diary entry by 4 p.m. on Wednesday before the subs go home. It'll go in this Saturday's edition.'

That quick! 'I'll get straight on to it,' she promised.

Cassie's mind was racing with things to put in the column. Maybe she could include a list of things to ask the photographer, or things that might go wrong. There must be some photographic disasters she could find if she did an internet search. She jotted down a few quick thoughts in her notebook, then pulled on a denim jacket and picked up her bag. She'd better get going. Sylvia would be annoyed if she was late.

She plugged in her satnav and keyed in the postcode to the I.D. Images studio. She'd heard the name, of course. The initials stood for Imogen and Daniel, who were a high-profile photography couple who covered all the top society and celebrity weddings and were only ever known by their first names. I should think myself lucky, she thought as she started up the car. Most girls would give anything for a dream wedding like this.

She'd never hankered after a big wedding; a quiet family affair was more her style. She wasn't one of those women who planned her wedding years in advance, flicked through bridal magazines, and chose the dress and bridesmaids' outfits even

5

before she had the groom. Not even when she had the groom, actually. So it was ironic that she was now planning a big wedding with all the pomp and palaver that came with it. She thought of the beach wedding she'd once dreamed of. Just her and ... she shook the memory from her mind. It was history. They'd been nothing more than kids. Today wasn't the day for a trip down memory lane and dragging up old heartache. Timothy was a wonderful, supportive, reliable fiancé who only wanted the best for her. And Sylvia might be a little over-enthusiastic – make that, pushy – but she meant well.

The traffic was horrendous. It took Cassie half an hour to drive to the studio and another ten minutes to find a parking space. By the time she arrived she had three missed calls – which she'd ignored but guessed (correctly) were from Sylvia. She parked the car at the back of the studio and hurriedly made her way to the front, where Sylvia was pacing around outside. She looked smart and stylish, dressed in navy trousers with a navy and white patterned blouse, navy and white pin-striped blazer, navy shoes, and a matching navy handbag, her ash-blonde hair immaculately coiffured in her usual 'just stepped out of the hairdressers' style. Cassie didn't need to be able to see her face clearly to know she'd be wearing a layer of make-up. Sylvia never left the house looking anything but her best – Cassie was sure that if anyone knocked the door before she was ready to face the world Sylvia would refuse to open it. She looked pointedly at her watch when she saw Cassie walking towards her.

'Cassandra, our appointment was five minutes ago,' she said irritably. 'I've had to apologise and assure them you were on your way. It's so embarrassing. You know how important punctuality is.' She was wearing her disappointed face. 'It took me considerable effort to get this appointment. Surely I don't need to remind you that I.D. Images is one of the most sought-after agencies in the country. Their photographers are booked up months in advance. In fact, if it wasn't for the cancellation we'd have no chance of getting an appointment at all.'

'Sorry, Sylvia. There was so much traffic,' Cassie apologised. No matter how hard she tried she always seemed to let Sylvia down.

'Well you're here now, but it's always best to allow that bit longer for traffic, dear.' Sylvia pursed her lips as she looked Cassie up and down, her feet resting a moment on the red nail varnished toes peeping out from her sandals. 'I thought you were going on to work? I must say you're dressed rather more ... casual ... than I expected. First impressions are so important, you know.'

Cassie felt her cheeks flush as she bit back a response. They were meeting the photographer to discuss the requirements for the wedding, not having a photoshoot! 'I've had to swap my day off so I can make this appointment,' she pointed out. 'I'm meeting a friend for lunch, so I didn't see the need to wear anything smart. We're just discussing arrangements, aren't we?'

'Yes, but ...' Sylvia waved her hand dismissively. 'Oh well, nothing can be done about it now, and that dress does have a certain charm.' Sylvia turned towards the door. 'Come along, dear, we have an appointment with their new photographer. J.M. Daniel said he's an award-winning photographer who normally works abroad and has joined them for the summer. We don't want to keep him waiting. There are plenty of other couples on the waiting list for a cancellation. We're lucky to get an appointment, you know.'

She wished Sylvia would stop telling her how lucky she was. Lucky that she was marrying Timothy, lucky that Sylvia was so well-connected and could pull so many strings. Lucky, lucky, lucky.

Don't be such a bitch, she told herself. Timothy was well aware how pushy his mother was and had begged her to be patient with her. 'I know she's annoying, sweetheart, but she means well,' he'd said when Cassie had mentioned that she felt like the wedding was being hijacked. 'Humour her for me, will you?'

Then she felt horrible for being so mean and grumpy and had instantly agreed. Timothy could always sweet-talk her in to

7

anything. He was such a charmer. He had a tougher side to him though, and a reputation for being deadly in the courtroom.

'Cassandra!' Sylvia's sharp tone jolted Cassie back to the present. The older woman was standing at the reception desk looking rather irritably at her. Cassie quickly joined her, trying not to be intimidated by the plush, brown leather seating, expensive prints hanging on the walls, exquisite figurines, and strategically placed vases of colourful, aromatic flowers. She wished now that she'd donned something a bit more sophisticated than the maxi dress she'd picked up in Puerto Banus market when she and Timothy were on holiday in Marbella last autumn. Come to think of it, Timothy had looked her up and down when she'd put it on this morning but he hadn't said anything. He seldom did; his look was enough but today Cassie had been too distracted to take much notice of it.

'Ah good, the bride-to-be has arrived,' the receptionist said. 'We're cutting it a bit fine, as J.M. has another appointment soon.' She picked up the phone and pressed a button. 'Mrs Campbell and Miss Tyler are here now, J.M.' She paused. 'Certainly.' As she put the receiver down she smiled at them. 'Do take a seat. J.M. will see you in a few minutes.'

J.M. Cassie hated it when people called themselves by their initials: it was one thing using initials for the name of the business, I.D. Images, but to refer to yourself as J.M. was ridiculously pompous. She hoped this photographer wasn't as pretentious as he sounded.

She idly picked up a copy of *Society Brides* and started to flick through it, almost choking at the price of some of the wedding dresses. You could put a deposit down on a house with that much money!

'J.M. will see you now, Ms Campbell,' the receptionist announced. 'Just along the corridor, second door on the right.'

'Thank you.' Sylvia set off down the corridor, leaving Cassie to follow her.

'I do apologise for keeping you waiting,' she heard Sylvia say as she walked into the room. 'I'm afraid that Cassandra was unavoidably delayed.'

'No worries, Mrs Campbell.' The man looked up from the computer screen and as his chocolate brown eyes rested on Cassie they widened in recognition

Cassie's heart flipped as she stared back in disbelief.

Jared.

Two

Jared must have seen the panic in her eyes because he quickly composed himself and shook Sylvia's hand. 'Delighted to meet you. And this must be the bride-to-be.' He smiled at Cassie as if he'd never met her before. Never held her in his arms, kissed her, made love to her, promised that he'd love her forever and then walked out on her.

She'd often imagined seeing Jared again, wondered how she'd react. Now it all came flooding back and all she could do was remember how utterly devastated she'd felt when he'd walked out on her.

Get a grip, Cassie told herself. That was years ago. You're over it now. You're marrying Timothy. Jared is history.

She was suddenly aware that Jared was holding out his hand to her and Sylvia was watching her curiously. She forced a smile on her face and shook his hand, desperately hoping she showed no sign that his touch still made her tingle.

'Miss Tyler,' he said smoothly.

'Call me Cassie,' she told him. 'Sorry I kept you waiting.'

'Not a problem.'

How she wished she'd arrived on time. Jared used to tease her about being late. He probably thought she was still as ditzy as she was back then. If only she'd put on one of her power suits instead of a maxi dress, then she would have looked sophisticated and professional. Like she'd changed; which she had.

11

Oh God, she was still holding his hand. What must Sylvia think? She quickly removed her hand, tore her gaze from those big brown eyes, and tried to act as if her body wasn't zinging at his touch. Just like it always had.

'Take a seat, ladies, and tell me exactly what sort of photographs you're looking for.' He glanced down at his notes. 'I see that the wedding is only two months away.'

'Yes, we decided against a long engagement,' Sylvia replied as if she was the bride. She sat down in one of the plush dark brown chairs and indicated for Cassie to take the other seat. 'Timothy and Cassandra got engaged on Valentine's Day and we thought a summer wedding would be lovely. Especially when we managed to secure Hollington Castle,' she paused to make sure this announcement had the desired effect.

Jared nodded, looking suitably impressed, and Sylvia continued, 'I know it's short notice but Daniel assured me you'd be able to fit us in.' She was letting him know that she was on first name terms with the director of the company.

Jared nodded again. 'We've had a cancellation for that date, so yes, we can accommodate you both.' His gaze flicked to Cassie then back to Sylvia. 'Would you like a cup of coffee while we discuss the arrangements?'

'Thank you. Black with no sugar, please.'

Jared raised an eyebrow questioningly at Cassie. 'And for you, Cassie?'

'Black with no sugar for me too, please,' she replied. That would surprise him. She always used to have white coffee with two sugars. The Cassie he used to know had a sweet tooth. At least that was one thing that had changed. Except it hadn't, really, she was only drinking black coffee to make sure she could get into her wedding dress. Well, to be honest she was drinking black coffee in front of Timothy and his mother because they would frown and remind her about needing to get into the wedding dress. When they weren't around she still took her coffee with milk and sugar. She thought longingly of the iced mocha she'd be enjoying with Sam later.

Jared pressed the intercom and asked the receptionist to bring in the coffees, then he leant forward, linked his hands under his chin, and gave Cassie the benefit of his full attention. Devastating. She quickly averted her gaze. 'Now, tell me about the wedding,' he said. 'It's important that I get a feel of the atmosphere you're trying to create so I know what tone to set with the photos. We aim to be professional but not intrusive. And please don't hesitate to ask any questions you might have. We want our clients to be completely happy and relaxed on their special day. We won't take offence at all if you decide that we aren't the right photographers for you.'

You're not! Cassie's mind was screaming. You're the very last person I want as my photographer. Ever. For a moment she feared she'd uttered the words aloud, but Sylvia was now talking to Jared, so clearly it was all in her head.

Luckily, Sylvia monopolised the conversation, or Cassie would never have been able to get through the next half an hour. She could hardly believe she was talking about her wedding to her ex, the man she thought she'd be with forever until he'd upped and left, breaking her heart in the process. It was surreal.

If Jared felt uncomfortable at all he certainly didn't show it, the rat, which proved that he was completely over her. Well, that was fine. She was over him too, and had no idea why his light touch on her hand should send familiar tingles up her arm or why his big brown eyes should still send shivers down her spine. She was over him. She'd been over him for years. So why did her treacherous body act as if she still fancied him?

It's just the shock of seeing him again, she told herself. It's bringing back all the old memories.

'We'd also like some pre-wedding photos,' Sylvia said. 'My son is anxious to have a few photos in the run-up to the wedding, and of the bride getting ready on the day. I presume you can accommodate that?'

'Certainly. Perhaps we could arrange an appointment for a more detailed consultation, Cassie, so we can go through all the options? I'm sure your fiancé would like to have input on that one. I can also take photographs of you on your honeymoon, if you wish? I.D. Images often makes a photographic record of the whole event – engagement, wedding, and honeymoon. We find that many couples appreciate that; it's a wonderful memory to look back on.' He was looking intently at Cassie. 'When did you get engaged? Did you use the services of a professional photographer then?'

'Valentine's Day,' she replied, avoiding direct eye contact. 'And no, we didn't. It was all … very spontaneous. I don't think Timothy had time to think about photographs.'

It had come as a total surprise. She had no idea that Timothy had been planning to ask her to marry him. They'd been going out together for two years, and living together for six months, but she hadn't thought any further than that. She was quite happy how things were and thought Timothy was, too. Then, on Valentine's Day he'd taken her to Alberto's for a meal and had been very attentive. She hadn't been that surprised when a bottle of champagne on ice was brought to the table, thinking that maybe Timothy was celebrating being appointed to a high-profile case as he often did. Then a violinist had walked over to their table, playing a romantic melody, and to her amazement Timothy went down on one knee, held out a heart-shaped box with a huge twinkling diamond ring placed on a red velvet cushion, and proposed. The whole restaurant had gone silent. She could feel everyone holding their breath, waiting for her reply. Timothy was gazing at her, willing her to say yes. So she had. How could she have done otherwise and humiliated him? Besides, she loved him; of course she wanted to marry him.

But not yet. There it was; that niggling little voice again. She refused to listen to it. Yes, the proposal had been unexpected, and it was all happening a bit faster – a lot faster, actually – than she'd expected, but she loved Timothy, so as he said, why wait?

'That is so typical of Timothy,' Sylvia cut in. 'He's such a romantic. I'm sure he probably would like some honeymoon shots too, Cassandra.'

Would he? Cassie had been hoping to spend some time together and relax on their honeymoon. Timothy was always so busy with his work that some days they barely had time to say two words to each other. She didn't really relish the thought of a photographer tagging along with them. Especially Jared. That would be seriously weird. Then she realised that Jared was talking to her. She looked at him questioningly.

'Where are you going on your honeymoon?' he repeated.

'We haven't discussed it yet. We only decided on the date yesterday,' she confessed.

'Really? How brave of you to be planning a wedding in such a short time; exciting too, of course,' he added. 'And I.D. Images will ensure that your photographic record of the day will be really special.' He handed her a glossy booklet. 'You'll find all the details of the services we offer in here. Perhaps you can talk to your fiancé about the available options. When you've decided what you both want, please book an appointment to discuss your requirements with me. The sooner the better as we're working to such a close deadline.'

'Thank you.' She took the leaflet, then remembered the list of questions she'd drawn up to ask him for her column. 'Actually I do have a few questions, if you don't mind.'

She heard Sylvia's sharp intake of breath, obviously annoyed that Cassie was daring to question such an illustrious company. Well, sod her! Cassie whipped the notebook out of her handbag.

'How many weddings have you photographed?' she asked. It was the first question she'd thought of and she actually really wanted to know the answer. She'd never thought of Jared as a wedding photographer.

'As I'm sure Mrs Campbell has told you, I.D. Images has been working in wedding photography for many years covering numerous society and celebrity weddings.' He picked up a cream leather album from the desk and handed it to her. 'Have a look through this, you'll see some of the weddings we've photographed.'

She took the book off him. 'Thank you, but I actually meant you personally.'

She saw the look of hesitation on his face before Sylvia cut in. 'It goes without saying, Cassandra, that Imogen and Daniel would not have taken J.M. on to their books if he wasn't superbly qualified. Their reputation is unrivalled.' Her voice was iced with reproach.

She fought down the anger at being chastised in front of Jared and Cassie went on to her next question. 'What's your working style? Do you like to blend into the background and take natural shots or to take charge and choreograph them?'

'I have to say my instinct is to take natural shots.' He smiled. 'However, it's your wedding, your decision. You tell me what style you both prefer.'

'Nat –' Cassie started to say but Sylvia cut in again.

'Choreographed, of course. It's important for the album to be perfect.'

Cassie counted to ten … slowly. Jared gave her a knowing smile. The kind of smile they used to share when they were together. They'd never needed words – they'd just look at each other and know what the other one was thinking.

'Perhaps you could discuss it with Timothy, Cassie, then let me know? I'll need to familiarise myself with the wedding venue, too. Could you both arrange to meet me there one day when you're free? You can show me around and we can discuss lighting, scenery, etc.'

'I think Timothy will be much too busy. As a partner of Campbell and Mason it is difficult for him to take time off, but I can always accompany Cassandra, she can always get time off from her … job,' Sylvia replied, before Cassie could open her mouth. 'I know my son's tastes very well.'

'I'm sure you do.' Jared turned his attention back to Cassie. 'What do you do, Cassie?'

'I'm a journalist. Well, more of a features writer at the moment.' That shouldn't surprise him. She'd studied journalism at the same university he'd studied photography.

'Really? How fascinating. What paper do you work for?'

She told him the name of the paper, wishing that it was one of the big names instead of the local evening one so she could show him how well she'd done in the years since he'd left, so that he could see he wasn't the only one who'd done good, moved on, and that she hadn't sat around moping for him. Only she had, hadn't she? She'd been heartbroken for the best part of two years, then she'd given herself a shake and forced herself to start living again. She needed to get away, so she'd replied to

Owen's advertisement for a features writer, got the job, found herself a flat share, and moved to London. Somehow she'd put herself back together and got on with her life.

The fact that she was marrying someone else proved that.

She was getting married. Jared stared out of the window, hands thrust in his pockets, watching Cassie and the stuck-up woman who was soon to be her mother-in-law walk over to the car park. They stood talking together for a few moments, then the snobby woman got into a sleek white Porsche while Cassie made her way over to a red MG sports car. Nice, and still in immaculate condition. Very Cassie.

He'd often wondered how he'd feel if he met Cassie again but hadn't expected to be so attracted to her, to feel the same desire he'd felt all those years ago.

When Cassie had followed Mrs Campbell into his office, he'd been stunned. She was the last person he'd expected to see. The first woman he'd ever loved. The only woman he'd ever really loved. The woman he'd walked away from seven years ago because he thought travelling all over the world taking photographs was more important. The woman he'd never quite got out of his mind; despite the long list of beautiful women he'd dated since. And now she'd walked back into his life and wanted him to be the photographer for her wedding. Or rather, her future mother-in-law wanted him to be the photographer. He was sure that it was the last thing Cassie wanted.

Cassie had been surprised to see him; that was obvious from the expression on her face. He'd quickly picked up that she didn't want him to give any indication that they knew each other, which had confused him. He wouldn't expect her to be delighted at bumping into him again but a brief acknowledgement was in order, *surely?* Didn't her fiancé know about their relationship? If not, why hadn't she told him? Was it because he was such an insignificant part of her past that she wanted to forget? Or because, like him, she'd never quite got over their break-up?

His decision to come back to London and work as a photographer for I.D. Images had been entirely financial. His time spent photographing in remote parts of the world had earned him many accolades as a photographer, but had also eaten into his bank balance. He needed some money behind him if he wanted to fulfil his dream of going to the Arctic to film polar bears in their natural habitat. It was something he'd wanted to do for years, the last on his 'must do' list. So when Daniel, a good friend and someone he'd worked with a few years ago, had offered him a substantial salary to join his elite band of photographers for the 'wedding season' – in Daniel's words, 'We've got bookings coming out of our ears and it's about time you got back to civilisation, mate' – he'd decided to take it. A few months as a society photographer seemed the quickest way to get the funds he needed. So he'd booked a flight back, rented a flat, and started clicking celebrities and socialites instead of remote tribes and endangered species. His bank balance was now looking healthier, but, boy the wanderlust was biting pretty hard. It had been a long time since he'd lived in a bustling city and he couldn't say it grabbed him. He was counting the days until he could get away again.

Cassie was driving now, the black leather hood down, her long hair blowing behind her like a golden streamer. It was lighter than he remembered. She'd evidently decided to do something about the strawberry blonde colour she had always hated but he had adored. She was even more beautiful than he remembered too. Those huge, cornflower blue eyes were the same but her bone structure was more defined, and that maxi dress clung to her figure in all the right places. It certainly stirred feelings that had been long buried in him.

He tore himself away from the window and walked over to the desk. But what could he do now? It would look totally unprofessional to back out, and Imogen would be furious. She hated being let down and there was no one else free to take over. He'd just have to deal with it. A few months at this job, and he would have enough for his Arctic trip, then he'd be out of here again. Cassie was in the past. Maybe photographing her wedding was just what he needed to stop thinking about her.

Three

'Jared!' Sam repeated, her loud squeal causing a few heads to turn and look at them. 'Jared's back and he's your wedding photographer?' She sat back in her chair and stared at Cassie in disbelief. 'Wow! And you really had no idea?'

'Of course I didn't! He calls himself J M, so why would I think it was my Jared?' Then she realised that she'd said 'her Jared'. He'd stopped being her Jared aeons ago when he'd decided that his career as a photographer was far more important than marrying her. What was she doing, thinking of him that way?

'I thought he was busy roaming the world taking photos of endangered species and far-flung places?' Sam said. 'Since when did he become a society photographer?'

'I've no idea.' The last she heard he was in South America. The breath-taking spread of the Amazon he'd done for *National Geographic* had won him a prestigious award. 'He's working at I.D. Images now and Sylvia's booked him to be our wedding photographer. He even offered to come along and take photos of our honeymoon. Apparently it's all part of the *service*.'

'I can't believe it.' Sam shook her head. 'What are you going to do?'

'What can I do? There isn't time to get another photographer, not one with such a fantastic reputation, anyway. It's no big deal,' Cassie shrugged her shoulders and concentrated on sipping her iced mocha.

She tried to ignore the fact that Sam was staring at her, all agog. 'How did you feel when you saw him again? Has he changed? Is he still a hunk?' she asked, curiously.

An image of Jared with his deep chocolate eyes, thick dark hair that made you want to run your fingers through it, cute goatee beard (that was new, and she had to admit it suited him), smooth olive skin, and lithe body flashed across her mind. Yes, he was still a hunk. In fact, he was even hotter than she remembered. 'It was a bit ... weird,' she admitted slowly.

'What did you say to each other? How did monster-in-law take it, knowing your ex is the great Jared Macey?' Sam leant forward, her eyes shining, eager to know all the details.

Cassie took a long slurp before replying. 'Sylvia doesn't know. We didn't say that we knew each other.'

'What?'

She couldn't meet Sam's gaze, didn't want to see the incredulous look on her face. She knew how stupid it sounded.

'You mean you didn't say hi, ask each other how you were, that sort of thing? You both pretended you didn't know each other?'

'It wasn't like that. I was stunned when I saw him, and I think he was too. Then Sylvia started talking and the chance had gone.'

There was a bit of a silence while Sam digested this. A silence in which Cassie wished she could rewind the clock, walk into the office of I.D. Images, and say breezily. 'Jared! Fancy seeing you again.' It's what she should have done. What anyone else would have done. Why hadn't she?

'Isn't it going to be a bit freaky having your ex, the one who broke your heart, as your wedding photographer? Surely when Timothy knows he'll want to get someone else.'

Cassie sighed and put the half-empty mug down on the table. 'The thing is, I never actually got around to telling Timothy about Jared,' she admitted.

'What?! Really?' There was a further silence as Sam digested this additional information. 'Awkward,' she finally said. 'What are you going to do?'

'What can I do? Sylvia's booked him; it's too short notice to arrange another photographer – at least a good one. Besides, if I cancel what excuse can I give? 'Oh, by the way, Timothy, I forgot to mention that I went out with a guy called Jared for years, and your mother's booked him to take our wedding photos?' She shrugged, trying to sound more casual than she felt, because to be honest the thought of Jared taking shots of their wedding was seriously freaking her out. 'It'll be fine,' she said. 'It was a long time ago and we've both moved on. Jared is just the photographer as far as I'm concerned. It's not a problem.'

'Don't you think you should come clean, though? Timothy might wonder why you didn't tell him if he finds out later.'

Cassie thought about it. She and Timothy had never actually discussed ex-lovers. When she'd tried to broach the subject he'd said, 'Look, we're both adults with history, let's leave it there. The past is the past.' Which had seemed very adult at the time. Sam was right, though, she should tell him their wedding photographer was her ex-boyfriend. No need to go into too much detail, of course.

'Sure, I'll mention it to him later. It's no big deal.'

Sam shot her a look that said she didn't believe her for a nanosecond but thankfully changed the subject. 'Well, you have had a busy weekend! I only saw you last Wednesday, and now you've arranged the wedding date, booked the venue, *and* the photographer. Talk about quick work!'

'I know, I'm a bit nervous, actually,' Cassie confessed. 'Sylvia and Timothy are planning a big, posh do. And you know me, Sam; I'd prefer a quiet affair. Just friends and family.'

'Well, that's what you get for marrying a hot-shot lawyer,' Sam told her. 'Can I help you with anything?'

'With everything!' Cassie pulled a notebook and pen out of her bag. 'I don't even know where to start. Could you help me write a list of the things I need to do? And maybe help me sort them out, too?'

Sam chuckled. 'So that's why you want me to be your maid of honour. OK, I'll rescue you. Now, let's see ...' She held up her hand and ticked the items off on her fingers as she listed them one by one. 'There's the invitations, the dress, the bridesmaids' dresses, flowers, wedding cake, reception – I guess you're having it at the castle?'

Cassie was busy scribbling it all down. She looked up and nodded. 'It's all part of the package.'

'OK, but there's still food, drinks, entertainment.'

Cassie groaned and sunk her head into her hands. 'It's too much. How can I do this all in time?'

'You can always get a wedding planner. I'm sure Timothy will cough up the funds.'

For a moment Cassie was tempted, then she shook her head. 'No, Sylvia is taking over enough, I'm not handing the rest to someone else to organise. I want some input in my own wedding.'

'Good for you. Well, don't panic, we'll sort it out together,' Sam reassured her. 'The first thing you need to do is buy some invites, and get them sent out so you know how many guests are coming. Next on the list is your dress. That's a priority. It sets the whole atmosphere and theme for the wedding. You can't plan anything else until you've got the dress. How about we go shopping for it on Saturday? I doubt there's time to have one specially made now, but there's some fantastic boutiques in town, you're bound to find something you like.'

'Oh, would you, Sam? That'll be great. I don't fancy wedding shopping alone.'

'Of course. That's what maids of honour are for,' Sam told her.

Cassie drained her coffee, just about resisting the urge to put her finger in the glass to scoop out and lick the milky liquid on the sides.

'It's been lovely to chat, Cas, but I've got to get back to work now. We haven't all got the day off.' Sam was the personal shopper of a large department store.

'Yeah, well, it's not *exactly* a day off. I've got to find some classy wedding invitations, then I've probably got a ton of emails to answer, and Owen's asked me to write a "wedding diary" every Saturday so I need to make a start on that.'

24

'What sort of wedding diary?'

'You know, relating my experiences of planning a wedding in two months. Trips to the photographer, sorting the flowers, etc. It's for the glossy weekend supplement. Owen's actually upgrading me.'

'That's fantastic.' Sam frowned. 'I'm surprised though, I didn't think Timothy would be up for it. Or you, to be honest, writing about weddings doesn't strike me as your kind of thing.'

'It isn't really but I can't turn it down, can I? It's my job. Timothy probably wouldn't approve but he doesn't know, and he won't find out as I'm using a pseudonym. It won't be too personal, of course. No names mentioned. Just a light-hearted humorous account with a bit of info and advice for other brides-to-be flung in.'

'Like not booking their ex as the wedding photographer?' Sam quipped. 'Honestly, Cassie, if you told the truth in this diary it would be hilarious. The paper would be a sell-out.'

'Tell me about it!' Cassie said with a grin.

Sam stood up. 'I've really got to go. Phone me tomorrow and let me know what Timothy says when you tell him about Jared.' She unhooked her bag from the back of the seat. 'Once he's got over the shock he's bound to be impressed that you two used to be an item. Not that Jared was famous then, but even so.'

By the time Cassie returned home, with a pack of classy invites, she'd decided that having Jared as their wedding photographer was no big deal, what happened between them was history. Actually the more she thought about it, the more it seemed like a good idea. Let Jared see what a splendid wedding she was going to have, how a prominent, successful lawyer like Timothy wanted to marry her. How completely she'd fixed her smashed heart, and was now totally over him.

She ticked invitations off her wedding list and put a star by wedding dress – she'd hopefully get that on Saturday. Now she should start making notes for her wedding diary while today was still fresh in her mind. She'd be at the Discover France show for most of tomorrow and Owen wanted the column by Wednesday. That didn't give her much time. She chewed her pen, trying to recall the wedding preparations she'd made to date. As this was the first column, she needed to really hook the reader. Maybe she should start with the title.

She scribbled down a few titles – *My Wedding Diary*, *Two months to plan a Wedding, Diary of a Bride-to-Be*. They all seemed so boring. This wasn't going to be an easy task. She tried to think of some key words that might attract the reader's attention. Secret, perhaps. *My Secret Diary. The Secret Diary of a Bride-to-Be.* No. She scribbled them out furiously. Perhaps she'd leave the title for now and get on with the content.

She'd only been writing a few minutes when her mobile rang. It was Craig, a photographer from the newspaper. They often worked together and he was accompanying her to interview a local-author-made-good tomorrow, after the Discover France show.

'Just checking that you're still on for tomorrow,' he jested. 'Owen told me you'd swapped your day off. What was the emergency?'

'No emergency. I had an appointment with the wedding photographer.'

'Now that is *really important*. No wonder you changed your shift,' he teased. 'I guess we'll have to expect this now you're almost a bride.'

Almost a bride! That was it. That's what she'd call her column. 'Craig, you're a star!' she said as she jotted it down on her pad.

'Oh, I know, but what have I done to make you realise it?' he quipped.

'Only given me a brilliant title for my new column on weddings,' she told him.

'You? Writing about weddings?' Craig laughed. 'Now that's going to be worth reading.'

'I know, but the boss has spoken. I'll try to be at the show as soon as it opens tomorrow. Owen said he wants lots of info, he's going to run some sort of holiday special next month.'

'See you there then, about 9.30a.m.,' Craig replied.

'Great.'

She was looking forward to the show. It was being held at a large hotel on the outskirts of London, and she knew from experience that there would be about a dozen exhibitors, and many of them would be offering food and drink samples. It should be an interesting morning, which meant she should type up her column now. She fetched her laptop and settled down to work.

She'd almost finished the first draft when she heard the front door open. Timothy was home early.

'Hi, I'm in the lounge,' she shouted.

He strode in and made his way straight over to the drink cabinet. He looked exhausted.

'Tough case?' she asked, saving her work on to a memory stick.

'Very.' He picked up a bottle of red wine and two glasses. 'Do you want one?'

'Not for me, thanks.' She shut down the laptop and slipped the memory stick into her handbag. She'd finish it on the computer at work tomorrow. 'Is the case almost finished?'

'We'll be summing up tomorrow so I need to work on my notes tonight.' He leant back against the cabinet and took a large sip of wine.

'How's it looking? Do you think you'll win?' she asked, quickly clearing her papers and laptop off the coffee table. Timothy never discussed the details of his cases with her because of professional protocol, but would remark if it was a tough case and how he felt it was going.

'I hope so, but it's touch and go. Have you started dinner yet?'

'No I wasn't expecting you home yet. I'll go and put the oven on now.'

'Don't worry, I had a large lunch. A sandwich will do, I'll take it in the study with me.' He kissed her on the forehead. 'Mother phoned and said it all went well at the photographer's, and you've brought some material home for me to look at?'

Trust Sylvia to get in with the news first. 'Yes, I have. I've bought some wedding invites too. We need to get them written and posted ASAP so we know who's coming, but I don't expect you have time to look at anything tonight?'

'Sorry, sweetheart, I must go through my notes. Denver's on the prosecution and he's like a dog with a bone. I need my summation to be water-tight.'

'That's fine, we can talk about it tomorrow,' she told him. 'I'll go and do that sandwich. Ham and cheese on granary?'

'Perfect. Thank you. Would you mind bringing it into my study?'

He disappeared with his glass of wine and briefcase and was engrossed in his notes when Cassie took his sandwich in, mumbling his thanks without looking up. He remained there for the rest of the evening.

It was almost midnight when Cassie knocked the door before cautiously opening it. Timothy hated to be disturbed when he was working but she didn't like to go to bed without saying goodnight.

'I'm off to bed now, it's almost twelve and I've an early start tomorrow. Can I get you anything before I go?'

Timothy glanced up from the pile of paperwork he was reading and smiled apologetically. 'Sorry, darling, but I need to get this finished. Don't wait up for me.'

She knew that there was no point trying to persuade him to come to bed. He was always like this when he was working on a case, determined to do whatever was needed to win. He was so dedicated to his work.

I'll tell him about Jared tomorrow, she thought, as she pulled back the duvet and climbed into bed. She'd been thinking about it that evening and had decided that the best way to broach the subject was to play it down. She'd smile and say 'You'll never guess what? Our wedding photographer is only someone I went out with years ago. Isn't that amazing? I had no idea he'd done so well for himself.'

There was no need to tell Timothy that they'd been inseparable for years, that she thought they were going to get married, have kids, the whole caboodle. And there was certainly no need to tell him how devastated she'd been when Jared had dumped her. So devastated that she hadn't been able to eat properly for weeks and it was a whole three years before she dated again. She was over Jared now, though. It was all in the past.

So why did she spend most of the night dreaming about him?

Jared tossed and turned, sleep eluding him. Ever since Cassie had breezed into his office that morning he hadn't been able to get her out of his mind. The way his body had reacted was like the last seven years had never happened. Her smile had the almost forgotten effect on his heart, the light touch of her fingers on his when she'd taken the brochures from him had sent familiar tingles up his arm.

Forget her. You walked out on her and she's marrying someone else.

He sat up, reached out for the switch on the stem of the table lamp, and with a quick flick, illuminated the room. There was no point lying in bed fretting all night, there was plenty of work that needed doing. He sat up and swung his legs over the side of the bed, grabbed his robe off the chair and tied it around his naked body, then padded barefoot across the floor to the spare bedroom he used as an office. A few minutes later, he was sitting at the computer editing some photographs he'd taken in the rainforest. He'd been asked to supply them for a commercial publisher and wanted to make sure he sent an impressive selection. The publisher had promised to credit him and publish a short biography if Jared supplied it. Not something he really liked doing – he found it much easier to write about the wildlife he studied than about his own achievements, but it was all publicity. And hell, he needed that if he wanted to get some funding towards this Arctic trip.

The next time he checked the time it was 2.30 a.m. Damn, he had to be up at 6.30 for work. He thought he'd better hit the sack. Leaving the computer on, he went into the kitchen to pour himself a glass of milk and headed for the bedroom. As he climbed into bed he absent-mindedly glanced at his phone and saw he'd received a message. He slid his finger across the screen to read it. It was from Savannah, his sort-of girlfriend of the past couple of years, and she'd sent it hours ago. He opened the message, and it was typical Savannah; brief and to the point. 'I'm back in London for a while. Fancy meeting up?'

They had a light, easy 'friends with benefits' relationship, picking up where they left off whenever they were in the same location. A sought-after model, Savannah often jetted off to exotic places. She was flirty and fun – most of the time. Like most models, she could be neurotic and self-obsessed. He smiled. Just what he needed to take his mind off Cassie.

Four

Cassie reached out for Timothy when she woke the next morning, but the other side of the bed was empty. He must have decided to sleep on the sofa bed in the study, as he often did if he was working late on a case. She was about to get out of bed and go down to him, when the bedroom door opened and Timothy came in carrying a tray complete with two bowls of cereal, a fragrant red rose in an exquisite crystal bud vase, and two glasses of orange juice. Her heart melted when she saw the rose. Timothy could be so thoughtful.

'Morning,' he said cheerfully, placing the tray down on the dressing table. He was already dressed for work in a smart pinstriped shirt, navy tie, and black trousers. He looked tired, and she wondered if he had slept at all. He sat down on the bed, leant over, and gave her a kiss on the lips. She entwined her arms around his neck and kissed him back. 'Sorry I didn't come to bed last night. It was really late by the time I finished and I didn't want to disturb you.'

'Don't worry.' She smiled at him. 'I hope it goes well today.' She'd be glad when the case was over and Timothy could rest a bit. He worked too hard.

'It's a tough one. I'm convinced my client is innocent, but to be honest I'm not sure which way the jury will go.'

A troubled frown creased his forehead and there were dark shadows under his eyes. Timothy hated to lose a case. It was a matter of pride to him – but even Timothy with his encyclopaedic knowledge of the law and eloquent rhetoric skills couldn't win them all. She hoped he won this one. He was always very quiet and withdrawn when he lost a case and she had to spend a lot of time and energy trying to jolly him up again. That's what you get when you're engaged to a successful, driven lawyer, she reminded herself. Timothy hadn't become a partner of Campbell and Mason without years of hard work and dedication.

He passed her the breakfast tray. 'I must apologise. I've been so preoccupied I haven't had time to discuss your visit to the photographer yet. Mother said she was impressed with all the options.'

'I wanted to talk to you about that. You'll never guess ...' she started to say, but the classical ring of Timothy's mobile cut her short – classical, literally. It was Bach's *Cello Suite*, which she only knew because Timothy had told her. He tried his best to encourage her to like classical music too, but she wasn't really in to it.

'Morning, Mother.'

Cassie stifled a groan. Sylvia could talk for England, and now there wouldn't be time for her to slip in that she knew Jared. She couldn't make out what Sylvia was saying but could tell from Timothy's end of the conversation that she was singing I.D.'s praises.

'Mother wanted to know if we've looked through the list of photographic services I.D. offer,' Timothy said when he'd finally managed to end the call – by which time Cassie had finished her bowl of muesli and low-fat yoghurt. 'We must go through them tonight. Is there anything you particularly wanted?'

'I like the idea of the pre-wedding shots.' She lifted the tray onto the bedside table. 'And they provide a mini studio on the day for guests, which might be fun. Oh and J.M. wants to do a venue visit, so he can get the feel of the place and work out where to take the best shots.' She hadn't meant to sound so enthusiastic, but it was difficult not to be. I.D. Images offered an enticing variety of photography packages to ensure its clients' wedding days were special ones. She'd be totally made up to have I.D. as their wedding photographers if it wasn't Jared taking the photos. She must tell Timothy about him and she had to do it now before she lost her nerve. She leant forward and touched him lightly on the arm.

'I couldn't believe it when I saw who the photographer was ...' she started to say, but Timothy stood up.

'Can we talk about this later, sweetheart? I really need to go. I've got a meeting with Felicity before court begins.' He bent over and kissed her on the forehead. 'We'll sit down tonight and talk about it, I promise.'

'Yes, of course, it's just that ...' she hesitated. If she insisted on telling Timothy about Jared now she would make it seem like their past relationship was important, and it wasn't. She and Jared were over long ago. Best to wait until tonight and casually slip it into conversation.

'No problem. I hope it goes well today.' She wrapped her arms around his neck and pulled him down towards her for a proper goodbye kiss. All she got was a quick peck and then Timothy was gone. Ah well, it was time she got ready to go to work too. She wanted to be at the Discover France show early as it was bound to be packed. Then she had to interview up-and-coming author Alex Hawkins, whose latest crime novel was racing up the charts. She got out of bed and headed for the shower.

The traffic was bad so it was a little after ten when she arrived at the plush hotel where the Discover France show was being held. Crowds of people were already milling around the thirty or so tables placed around the outside walls of the room. Craig waved to her over the crowd.

'Anything interesting?' she asked as she joined him.

'There's some fantastic venues. I've left my card with some exhibitors. I'm hoping to get a free press trip.'

'You and me both.' She grinned. 'A few days in France is just what I could do with right now.'

'Go for it. I reckon you could talk a few of them here in to buying advertising space in your column. They could bill themselves as honeymoon destinations,' Craig carefully placed his camera in its case and zipped it up. 'Oh, and there's a stand advertising wedding venues so that must be worth a look. I can't think of the name but it's near the back of the room.'

'Really? Brill, I'll certainly check them out.'

'I've got to go. I've got a couple of jobs to do before the author interview. I'll see you there at 2.30.' Craig disappeared into the crowd before she could reply, anxious to get to the next job, as usual. As they both worked on a small local paper, there was always plenty of work to do and they both often flitted from job to job.

She wanted to spend a bit of time here though, to see if she could get a couple of advertising features out of it for the Summer Wedding Supplement and bring in some much needed income for the paper. That would please Owen. So she wandered around, stopping to talk to a few of the exhibitors, swapping business cards with those interested in advertising space and noting down information of others that she thought Owen might be interested in doing a feature on. As she passed an exhibition near the back, a poster of a medieval château set in beautiful countryside caught her eyes. Beneath it was another château, this time by a lake. Intrigued, she looked at the name of the stand Romantic Wedding Venues. That must be the one Craig mentioned, and he was right. It was ideal for her column.

A young couple sat on the chairs at the table, talking to the fair-haired woman behind it, so Cassie took a handful of brochures to glance through while she waited. The company, L'Amour, was based in the Dordogne region. It looked stunning. Now she wouldn't mind going there.

Finally the couple got up, shook hands, and left. Cassie sat down, smiling brightly.

'Hi, I'm writing a wedding diary for the local paper,' she explained, handing the woman her card. 'We'd be very interested in writing a feature on you.'

'That would be excellent. We're hoping to organise a press trip in a few weeks,' the woman replied. 'Let me tell you a bit about our company and I can contact you once the trip is organised.'

Cassie listened fascinated as the woman, Adele, showed her the photos of the different châteaux they represented, and outlined the services they offered. One château, a seventeenth century castle in the Champagne region, was particularly gorgeous. A dream wedding location. If only she and Timothy hadn't rushed their wedding plans they could have done something like that, she thought wistfully. They hadn't even had chance to discuss wedding options. Sylvia had heard about the cancellation at Hollington Castle and pushed them in to booking it. Pushed them into everything.

'It's beautiful, isn't it?' Adele said. 'The hosts have only recently joined our list. The château was refurbished last year and then opened for wedding functions. They're offering very good rates at the moment. Would you be interested in visiting it and including it in your wedding feature?'

'Definitely,' Cassie nodded. A few days in France were just what she needed. Of course, she'd have to sell it to Owen and persuade him to give her a few days off work to go but she didn't think that would be a problem. She could get several holiday and wedding features out of the trip, enough to supply the weekend section for a few weeks at least.

Adele promised to email her within the next couple of weeks with more details so Cassie picked up a few brochures to take back for Owen then moved on to the other exhibitions. She left a couple of hours later with a goody bag of French chocolates, pens, bookmarks, and brochures. She'd thoroughly enjoyed the morning but now it was time to meet Craig and interview Alex

It was a difficult interview. Alex liked to talk and the success of his book had obviously gone to his head. Cassie had trouble keeping him on track and he refused to answer some of her questions, such as what difficulties he'd encountered or any negatives he'd experienced or rejections he'd had. Alex was determined to portray himself as a successful author whose star had always shone bright. Which was a shame, as readers preferred to read about the struggles people had overcome to get where they were – it made them appear more human. Still, she recorded the interview – with Alex's permission – ready to write up later. Rather than pose for a photograph Alex insisted on handing them a publicity one, along with a promo sheet so they could write a short biography about him, which seriously peeved Craig off. He complained loudly as soon as they got out about how it was a waste of his time when he could have been doing another job. All in all, Cassie was glad to call it a day.

Timothy was already home when she got in and she could tell by the big grin on his face that he'd won the case. He was sitting on the cream leather sofa in the lounge flicking through the leaflets Jared had given her yesterday. 'There's a good choice,' he said. 'The Story Book albums are nice, but I prefer the traditional style. They offer a bespoke service too, which sounds ideal. We can design our wedding album exactly how we want it. What do you think?'

She preferred the traditional style too and had been quite taken with the bespoke albums. There was a variety of page plans to choose from, even some vignettes. 'Yes, that would be lovely. Perhaps we could match the album cover with our wedding theme?' she suggested.

'Good idea. Have we decided on a theme yet?' Timothy's voice was laced with amusement.

Of course they hadn't. Timothy had been too wrapped up in his court case but now it was over perhaps they could start planning the wedding together without Sylvia butting in. 'No, it's on our to-do list. Along with wedding invites. We really need to send them out as soon as we can.'

'Yes, we do. How about we discuss it over dinner? I've booked us a table at Alberto's for eight. That should give you plenty of time to shower and get changed.'

'Really? Oh, lovely.' They hadn't dined out for a while and Alberto's was their favourite restaurant. It was where Timothy had taken her on their very first date, and where he'd proposed, of course. It was evident that he wanted this to be a special occasion.

'I thought that emerald green dress might be nice. Up to you, of course. Wear whatever you feel comfortable in.'

'I thought the red one …' She saw the frown cross Timothy's face and quickly retraced. 'Maybe it's a bit bright. I'll try them both on and see.'

In the end she decided on the green dress. She knew that Timothy liked it and she wanted tonight to be perfect. It was the first chance they'd had to talk to each other properly for ages and she was really looking forward to it.

Jared noticed her as soon as she walked in. She looked sensational in a long, emerald green dress that clung in all the right places. She looked happy too – her eyes were bright, sparkling, and she was laughing at something her companion was saying, a laugh that spread to her eyes. She was leaning very close to him, her arm hooked through his, her whole body language saying that she was in love. So this must be Timothy Campbell, the man she was going to marry. Tall, immaculately groomed, his fair hair obviously styled by a professional, his suit expertly cut. His whole manner shouted both money and authority. This was a man used to getting what he wanted.

They were so engrossed in each other that she didn't notice him sitting at the table in the corner. She floated past, still talking animatedly to the guy on her arm.

'Someone you know?' Savannah asked curiously.

Jared nodded. 'Clients. I'm going to be photographing their wedding.' He forced himself not to stare at the seductive way the silky material clung to Cassie's hips as she sashayed over to the table in the window and turned his attention to the beautiful, perfectly groomed brunette sitting opposite him. 'It's good to have you back. How long are you in London for?'

'Only until the weekend. I'm off to Cape Verde on Saturday. I'm modelling beachwear so we'll be there for a couple of days. It'll be exhausting, of course. People think it's so easy to be a model but they don't realise just what's involved.'

Jared tried to pay attention as Savannah related all that was expected of her during a photoshoot and not to let his gaze wander over to Cassie, who fortunately had her back to him. Even if she hadn't, he doubted she would have noticed him; she was too wrapped up in Timothy. Well, he was glad she'd found happiness, it made him feel less guilty about breaking her heart all those years ago. It just proved he'd done the right thing for both of them. It would have been a disaster if they'd married.

'Jared?'

Savannah's petulant voice broke through his thoughts. 'You haven't been listening to a word I've been saying, have you?'

'Of course I have, you were telling me about your modelling trip.' He smiled and gazed straight into her eyes, knowing she could never resist that. 'Sorry if I seemed a bit absent, I was thinking how lucky the photographers were. That's one photoshoot I'd love to be on.' Women like Savannah always liked lots of flattery.

'Really? Well, maybe I could recommend you to the agency for my next shoot.' She leant forward and clasped his hand. 'It would be lovely to work together. And we'd have the evenings free so we could spend some time together, instead of snatching a couple of hours here and there.'

'Sounds good to me. And talking about spending the evening together, how about I get the bill and we head back to mine? I've a bottle of very nice white chilling in the fridge just waiting to be opened.'

She clasped his hand tight, her heavily mascaraed eyes gazing into his. 'Sounds perfect.'

The last person Cassie had expected to bump into was Jared. When she'd spotted him sitting at the table with the stunning brunette she'd wanted to walk right back out again. She hadn't seen him for seven years and now he was everywhere she turned. Well, she wasn't going to let him know she'd noticed him. Then she wouldn't have to acknowledge him. Clutching Timothy's arm tightly she'd fixed her attention on her fiancé and glided past Jared's table without even a sideways glance.

Timothy had reserved them an intimate table in the corner of the restaurant, lit by the warm glow of a thick white candle in a red hurricane lamp. A single red rose was placed in a bud vase by her place, reminiscent of their engagement night. Cassie felt a thrill of pleasure as she sat down, her back to Jared. She could feel his eyes on her but refused to look around, focusing all her attention on Timothy. This was their evening and she wasn't going to let Jared spoil it. She couldn't be happier. She was marrying the man of her dreams. He was kind, considerate, understanding. All she ever wanted in a partner.

As the evening passed she toyed with the idea of glancing around to look for the loo, pretending to notice Jared for the first time and introducing him to Timothy. Casually telling him that Jared was going to be their photographer, of giving a little laugh and saying 'Would you believe it? Jared and I actually dated for a while many years ago, didn't we, Jared?' It's what she should do. It was the perfect opportunity, but she just couldn't. She didn't want anything to spoil this evening. She and Timothy had hardly spent any time together for ages. She'd tell him tomorrow.

Five

The news room was buzzing when Cassie walked in the next morning. Owen called her before she even got to her desk – there had been a smash and grab at a local jewellers and he wanted her to chase up the story. She spent the morning interviewing the staff and witnesses and then typing up a report for the next day's paper. By the time she'd sent it over to Gary, the sub-editor, it was almost time for lunch.

'How's the wedding diary coming on?' Owen asked, coming out of his office. 'I need it by four.'

'You'll have it,' she promised. She'd brought her memory stick with her. It wouldn't take long to finish what she'd started Monday night. She'd do that now and then go to lunch.

Owen gave her the thumbs up and went back into his office.

'Lucky you, having a regular column.' Beth sat down at the desk next to her. Beth worked part-time and had just arrived for her shift. 'How are you getting on with it?'

'OK, but I wish it was about something more exciting than planning a wedding.' Cassie slipped her memory stick into the hard drive.

Beth grinned. 'I have noticed you don't seem as carried away by all the preparations as brides usually are. I don't think there's any danger of you turning in to a bridezilla.'

Cassie selected the 'Almost a Bride' file, opened it, and saved it to her computer. 'No chance. I mean I'm looking forward to marrying Timothy, of course I am, but I think there's far too much fuss made over weddings. It's almost as if it's all just about the day and it isn't, it's about the rest of your lives together.' As she said the words her future life with Timothy flashed across her mind: living in his minimalist apartment, hosting stuffy dinner parties, putting up with Sylvia interfering with everything they did. She shook her head. It wouldn't be like that at all. They'd buy a house together, make it theirs. Not that they'd discussed that yet, they'd hardly had time to discuss anything but she was sure Timothy would want that too. As for Sylvia, like most mothers, she was trying to help because she wanted the wedding to be perfect. She'd be fine when it was over.

Cassie read through the draft she'd written yesterday. Owen had told her he wanted the column to run for eight weeks and to cover at least one topic each week, so she started by saying she had two months to plan her wedding and her first step was choosing the venue. She chatted on about deciding whether to get married abroad or at home, whether to have a small family wedding or a larger one, giving the pros and cons of each. She ended by giving a few hints about how to decide what venue to choose then read it through. The style was light, chatty, informative – and made it sound like planning a wedding was no bother at all.

Not at all what planning a wedding was really like! Well, planning her wedding anyway. She sighed, leant back in her chair, and flexed her shoulders.

'What's up?' Beth glanced over.

'I'm not sure about this column. It sounds boring.'

'Let me take a look.' Beth leant over her shoulder. 'It sounds fine, and I like the options you've given the reader at the end. It's a good idea to ask them to choose what sort of wedding to have. If I ever got married again I'd opt for a wedding abroad – it saves a lot of expense and drama.'

That's exactly what Cassie had planned to do. What she'd still like to do.

Beth picked up her bag. 'Right, I'm off to cover the Education Show. See you later. And try to look more enthusiastic about your column!'

The trouble was Cassie didn't feel enthusiastic about it. It sounded so dull and bland, when actually planning her wedding was turning in to a right drama. If only she could tell the readers that version! Maybe she'd write it up just for fun. She created a new document, and using the same title and pseudonyms she wrote a more-true-to-life version of her wedding arrangements then sat back and read it, a smile playing on her lips. Now that was what she called interesting!

'Have you got a moment, Cassie?' Owen was standing in the doorway of his office.

'Coming!' Cassie hit the 'save' button then grabbed her notebook.

'Cassie, is that column ready yet? I need to sub it!' Gary shouted to her.

'Sure, I've saved it to my desktop. I'll send it over in a minute.' She told him as she followed Owen to his office.

'What's up?' she asked.

'Alex Hawkins has been on the phone, complaining about the interview you did with him.' Owen perched on the corner of his desk, not an easy task with his portly frame. 'He said he's been misquoted. Have you got your notes?'

'Of course.' Cassie flicked to the relevant page in her book. 'I recorded the interview too so I can back it up.'

'Fab-tastic.' Owen skimmed the notes. 'He obviously doesn't like the way he thinks he's come across but I can see you've quoted him ad verbum. Well done.'

'He was a bit up himself, to be honest, but I tried not to make that come over too much,' Cassie said.

'No problem, I'll get back to him. Hold on to the recording just in case.'

'It's in my desk drawer,' she told him.

Owen nodded. 'Good. Now can you cover the demonstration outside the council buildings about the rates rise this afternoon? Get a few statements from people?'

'Sure. I'll grab some lunch then get on to it.' She turned to leave.

'Hang on – what about your wedding column? Have you finished it?' he asked. 'Can you send it to sub before you cover this?'

'It's finished and I was about to send it when you called me. I'll go do it right now.'

'Sending the column over in a mo,' she called over to Gary as she walked back into the news room.

'It's OK, I saw it on your desktop and sent it over myself,' he told her. 'It's already subbed and gone to print.'

'OK, thanks.' She grabbed her jacket, slipped her notebook in her bag, and set off.

Sylvia dropped by that evening to inform them that she'd booked them a consultation appointment with J.M. for Saturday morning. 'Then you can discuss with him the services you want, the type of album, and anything else.' She turned to Timothy. 'Don't tell me you can't make it, the wedding is just under two months away so we need to get this finalised. There's still a lot to sort out.'

Oh shit, she still hadn't told Timothy about Jared, Cassie thought in dismay, and now they both had a meeting with him on Saturday. She had to find a way to broach the subject when Sylvia had gone. She didn't want to tell him while she was here: she had a strong feeling that Sylvia didn't really think she was good enough for her son and didn't intend to give her any more ammunition. Not that it should matter, everyone of their age had past relationships, didn't they? It's just that Sylvia might make more of it … and mention that Cassie and Jared had made no sign they knew each other, which she had to admit could look suspicious – especially the way Sylvia would tell it. She'd definitely tell Timothy tonight when Sylvia had gone.

Sylvia showed no sign of going, though. She'd brought a 'suggested guest list' with her and seemed intent on spending the evening discussing it, and other wedding preparations. 'A small glass of chilled white would be nice, dear,' she said to Cassie. 'Just the one as I'm driving. And a sandwich if you have some granary bread.'

44

'There's a bottle chilling in the fridge.' Timothy got up to fetch the wine and three glasses while Cassie went to check what was in the fridge for a sandwich.

'Smoked salmon or Parma ham?' she called from the kitchen.

'Smoked salmon, please, with just a smidgen of butter on the bread and a couple of wafer thin slices of cucumber.'

Cassie set about making a sandwich. She had a feeling this was going to be a long night.

'We'll need a girlie meeting, dear, so we can talk about the dress and flowers,' Sylvia told her when she returned with the sandwich, crusts trimmed off and cut in to quarters, just how Sylvia liked it, with a bit of salad on the side of the plate and a fresh white napkin too. 'It's bad luck to discuss all that in front of Timothy. Have you chosen your wedding colours yet?'

'Yes, Timothy and I discussed it last night and we both decided we'd like a pale blue,' Cassie told her.

'Pale blue? That's an *interesting* choice. Pastel colours are pretty for summer weddings.' She took a nibble of her sandwich and swallowed it daintily before continuing. 'What about bridesmaids, dear? Two or three little flower girls would be nice. And a page boy, maybe? Then there's the maid of honour, of course.'

Cassie hesitated. She knew that Sylvia was anxious for Amanda to be her maid of honour. She'd dropped enough hints, as had Timothy.

Surprisingly, Timothy came to her rescue. 'Cassie has asked Samantha, her best friend, to be her maid of honour, which only seems fair as I'm having Philip, my oldest friend, as my best man.'

Cassie could have hugged him. 'We decided to have two flower girls. One from each family.' She turned to Timothy for support. 'We thought Sophia and Estelle. They're similar in age and will make lovely flower girls.'

Four-year-old Sophia (her sister Ellen's daughter) and five-year-old Estelle (Amanda's daughter) would look so cute with a pretty tiara in their hair and holding a basket of flower petals to scatter. And hopefully having Estelle as flower girl would make up for not having Amanda as maid of honour.

'That sounds sensible, dear.' Sylvia's smile was a bit forced. 'I presume your parents will be attending the wedding?'

'Of course, my dad's giving me away. And my mum and stepdad will be flying over from Cyprus the day before.'

'Would you like me to arrange accommodation for them? I'm sure we could arrange special rates at the castle for our wedding guests.'

Even with special rates, Cassie doubted if her mum and stepdad could afford to stay at Hollington Castle. The return flights and new outfits would make a large enough dent in their bank balances. Although they'd told her not to worry about that, assuring her they'd manage fine.

'There's no need. They'll be staying with Ellen,' she told Sylvia. 'They're looking forward to spending some time with her and Sophia.'

'Really? How cosy. Well, the next important thing is the dress. We really need to order that as soon as we can. Now, I just happen to know the assistant to Leah Maylin, the designer, dear,' she explained as if Cassie had never heard of the top designer. 'She has a fabulous wedding collection, and although it's short notice, she said she can slot you in as a special favour to me. I could book you an appointment with her for next week. Which days are you free?'

Was the perishing woman arranging everything? Didn't she think Cassie was capable of making suitable choices? Count to ten, Cassie. One, two, three … 'It's very kind of you but I've arranged to look for a wedding dress with Sam on Saturday.' OK, she'd have to make it afternoon seeing as Sylvia had booked them an appointment with Jared again, but she was going. This is one thing she was determined to stick to her guns about. If Sylvia had her way she'd be wearing a floaty meringue that costs thousands. Cassie was going to choose her own wedding dress.

'Are you serious, dear? You're actually going to wear an off-the-peg dress for your wedding?' Sylvia gave a little shudder, which made Cassie even more determined to choose the dress herself.

'There are lots of lovely wedding boutiques in town, most of them have a designer section,' she said. 'I'm sure I'll find something suitable.'

Sylvia pursed her lips and shot Timothy a reproachful glance, obviously expecting him to agree with her. Timothy pretended he was busy reading the newspaper. Although Cassie was grateful he hadn't taken his mother's side, she wished he'd backed her up. They should be united about the wedding. It was bad enough that Sylvia had given them a list of who they should invite and hijacked both the venue and photographer.

Sylvia left a little while later, making it quite clear that she wasn't very happy.

'I think Mother's a bit upset. I know she tends to interfere a bit but she's only trying to help,' Timothy said reproachfully. 'The wedding isn't far away, and there's such a lot to do, so it would be wise to take her advice. Mother has so many connections and is an expert at planning events like this.'

That meant she wasn't. Cassie wanted to scream, but she kept calm. Timothy hated raised voices or arguments of any kind. 'I realise that but I am capable of choosing my own wedding dress.'

'I know, sweetheart, I'm not suggesting otherwise.' He leant over and placed his hand on hers. 'Perhaps you could ask Mother to come with you and help you choose your dress? I'm sure that will make her feel better. She just wants to be involved a bit.'

He picked up the remote and switched on the TV for the news. That was it, matter closed. He was obviously confident that Cassie would do as he wished, as she always did.

Only this time she wasn't. Sylvia had taken over the wedding enough. She was not choosing Cassie's wedding dress. Absolutely not.

Six

They'd be here in a few minutes. Jared had been thinking about this meeting all week, wondering if Cassie had told Timothy about their romance yet. If so, how would he feel about his fiancée's ex-lover taking their wedding photographs? Would he object? After seeing Cassie with him in the restaurant the other night, he hadn't been able to resist looking up Timothy Campbell on the Internet, curious what this smug, smooth-looking guy who'd stolen Cassie's heart did for a living. He hadn't really been surprised to discover that he was a rich, hot-shot lawyer with an impeccable record. He'd seemed full of confidence – clear in the way he walked, dressed, and conducted himself. Not the sort of guy that would regard anyone as a rival. He probably wouldn't be at all bothered that Cassie and Jared had been lovers, confident that he was far superior. In fact, Timothy would probably go all out to show how much better, richer, and cleverer he was than Jared.

Jared reached in the jacket pocket of his worn brown leather wallet and opened it up; feeling inside the small inner zipped pocket he took out a photograph. It was a bit crumpled and tattered now but the picture was still clear. Him and Cassie, taken on their first holiday abroad together. Nine years ago. They'd gone to Cyprus and in this photo were at Aphrodite's beach. Behind them was Lover's Hill. He'd made a heart there with their initials inside, using tiny stones off the beach. J.M heart C.T. He wondered if the heart was still there, an eternal testament to the love they had once shared.

He studied their faces beaming out from the photograph. They'd looked so carefree and happy. So much in love. He'd ruined that. He was the one who'd torn them apart.

Still holding the photograph, he sat down at the desk and leant back in the chair, his thoughts casting back to the Jared who'd walked so casually away from the love of his life because he didn't want to settle down, to go along the mortgage and kids route. He'd desperately wanted to fulfil his dream of becoming a serious photographer, of travelling the world and filming the amazing things he saw, of going that extra mile to see an Emperor penguin hatching an egg in its natural habitat, an elephant nursery, the sun rise over the Sahara desert, the spectacular Northern Lights. And he didn't regret it – he'd had some amazing experiences. But he always carried this photo with him. Wherever he went, Cassie always lurked in the back of his mind, tucked away but never completely gone. Often, when he was in an isolated place, just him and his thoughts, waiting for the sun to rise or the animals he wanted to photograph to show up, he'd taken the photo out, looked at it, and wondered if he'd done the right thing.

Then Cassie had walked back into his life and turned it upside down. He hadn't expected to feel like this when he saw her again, the familiar ache in his heart. It's just nostalgia, he told himself. You know what they say, you never get over your first love. And Cassie had been his first love. There had been plenty of others since but none of them had ever touched his heart like Cassie had. Which is why he was still single, he guessed. No one had ever matched up to Cassie. He dated women like Savannah for company and fun but had never wanted a serious relationship with any of them.

Cassie had found someone to replace him, though. Someone rich, influential, clever. Jared had never been clever. He'd struggled to get through his exams at school but somehow he'd gained enough qualifications to get him on to the photography course he coveted at university. Cameras and photographs he understood, and the longing to travel had always coursed through his body. His career was his life. He couldn't give it up. Another couple of months and he'd be off again. So it was a good job Cassie had found someone else, and was planning a wedding, because he daren't get involved with her again. He still wanted his dream.

The trouble was that he wanted Cassie too.

The intercom buzzed. 'Mr Campbell and Miss Tyler are here, J.M.,' the receptionist announced.

'Show them in, please,' he told her.

He'd felt a bit pretentious calling himself J.M. but he'd wanted to keep his society photographer persona separate from his real job. He'd prefer people not to know that J.M. from I.D. Images was Jared Macey the wildlife photographer. For now, he was glad to hide behind the initials, a cloak of anonymity.

He slipped the photograph back into his wallet as there was a knock on the door and the handle turned.

'Come in,' he called as Timothy strode in. Suave, confident, expensive but not flamboyantly dressed; everything about him screamed money, social standing, a man to be looked up to. And one who was used to being in control too, he'd wager on it. The Cassie he'd known was feisty, free-spirited. Did she and Timothy clash a lot, he wondered?

Cassie followed him, looking stunning in a white trouser suit and blue lacy top. He guessed by the panicky look she shot him that she hadn't told Campbell they knew each other and didn't want him to give her away. Why not, he wondered. Was her fiancé the jealous type?

'Delighted to meet you J …' Timothy held out his hand, leaving the question floating in the air. He obviously wasn't comfortable with calling Jared by his initials; something about the way he spoke irritated Jared but he forced a welcoming smile on his face. He needed this job.

'J.M.,' he said. 'Do take a seat.'

'What exactly does J.M. stand for?' Timothy pursued as he pulled a chair out for Cassie, then sat down himself.

'It's how I'm known professionally. I prefer to use my initials rather than my full name.' Jared smiled again, and held Timothy's gaze just long enough to register the irritation in the other man's eyes, before looking down at the open folder on his desk. Timothy was obviously annoyed that Jared hadn't

51

answered his question, which probably didn't happen to him often. 'I took a few notes from my preliminary meeting with your mother and Cassie so I've a broad idea of what you're looking for. Have you had a chance to look through the brochures and come to any decisions?'

'Yes, Cassandra and I decided on a bespoke album in the traditional style. We've a few particular shots we'd like taken on the day.' As Timothy rattled off their list of requirements, Jared suppressed a sigh. This was not going to be one of his easier bookings. Only the thought of his impending trip to the Arctic was going to see him through this.

'I must say that photographer seems to know his stuff, although he seemed rather arrogant to me,' Timothy said as they left.

Cassie squeezed his arm. 'Well, at least we've got our photographer sorted out. That's something we can tick off our list; although I meant to ask him if we could look at some samples of the albums and I forgot.' She'd been too nervous in case she or Jared let slip that they knew each other, that's why. 'I'll ask him to bring some to the venue when we visit and then we can look through them. It might give us more ideas for the sort of cover and photos we want.'

'Good idea. I've been thinking I'd rather like a photographic record of our honeymoon. Perhaps the photographer could join us for a few days? He could take some professional shots of us walking along the beach at midnight, having dinner on the beach, that sort of thing.'

No way was Jared coming along on their honeymoon. She had to tell Timothy about him now, before this got out of hand.

'Look, there's something I've been meaning to mention,' she said but before she could continue Timothy's mobile rang.

'Sorry I have to take this, it's a very important client.' He flicked open the phone. 'Timothy Campbell speaking.'

Cassie sighed as she listened to Timothy's side of the conversation. It was obvious he was going to have to go into the office. She'd have to leave it until tonight.

She took out her own mobile and texted Sam asking if she had time to meet for coffee that afternoon.

'Usual place, 2.30 p.m.,' came back the reply.

Thank goodness. She really needed someone to talk to. She'd stop at the office and pick up a copy of today's paper first. She was dying to read her wedding piece.

'You've got to be kidding!' Sam stared incredulously at Cassie. 'You still haven't told Timothy about Jared? What are you playing at?'

'I didn't deliberately not tell him,' Cassie protested. 'I kept trying to but it never seemed to be the right time.' Honestly, she felt guilty enough without Sam staring at her like that. 'It's not a crime, is it? We haven't seen each other for seven years.' Seven years, two months, and three days, to be precise. She could still remember the exact day Jared walked out of her life.

'Timothy's bound to find out, and then what will he think?' Sam shook her head. 'You are over Jared, aren't you?' She looked Cassie straight in the face. 'You haven't still got feelings for him?'

'Of course not!' She retorted quickly. 'Stop making such a big deal out of this. Jared and I were over years ago. So what if I haven't mentioned it to Timothy? We haven't shared a list of our past relationships. As far as we're concerned the past is the past. It's now that matters.'

'You should still tell him though, it looks like you're keeping it a secret and he'll wonder why.'

'He won't be the slightest bit bothered. That fact that I didn't mention it and that Jared and I didn't chat about old times proves just how much we are over it. Timothy will realise that. In fact, if I do mention it he'll wonder why I'm making such a big deal out of it.' As soon as the words were out of her mouth she realised she was right. Timothy wouldn't expect her to tell him that she dated Jared many years ago. It was history. Jared was working for I.D. Images and had been appointed to take the photos of their wedding. It was as simple as that.

Then she realised Sam had opened the paper she'd placed on the table and was staring at it. 'What?'

'This is yours, isn't it? You're Paige Stevens?'

Cassie was stunned. 'How did you know?'

53

'Because it's all there. Paige who's about to be married to Ian, the hot-shot business man with his interfering "monster-in-law" who's only gone and arranged Paige's ex to take the photos. I quote, "Blake broke my heart and now he was going to photograph our wedding. What should I do?" The reader has to decide whether Paige should tell Ian about him or not.'

What? 'Give me that!' Cassie grabbed the paper and quickly scanned the page.

Almost a Bride

When I agreed to marry Ian, my fiancé, a couple of months ago I was imagining us getting married next year. Or the year after. Not in less than two months' time thanks to my monster-in-law-to-be hearing about a cancellation at the 'perfect venue'. I'm in a right panic. There's so much to do. The wedding dress, bridesmaids' dresses, flowers, invitations, favours, photographs ... and that's just for starters.

*Just in case you're planning a wedding too, I thought I'd keep a diary to record all the things I've learnt and found helpful. You can write in and tell me your tips too. One tip I'd really like is how to stop your future mother-in-law completely taking over. I mean, I'm glad of her help, really I am, especially with the wedding so near, but I wish she'd remember that it's **MY** wedding not **hers.***

We hadn't even got around to thinking about venues when monster-in-law phoned us to say she'd booked our venue. That's right, booked it without even a mention to us. And yes, it's lovely but she actually booked it without asking us first. She heard that there was a cancellation and didn't want it to get snapped up. And then she booked us a wedding photographer. I literally had to grit my teeth and count to ten zillion. Ian doesn't seem to mind at all, and keeps telling me she's only trying to help, and we should be grateful.

Help? She's taking over. She frowns if I have milk and sugar in my coffee or the tiniest morsel of cake. 'Think of the wedding dress, dear,' she mutters through pursed lips. 'You don't want to have to let it out, do you?' Let it out? I haven't even ordered it yet. She's put me on a pre-wedding diet so I don't look too fat in the photos. And in her book anything over a size ten is fat. If it wasn't for my illicit iced mochas with my best mate Andrea, and the secret sash of chocolates in my shoe cupboard, I'd have keeled over with starvation by now.

And to top it all off, when we walked into the photographer's I nearly fainted with shock. Honestly, I could have died right there and then! It was only Blake, my ex. The ex I had a mad, passionate affair with years ago and that I haven't told Ian about yet. I don't know how I did it but I managed to totally blank him like I'd never met him before, and left monster-in-law to talk to him, but all the while I could feel his eyes boring into me. And the very worst thing was, as Blake shook my hand when I was about to go, I felt a sort of tingle shoot up my arm, just like it used to; which is ridiculous because I love Ian and have absolutely no feelings for Blake at all.

What am I going to do? If I say I want to change the photographer, Ian and monster-in-law will want to know why, because this is one of the best wedding photography firms around and we're lucky to have got them (monster-in-law's words). And they'll wonder why I didn't say anything when I saw him. But how can I let my ex photograph our wedding? What should I do?

There were three questions at the bottom of the column: should she insist on changing the photographer, tell Ian about their affair, or keep the photographer and don't say anything? The readers were asked to email what they think she should do.

Shit. Shit. Shit. Sam was right. It was all there. But this was the piece she was messing around with. How the hell had Owen got hold of it?

Seven

'Whatever made you write all that?' Sam asked her. 'I mean, it's fantastic. You're going to have the whole nation gripped, but if Timothy reads it it'll be goodbye wedding.'

'I didn't write it. Well, I did, but not for publication. This isn't the copy I sent over.' Cassie exclaimed, reading the article again. 'I don't understand … oh shit!' She clapped her forehead with her hand. Owen had called her into the office just as she'd been about to send over her column. And when she came back Gary had told her he'd collected it from her computer and sent it over to sub himself. He'd obviously collected the wrong column. He must have glanced at her screen, saw the file, and used the latest version. She remembered it now, she'd just hit save when Owen had called her into his office! Damn, damn, damn. What had possessed her to write that fake column and save it to her desktop instead of her personal files?

She quickly explained. 'What am I going to do? The one they were meant to print was nothing like this. And the voting options were whether we should have a big wedding or a small family affair, not whether I should tell Timothy – I mean Ian – about Blake or not. What if one of Timothy's friends or colleagues reads this? They'll know I've written it.'

'They won't if they don't know about Jared,' Sam pointed out. 'Ian the stuffy businessman and his interfering mother could be hundreds of people. Love the way you used "monster-in-law" for her, by the way.' She grinned.

'Timothy and his mum will know I've written it if they see it. It's so obvious. Hello, I'm about to get married, Sylvia found the wedding venue and the photographer for us. What am I going to do? Why didn't I check what version Gary had sent over?' Because she'd been busy covering the demonstration at the Council building, that's why.

'Look, I'm sure Sylvia never reads this paper, she's more of a *Times* reader, isn't she? And Timothy must be, too. Or do they read it to see your stuff?'

Cassie shook her head. 'No, Timothy never reads any of my articles. And his mother, well, she just thinks it's a hobby of mine and would never stoop so low as to read the local newspaper.' She felt a bit calmer now. There was no need to panic, she could put this right. 'I'll talk to Owen on Monday, explain what's happened, and tell him we need to write it differently next week. I'll just say we've changed the photographer then concentrate on other wedding stuff. Keep the interfering mother-in-law in the background. It'll be fine, Owen'll understand.' He had to. This was her future at stake. Her happiness.

'Will he do that? It says that the column will be every Saturday for the next couple of months, until Paige's wedding. And there's a vote opening. People will be voting for what they want you to do. What if they want you not to tell Ian and keep Blake as the photographer?'

'Well, I bloody well won't, I don't care what Owen says.' She shook her head in disbelief as she looked at the article again. 'I can't believe this has happened. Thank goodness I didn't tell Timothy about Jared. If I had and he saw this article he'd know it's me writing it. Then he'd be mad about all the stuff I wrote about him and his mum. Timothy's a very private person. I don't think he'd understand about artistic licence and keeping readers hooked.'

'I guess you're right,' Sam grinned. 'Anyway, it's a kind of karma that Jared is photographing your very expensive wedding to a high-flying lawyer. Serves him right for dumping you.'

Cassie had to admit, that did feel good. Sam was the only one who really knew how totally heartbroken she'd been when Jared dumped her.

'Maybe you don't need to tell Timothy. You've sorted out the photos and albums now, haven't you? So you'll only be seeing him on your wedding day and you'll be too loved-up to be bothered by who's taking the photos.'

'Actually, we've got a couple of appointments with him before then,' Cassie confessed. 'Jared wants to familiarise himself with the venue so we're meeting him on Thursday, and we're having some pre-wedding shots, and an engagement photo – yes, I know we got engaged Valentine's Day but we're going to recreate the scene, wear the same clothes.'

'That little lot must be costing a fortune,' Sam said admiringly. 'Lucky you.'

She was lucky, Cassie thought. Not because Timothy was rich, she wasn't that mercenary, but because he was such a nice guy. He adored her and she adored him. That's all that mattered.

'Timothy did mention having some honeymoon shots as well, but I don't think I can handle Jared coming with us.'

Sam almost choked on her chicken salad wrap. 'Absolutely not! You can't be serious.'

'Don't worry. I told Timothy that I wanted the honeymoon to be an intimate affair, just the two of us, and he's agreed. Let's finish lunch and see if we can at least nail the wedding dress today.' She finished her coffee. 'Do you realise that there's only seven Saturdays before the wedding?'

'I know and I can't believe that you've no idea what you want to wear,' Sam told her. 'I've had my wedding dress planned for ages. I know exactly what I want. I just need Paul to pop the question.'

'I'm sure he will soon. You've been together for ages,' Sam reassured her. Sam was such a romantic. She could imagine her wedding. It would be all hearts and flowers, silk, and lace.

'Oh, there's no rush. I'm happy as we are, really. Although I do want to get married one day, and when we do I want lots of white lace and net. I intend to look like a princess. It's the only day I get to be the main attraction and I'm going to milk it for all it's worth.'

'I don't want anything too fussy. Definitely not a meringue,' Cassie said adamantly. 'You'll never believe it, but Sylvia was trying to talk me into going to see Leah Maylin and having my dress specially made. Of course, she knows the designer personally and between them they'd choose the dress for me. I wouldn't get a look-in. Thank goodness Timothy backed me up when I said no, although I could tell he thought it was a good idea.'

Sam stared at her, mouth open in a big O. It was as if she was trying to speak but couldn't get the words out. Finally, she managed it. 'Sylvia was going to ask a top designer to personally make your wedding dress and you said no?' She shook her head. 'Now I know you're nuts.'

'It's not that I don't want a designer dress, it's that I don't want Sylvia running the show and making all the decisions. You have no idea what she's like. Every dress I try on she'd frown at, or purse her lips or ask "Are you sure that is the one you want, Cassandra?" In that patronising voice, making it clear she doesn't approve and I'll end up doubting my own taste and having what she wants. I want to choose my own dress. Plan my own wedding. She's driving me nuts.' She hadn't meant to rant so much but the words just came pouring out. She'd been bottling up her irritation with Sylvia for weeks now and once she let it out she couldn't seem to stop it.

'Good for you.' Sam clapped enthusiastically, causing a couple of people to glance over at them. 'We'll show her. Come on, let's go wedding dress shopping.'

'She's not as bad as all that,' Cassie said, feeling guilty as they got up from table. 'It's just that she's so controlling.'
'Yes, and Timothy lets her be. I'm glad you're standing up to her. If you don't, she'll be a nightmare once you get married. You need to nip her interfering ways in the bud before she gets worse.'

Cassie was worried about that herself. There wasn't a day that went by when Sylvia didn't ring Timothy at least twice, and she always seemed to know more about his life and whereabouts than Cassie did.

'I guess your column next week will be about buying the wedding dress,' Sam said as they left the café. 'You'd better not put anything horrible about me in your articles. I'll be reading them, you know!'

'As if!'

'Good. Well, as I'm the maid of honour it's my responsibility to make sure you get the dress you want,' Sam said. 'So I've drawn up a list of bridal shops to visit and we're not coming home until you've found your dream dress.'

'We're in for a long afternoon, then,' Cassie said with a mock groan. The truth was that she did need someone to organise her. Left to her own devices she'd be doing everything at the last minute.

Left to her own devices she wouldn't be getting married yet. She shoved the thought out of her mind. OK, yes, she had thought it would be a year or two before they tied the knot but what did it matter? And at least this way it was more exciting and there was less time to have an attack of nerves. The last thing she wanted to turn into was a bridezilla.

Sam was a woman on a mission and she'd certainly done her homework. The first bridal shop she took them into had a stunning array of designer dresses, ranging from the more formal wedding gowns to Grecian goddess-styles. Sam was practically drooling over them.

'What about this?' she asked, holding up a classic gown with a high waist and full skirt. 'Very Audrey Hepburn. You'll look sensational in this.'

'It is lovely,' Cassie agreed. 'But it isn't really the style I'm looking for.'

'Try it on, dear. The dresses look so different on,' the owner told her, leading the way to a large cubicle. 'Take your time, try on as many as you like. We offer a wide range and our skilled seamstresses can do any alterations you wish.' She pulled open the red velvet curtains that enclose the changing cubicle. 'When's the wedding?' she asked.

'June 26th,' Cassie told her.

'Less than two months away? Don't worry dear, we can sort you out.'

Cassie selected an assortment of dresses and the elegant lady hung them on a rail outside the cubicle, passing them to her one by one.

Sam sat down on a pouffé and waited for the fashion show to begin. First, Cassie tried on a white satin dress with lace detail and a fishtail. It looked gorgeous but she found it difficult to walk in. 'I feel like I'm waddling,' she told Sam, who grinned.

'You look sensational. It really shows off your curves.'

The next dress was an exquisite floral lace number with a sweetheart neckline and capped sleeves. Cassie loved it apart from the neckline. Then she tried on a flowing full-skirted dress with a fitted corset that made her look like she actually had boobs, which Sam was ecstatic over. In fact, it was very Sam. But not at all Cassie. A succession of other dresses followed: long sleeves, short sleeves, sleeveless, backless, corseted ...

Sam gasped in awe at all of them, exclaiming that each one in turn was totally divine, but although Cassie liked them all none of them was 'the one'.

'I'm sorry,' she told the woman. 'They're all really gorgeous. But ...'

'But not for you.' The woman patted her on the arm. 'Don't apologise. Your wedding dress is the most important dress you will ever wear. It must feel right. You must feel like a princess in it. Like the most beautiful woman in the world. Don't settle for a dress that makes you feel anything less.'

'Thank you.' Cassie could have hugged the woman. She was right, what she was looking for was the dress that made her feel like the most beautiful woman in the world.

She found it; three hours and six bridal shops later. A stunning lace and satin wedding gown with a scalloped lace neckline, three quarter sleeves, and a keyhole back. It fitted over the hips and flared out from the knees. It made her look elegant, sophisticated, and sexy.

'It's perfect!' Sam clapped her hands, almost squealing in delight. 'You've got to have it, Cassie.'

Cassie stood in front of the mirror, staring at her reflection. It was a wonderful dress. Sam was right, she had to have it.

She looked at the price tag and hesitated. It was a lot of money but Timothy had opened a special wedding account for her and told her to spend as much as she needed. 'What matters is that you get the dress you want,' he'd insisted. 'Don't even think about the expense.'

Well, this was it.

'You've got to have it,' Sam repeated. 'Timothy's eyes will pop out of his head when he sees you in in this. And it will look absolutely amazing on the photographs.'

But as Cassie looked at her reflection in the mirror the question that popped into her mind was what Jared would think when he saw her in this dress.

Eight

Cassie went to the office early on Monday morning, hoping to catch Owen in a good mood. She'd practised the speech she was going to make and was pretty sure she could talk him around. It was likely that hardly anyone had read the column and voted anyway, she thought. People were so busy at the weekends and it was only the local paper, not one of the big dailies, she reminded herself.

As she walked through the door she was astonished to be greeted by a chorus of cheers and clapping.

'Wow!' She gaped at them all, stunned. 'What did I do?'

Owen came out of the office, beaming. 'Your wedding column, that's what. It's got everyone talking. There's an inbox full of emails for you to answer and sales on Saturday doubled.'

'Really?' She grinned in delight until she remembered that the wrong column had been published. Damn. She hadn't expected it to be such a success. Now it was going to be even more difficult to talk Owen into letting her change the way she wrote it. She had to do it though. What if someone Sylvia or Amanda knew had read it and told Timothy? 'That's great, but I need to talk to you about the column, Owen,' she said as firmly as she could.

'Sure. Let's go into the office, shall we?' He looked over at Sally. 'Bring us a coffee, will you, Sal?'

Owen was asking her to sit in his office and drink coffee with him? Her column must have been a success. She couldn't help feeling proud. Your wedding is at stake, she reproached herself. You can't let Owen sweet-talk you in to continuing to write such a personal column.

'Sit down.' Owen actually pulled out the chair for her. He obviously meant business.

She sat. 'Owen ...'

He beamed at her in delight. 'Take a look at this.' He pointed to the computer, which was open on the email inbox. She was astonished to see row upon row of emails addressed to Paige Stevens, with 'Almost a Bride' in the subject bar.

'Wow!' She couldn't even begin to count them. 'How many are there?'

'A few hundred. And this is only the first week. We're on to a winner here, Cassie.'

Now she felt really guilty. 'I'm pleased the column was so successful but the thing is ...' Her mouth felt dry. She licked her lips, swallowed. *Spit it out, for goodness' sake!* 'Gary subbed the wrong column. This is one I was just messing around with, writing for a bit of fun. It wasn't the one I meant to submit.'

Owen frowned. 'What do you mean?'

'Well, I was writing the column and I thought it sounded a bit boring; nothing like the sort of stuff that really happens when you're planning a wedding. So I thought I'd up the drama a bit. I don't know why I did it. It wasn't meant to be published. I told Gary I'd finished the column and was just about to send it over when you called me into the office. When I came back out Gary said he'd collected the column and subbed it. He must have collected the wrong one. I never thought to check as I had to go straight back out again.'

Owen looked puzzled. 'OK, so you never meant to send this one, but so what? It's a success. Well done! You've found a winning format. It's exactly what we want. Our readers love it. And the title "Almost a Bride" is fab-tastic. Sheer genius.'

'Owen, I can't write another column like this. I shouldn't have written this one and it definitely shouldn't have been published. We have to change the format!'

Owen gave her a scrutinising look. 'And the reason why we have to do that is …?'

Cassie stared at him in dismay. What could she say? She was going to have to admit that it was true otherwise he'd be pushing her to continue with the same story.

'Look,' she swallowed. 'Some of it is … er … true.'

'Well, I guessed that, you're always going on about what a nightmare your chap's mother is. Don't worry, you'll be using a pseudonym. No one will know it's you. And we'll pretend the wedding is six months away instead of two. That should throw them off track.' He narrowed his eyes. 'The rest of it isn't true, is it?'

'What?'

'The bit about the photographer?'

She wanted to deny it but knew that the sudden hot surge to her cheeks had given her away.

Owen whistled. 'Fan-bloody-tastic! We really need this, Cassie. This will push our circulation through the roof. It's reader-grabbing stuff.'

'It's my life!' Cassie retorted. 'I don't want it plastered all over the paper.'

'I see.' Owen perched on the end of the desk and adopted his best 'fatherly' mode. 'Look, Cassie, I'm going to be straight up with you. The paper's in trouble.'

Cassie stared at him suspiciously. 'If this is a sob story to get me to agree you might as well stop now, because I'm not going to.'

'It's the truth. It's the curse of the bloody digital revolution with all the free bloody e-papers. Print sales have gone through the floor. Everyone knows that. And a small paper like this, we just can't sustain such a loss. I'm going to have to start laying people off if sales don't pick up soon. Your "Almost a Bride" column could make all the difference to whether we go under or not.' He sounded genuine.

She fidgeted under the 'Please agree to this' look he was giving her. 'That's not fair. You're trying to guilt-trip me. I'm not a big name, I'm not going to draw people in.'

67

'No, but this stuff will. It's got the personal angle that people love. You're not only giving the other wannabee brides the benefit of your experience, you're giving them a dilemma. They'll be wanting to buy the paper every week to find out what happens next: if your fiancé finds out about your ex, what he says, what his stuffy mother does, and how you manage to hold it all together.'

'I can't do it.'

'Why not?' Owen demanded. 'What's the big deal? We've all got exes and interfering relatives. No one will know it's you.'

'If Timothy gets wind of this we're through.'

'I thought he doesn't read your pieces? Bit beneath him and all that. Hot-shot lawyers like him read the *Times,* not the local rag. Anyway, it's not written under your name.'

'No, but it's obvious I wrote it to anyone who knows us. What if one of our friends or family read it and told him?'

'They won't guess it's you, why should they? People will think it's made up, just a filler piece for the paper. Even if they did think it was true, hundreds of people will be getting married in the next few months, this could be about any one of them.'

Unless they knew about Jared. Anyone who knew about Jared would know that Cassie had written this piece.

'Hundreds of people aren't having their ex photograph their wedding,' she pointed out.

Owen met her gaze. 'Does Timothy know this photographer chap is your ex?'

'No,' she admitted. 'I haven't got around to telling him yet. So, you see, if he reads this we'll be finished. I need out, Owen. We have to go back to the format we agreed.'

He thrust his hand over his balding head. 'How can we do that now? Look at the response we've had. People will be waiting to read more. They want to know what decision you – Paige – make. They're voting on it.' He switched screens to the online version of the newspaper and scrolled to the voting option asking readers what decision they think Paige should make. So far five hundred people had said she should tell Ian about Blake and three hundred said she shouldn't.

She repeated what she'd told Sam. 'That's not a problem. We'll say that I've decided to tell Ian and we're changing the photographer. Then I'll write the piece how I was originally going to do it: giving advice about planning a wedding. I was planning to write about choosing the wedding dress this week.'

Owen looked aghast. 'I'm begging you, Cass. We're going under, we need your column.' He leant towards her. 'This could be big, Cassie. It could save all our jobs.'

Cassie's mind was racing. She thought of Beth, a single mum to her two kids who definitely needed her job, and Craig, who'd been out of work for eighteen months before he landed a job on the paper six months ago, and of Owen who'd been in charge for twenty years now, and would probably struggle to get another job at his age. And yes, part of her was excited at writing such a popular column. The public response was fantastic.

What if Timothy read it?

He had never read her any of her stuff, why would he start now? And in the unlikely event that any of his friends read it, surely they wouldn't think it was her? She doubted if any of them knew the name of the paper she worked for and it wasn't written under her name anyway. Besides, she could exaggerate, embellish, and disguise the characters so that no one recognised it, and keep Jared out of it as much as possible. Dare she risk it?

'Think about it, Cassie. All our jobs are on the line.'

It was sheer blackmail.

'OK,' she nodded. 'But I get to check the final draft before it goes to print, every week. Deal?'

'Deal.' Owen held out his hand, she took it, and shook it. 'I knew I could rely on you. This is going to be dynamite.'

She still wasn't sure she'd made the right decision, Cassie thought as she walked back into the news room, but what else could she do? And she had to admit that it did feel good to write such a popular column. The feedback had been amazing.

'I'm sorry, Cassandra, but I've got an urgent meeting tomorrow afternoon. I won't be able to make the venue appointment after all,' Timothy informed her as they ate supper together on Tuesday evening.

Cassie stared at him in dismay. That meant she'd be alone with Jared. There's no way she could deal with that. 'I can't cancel it now, it's all arranged,' she pointed out. She'd even asked to be on the early shift tomorrow, which meant being in the newspaper office at the crack of dawn, so that she'd be free in the afternoon. Of course if she'd told Owen he'd have let her go anyway, considering it material for her 'wedding piece', but she was determined not to write about Jared this week so she didn't want him to know.

'I'm sorry, but I can't get out of it. It's a meeting with a potential client that could put a lot of business our way.' Timothy took a sip of his wine. 'Surely there's no need to cancel? All you have to do is meet the photographer at the venue, let him look around and check out whatever he needs to check.' He must have seen the look of panic on Cassie's face because he reached over and placed his hand on hers. 'You seem a bit worried about it. Would you like me to ask Mother to come with you?'

For a brief moment – a very brief moment – it was tempting. She shook her head; spending another afternoon with Sylvia wasn't high on her wish list. 'No, I'll be fine. I was just disappointed as I was hoping we could go together. It doesn't matter, of course your meeting must come first.'

'If you're sure …' He looked at her, puzzled, and no wonder. She worked for a newspaper and was used to interviewing lots of different people, so why was she flapping about showing their photographer the wedding venue? She was being stupid. She was an adult, for goodness' sake. Of course she could handle spending an hour with an ex-boyfriend. She smiled brightly. 'No problem. Of course, it would have been nice if you could have come too, but I can handle it.'

To be honest, she was dreading being alone with Jared. It would be so awkward. While she was with Sylvia or Timothy, she could avoid talking to him about anything personal, she could pretend that they'd never met. On their own it would be there, hanging in the air like a storm cloud ready to burst.

70

I'll keep it strictly professional, she decided. I won't even ask him how he is and definitely won't discuss our past. If he mentions it I'll say that I haven't told Timothy because it isn't important. We both moved on years ago.

The next morning was hectic. From the minute she got into the office it was all systems go. She'd no sooner set foot through the door when Owen called. 'Do the police, fire, and hospital checks, will you, Cass? And don't forget I need your wedding piece this afternoon.'

She picked up the phone and dialled the police PR office to see what had gone on during the night – several fights, a road accident involving three cars, a few burglaries, one at a local jewellery store. A typical night, really. She scribbled down details of them in shorthand, ready to write up a report, repeated the same with the fire brigade and local hospitals. Then she filled Owen in on what had happened.

'Follow up the burglary at the jewellers, will you?' h said. 'You know the drill. Take Craig with you to get some shots, interview the locals, see what info you can get me. We might run with that as the lead.'

She nodded, grabbed her jacket and bag, and went to find Craig.

Jared read the piece for the fourth time. Cassie had written it, he was sure. He remembered her telling him the name of the paper she wrote for, so he'd picked up a copy on Saturday, after their meeting, and shoved it in his bag. He'd forgotten all about it until this morning and then he'd decided to read it before he met her and Timothy at the venue. It would give them a bit of common ground, perhaps, if he could tell her he'd read one of her pieces in the newspaper. He'd read all the way through looking for her name, then he'd found this in the Femail section. 'Almost a Bride', it was titled, supposedly written by Paige Stevens. It was quite funny too; he'd smiled as she'd described her snobby interfering soon-to-be mother-in-law, her secret mocha drinking and chocolate nibbling, her fiancé who was too busy to deal with the wedding. As he read through he'd

71

started to wonder if it was written by Cassie, and then he'd come to the bit about the wedding photographer being her ex-boyfriend and he'd known it was. It had to be. She was taking a chance writing personal stuff like this. She was even asking readers to vote whether she told her fiancé about her affair with the photographer or not. He knew this was fairly common stuff for a journalist, they'd sell their granny down the river to get a story, but Timothy Campbell didn't strike him as the sort of man who'd like his private life lightly mocked in the Saturday supplement pages of the local newspaper. Had he read it? And as she was writing about it did that mean Cassie had told him about them? He had a meeting with them both soon and had no idea how to react.

He tossed the paper onto the coffee table and walked over to the window. He hadn't been looking forward to meeting Cassie and her fiancé again, and after seeing her wedding diary in the paper he was looking forward to it even less. This was something he could do without. He sighed. The last thing he expected when he took this job was to bump into Cassie, never mind be asked to take the photographs of her wedding. He just had to get through it the best he could and remind himself that it all added to his Arctic fund.

He picked up his Nikon and slipped a couple of spare lenses in the case. He wanted to get a couple of shots of the venue so he could study them and consider the best locations and angles. He was a perfectionist at the best of times, but this was Cassie's wedding, and he was determined that the photos would be fantastic. His pride wouldn't allow him to do any less.

Cassie's wedding. He'd wondered over the years if she'd got married, had a couple of kids, maybe. Sometimes, when he'd been waiting all day for 'the perfect shot', his mind had drifted to Cassie and remembered how happy they'd been, how in love. There had been times he'd wondered if he'd done the right thing by walking away. Then the animal he'd been waiting for had appeared, he'd got the shot he wanted, and he knew that he'd made the right decision. They'd been too young. If they'd married back then he'd have never been able to fulfil his dream and would have resented it, he was sure.

They weren't too young now. He was thirty soon and Cassie just a year younger. Supposedly the right age for settling down; except he'd still got such a lot to do. It's a good job she is marrying someone else, he decided, as he packed his camera into the small black leather holdall he always took to photo shoots. It would be so easy to fall for her all over again. And that's the last thing he wanted.

Nine

It was beautiful, Cassie thought, as she pulled up in the car park in the grounds of Hollington Castle. The castle, built on the ruins of a former medieval castle destroyed in the Civil War, was very French in design, thanks to the influence of Lord Hollington's French wife, Colette. She couldn't even guess how many rooms it had, but judging by the row of windows across the front it was at least twenty and of course there would be rooms at the back and sides, too. The majestic building was surrounded by an immaculate lawn, a spectacular water fountain, orchards, and flower gardens.

It was the middle of May now, so the flowers were blooming, the trees bursting with green leaves. Everywhere looked so fresh. She imagined herself pulling up outside in a horse and carriage – actually, she'd only just thought of the horse and carriage: she had been planning a sleek white limo but looking at the castle now, a horse and carriage was far more suitable. She imagined the guests arriving, parking in the huge grounds, gazing at the picturesque white building with its fairytale towers and balustrades, wandering around the immaculate lawned gardens with the fragrant flower borders. She imagined the photos taken over by the fountain, in the wonderful summerhouse, or standing by the lake. If only Timothy was with her today. It didn't seem right to be showing Jared around alone. Maybe she should have asked Sylvia to come as Timothy had suggested.

'It's beautiful. A perfect place for a wedding.'

She jumped at the sound of Jared's voice behind her, turned, and almost collided with him. He was so near she could smell his aftershave, the tang of his own male scent. One more step and she would be in his arms. Instinctively, she took a step back.

'Sorry, I didn't mean to startle you.' He looked around. 'Where's your fiancé?'

'Oh, er, Timothy couldn't make it.' Stop stammering and pull yourself together. 'He's got an important court case coming up so had to meet a new client. Obviously he'd have come if he could. That's not a problem, is it? I can show you around. It won't take long.' Great, she'd stopped stammering and was now rambling instead. Why did she have to sound – and probably look – so nervous? Whereas Jared looked perfectly relaxed: his hands in the pocket of his beige chinos, his white no-collar shirt unbuttoned at the neck, revealing a smattering of dark curly hair. Still the same Jared, she thought. His clothes might be designer but he wore them with his trademark casualness.

And he still oozed with sex appeal.

He grinned, the familiar lop-sided grin she remembered so well, and she felt the years fall away. It was as if they were twenty-one again.

'Not a problem at all. In fact, it might be nice to have a couple of hours alone to catch up. I find it difficult acting like we've never met, but if that's the way you want to play it then that's fine by me.'

'I'm not *playing* anything,' she retorted. 'It just took me by surprise seeing you when I first walked in. I decided it would be best not to say anything until I told Timothy. I didn't want him to find out second-hand from his mother.'

'Find out what? That your ex was going to photograph your wedding? An ex that you had a long relationship with, who had …' he made quote symbols with his fingers, "Broken your heart and you'd forgotten to mention to him?"'

Oh shit, he'd read her article. She stared at him dumbfounded, her feelings quickly changing to mortification as she watched him take a copy of the paper out of his bag, and open it at her column. '"Almost a Bride" by Paige Stevens. Very entertaining. I know it's your column, so don't deny it.'

Damn Owen! She glared at Jared. 'Yes, OK. It's my bloody column, but it's been hijacked by my editor. I didn't write all that stuff. It wasn't meant to be published like that. Owen saw a chance to improve the circulation figures and seized it. He didn't even run it by me.'

Jared tilted his head to one side. 'Well, where did he get the information from? How did he know about us?' A smile played on his lips. 'Your portrayal of Sylvia is very good, by the way.'

This was so embarrassing. There was no way she was going to admit to him that any of the stuff she wrote was true. 'The sub-editor uploaded the wrong file by mistake. I'd just made a mock-diary because the wedding diary he wanted me to write sounded so boring. When I was away from my desk the sub-editor saw it on my screen, thought it was the proper column, and subbed it. I didn't even know about the mistake until I read Saturday's paper.' She crossed her arms and scowled at him. 'So don't go reading anything into it. I am so over you.'

'I'm glad to hear that, as you're getting married in a couple of months.' His expression softened. 'For what it's worth, I'm sorry for the way I left. For breaking your heart. If I did,' he added quickly.

'You didn't.' She snapped. *You smashed it into smithereens, shattered it almost beyond repair.*

'I'm pleased to hear that, really I am.' He sounded sincere. 'And have you told Timothy about us yet? Because if he reads this column he'll soon find out.'

'No, not yet. It's no big deal. We went out for a few years when we were kids. End of. Timothy and I don't feel the need to tell each other about every relationship we've had. We're far too adult for that.' There, that told him. 'Anyway, he never reads any of my stuff, so he won't see it. After this week the column will return to a normal wedding diary. I've put Owen straight on that.'

'I bet you have. Although it might not be popular with the readers. According to the internet poll the majority want you to tell Ian about me. I get the impression they're eager to see what happens when he finds out.' A smile played on his lips. 'One reader even suggested that you dump Ian for me.'

She shot him a furious glance. 'As if! Now can we please stop talking about that stupid column and get on with discussing my wedding photographs? Which is what you're here for.'

He shrugged. 'Sure. Lead the way.'

She flounced off, determined to keep a few steps in front of him. This was an impossible situation. Why hadn't she organised the photographs herself instead of allowing Sylvia to take over? Then she remembered; it was because trying to stop Sylvia from doing something was like trying to stop a tornado.

'Look, I'm sorry. I didn't mean to upset you.' Jared caught up with her, matching his stride to hers, so they walked along the driveway together. 'You're right. It's all in the past. No need for anyone to know. I need this job and you need a good photographer at short notice. And I am good.' He said this with no hint of conceit.

'I know you are. I've seen some of your photos.' That's right, Cassie, let him know you've been following his career.

'Good. Then can we agree to start again. Move forward on a bride-to-be and wedding photographer basis. Strictly business?' He held out his hand.

She blanked it and kept her gaze fixed firmly ahead, keeping her voice crisp and polite. 'That seems the most sensible thing to do.'

Tessa, the receptionist, greeted her with a big smile. 'Miss Tyler. How lovely to see you again.' She looked beyond her, questioningly. 'Is Mr Campbell not with you today?'

'No, he's working. This is our wedding photographer, Jar ... J.M. As I mentioned on the phone he'd like to look around the venue and take some preliminary photos.'

'That's absolutely no problem. I'll just let Katrina know you're here. If you wouldn't mind taking a seat for a moment.'

'Of course.' Cassie walked over to the plush green velveteen seats and sat down on one. Jared took the seat opposite.

'I take it Katrina's the one who deals with the wedding bookings?' he said.

'Yes, she's lovely. She'll show us around and you can ask her any questions you want. Timothy and I have thought of a few ideas for photos, but obviously you're the expert.'

'Not at weddings,' he admitted. 'But I promise your photos will be spectacular.'

'Good to see you again, Cassie.' Cassie looked up as Katrina walked over to them, her face wreathed in a welcoming smile. 'What a shame Timothy couldn't make it, but I'm sure we can manage between us.' Katrina was über-friendly, and had quickly established first name terms when they'd had their first appointment to look around the château, and surprisingly, Timothy – who always liked to be treated with a bit of respect and deference – hadn't objected. 'You must be the photographer.' She beamed at Jared.

He stood up and shook her outstretched hand. 'J.M. of I.D. Images. Pleased to meet you. You've a lovely place here. The ideal venue for a wedding.'

'Thank you, we pride ourselves on being one of the more exclusive wedding venues,' Katrina said. 'We like to offer our client a professional service that ensures their wedding day is full of wonderful memories.'

'Indeed.' Jared nodded. 'Now can you talk me through the day? Show me the entrance where the bride – and groom – come in? The room where the ceremony is actually taking place? The reception area?' He turned to Cassie. 'Will you want some pre-wedding photos in your room? Some of you and the bridesmaids getting ready?'

It was surreal, Jared photographing her getting ready for her wedding. Sod it, if he could handle it so could she. 'I don't think so ...' she hesitated. It might be a nice touch. 'Well, maybe a couple but we'd like most of the photos of the wedding itself.' She turned to Katrina. 'Would you mind taking us on a tour so we can discuss the best locations for shots?'

'Certainly. Let's start with the chapel where the ceremony takes place, shall we?' Katrina led the way.

Cassie had loved the little chapel in the grounds when Katrina had shown it them on their first visit, and that had been a dull, grey day. Today, with the sun glistening on the lake behind the chapel and dancing over the sparkling stained glass windows, it looked almost magical. It was all she could do not to clap her hands and squeal in delight. Jared seemed impressed too, and spent several minutes working out the best angles for the shots.

'I'm presuming you want photographs of the wedding service?' he asked. 'Will it be a civil ceremony?'

'A civil ceremony then a blessing. One of my friends is a lay preacher and will do the blessing for us.' Sylvia had been outraged when she mentioned it.

'A woman priest? And not even from the established church,' she'd protested, but to Cassie's relief Timothy had come down on her side.

'If it's important to Cassie then it's fine by me,' he'd said. Cassie could have hugged him. Sylvia had been quietly furious.

The chapel was small but beautiful, with vases of flowers strategically placed, and a huge stained glass window at the front of the church, where the sun shone through and illuminated the exact spot where the bride and groom would be standing. The ceremony being held here would make the wedding so special.

Jared walked around, stopping every now and again to look through his camera, obviously assessing the best position for photos. Cassie stood at the altar, imagining her and Timothy standing there, saying their vows, promising to love each other forever.

Forever was a long time.

'Roughly how many guests are you expecting?' Jared called, interrupting her thoughts.

Roughly? She knew exactly. Timothy had set the limit. 'It's a small private ceremony for family only, so twenty-five. There'll be eighty guests at the reception, though.'

'Are you staying here the night before?'

She shook her head. Timothy and Sylvia had wanted her to but she didn't want to be alone in this castle. She thought it would be far more relaxing to be at home with all her things around her. Sylvia was appalled. 'You can't be serious, dear.

It's bad luck for the groom to see the bride before the wedding,' she'd pointed out. Surprisingly, Sam had agreed.

'Come and stay at mine,' she'd offered. 'Paul won't mind, he'll stay over at his brother's. They love a chance to watch footy and drink a few beers.' Cassie had readily accepted.

'No, I'm staying at Sam's, she's a friend,' she added, then realised that she didn't need to explain who Sam was. Jared would remember her. They were all at college together.

He did, she could see by the smile in his eyes. 'How are you arriving?'

'In a horse and carriage,' she told him, crossing her fingers as she'd only decided that this morning, and wasn't sure whether she'd be able to find one in time, although Sylvia was bound to know someone.

'Nice.' He nodded approvingly. 'We'll have some shots of you arriving, then stepping out of the carriage. Some of the guests arriving ...' He rattled off a list of suggestions for photos and Katrina oohed and aahed, clearly impressed. Cassie was impressed too. It was obvious that Jared was a professional and would ensure they had some fabulous photos of their special day.

When they'd seen everything Jared needed to see, they returned back to the reception where Katrina showed them to a private table in the corner. 'I'll leave you to discuss the photographs further,' she said. 'Would you both like coffee?'

'Please, milk and one sugar,' Jared told her.

'Black ...' Cassie hesitated as Jared raised his eyebrow questioningly, the corners of his lips lifting into a playful smile. Damn it, he'd read her column and knew her secret sugar and chocolate consumption. 'The same, please,' she said.

'Better not let Timothy and Sylvia know,' he teased as Katrina went off to get the coffees.

'Oh, shut up!' She retorted, then seeing the twinkle in his eye she couldn't help breaking into a grin. Honestly, he made her feel like a naughty schoolgirl.

It was a mistake to let her guard down and smile at him, because now he leant forward and held her with his gaze. 'It's been a long time, Cassie. How have you been?' He sounded like he genuinely wanted to know.

She really didn't want to do this. 'Fine. How about you? Is wedding photography your new direction?'

'Only temporarily, until I've earned enough to fund a visit to the Arctic.'

Still the same old Jared, dashing off all over the world to take photographs. The next words were out of her mouth before she could stop herself. 'I take it you aren't married then? Or you have a very independent wife.'

'Nope, still single and fancy free. I don't think my job fits with married life.' He looked at her seriously. 'If it did, I would have married you.'

She was stunned. She stared at him wordlessly, trying to find suitable words to reply. Why did he have to say that?

'I'm sorry, Cassie. I know I hurt you, but honestly, if we'd stayed together you'd have been hurt even more. This job, it's in my blood. I need to do it as much as I need to eat, to breathe.' Finally, she forced a brittle smile on her face. 'Forget it, it was years ago. We were just kids. If we'd have stayed together I'd never have met Timothy, would I? And he's the love of my life.'

For a fleeting moment she thought she saw pain in Jared's eyes, but then it was gone. 'I'm so pleased for you. Really, I am. I've felt guilty about how I let you down for years but now I can be at peace about it. Let's put it all behind us and get on with the job you're paying me for.' He rummaged in his bag for his notebook. 'I'll make a few notes so I know exactly what you want. Do you want me to get them typed up and sent to you so you can run it all by Timothy?'

'No, he's left organising the photographs to me.'

'You and Sylvia?' Jared gave her a lopsided grin and she giggled.

'Definitely not, she's taken over enough. This is my call.'

It was as if a cloud had lifted. Suddenly they were talking and laughing together as they had years ago. Katrina arrived with the coffees, so Jared read his notes out to them both.

'How does it all sound?' He looked questioningly from Cassie to Katrina.

'Wonderful.' Katrina clasped her hands and smiled broadly, her eyes wide as she gazed at Jared. She obviously had the hots for him. Not that Cassie was jealous, Jared had always had that effect on women.

'Cassie. What do you think?' Jared's voice cut through her thoughts.

'Perfect,' she nodded in agreement. Her wedding day was going to be perfect.

They walked back to the car park together, still chatting easily. She'd always loved the way she and Jared had been so relaxed in each other's company. They'd been able to talk about anything. Timothy could be loving and attentive at times, but he wasn't much of a talker. He was quite a serious person and didn't really indulge in 'idle chatter'. His conversations were always about something. Which wasn't a bad thing, of course, but she and Jared had always seen the absurdity in things and had their own crazy sense of humour.

'I'm glad we cleared the air. I've got to admit I was a bit worried about doing this job,' Jared told her. 'I feel better about it now. And look, I'm sorry I teased you about the newspaper article. If you don't want to tell Timothy, it's up to you. As you say, it was years ago.'

'I think it's probably best not to tell him now. It would only complicate things. Do you mind? Will it make you feel awkward?'

'Not at all. It's your call.' They were standing by his car now. 'Hang on a minute, I've just remembered that I brought a couple of the photo albums with me for you to look through. It'll give you an idea of the designs we can do. I was expecting Timothy with you so I thought we could look through them together and decide today.'

'Oh great, I meant to phone and ask you to bring some.' She frowned. 'I wouldn't really like to choose without Timothy's input though, it should be a joint decision. Could I possibly take them home with me or do you need them?'

'Of course, take them.' He opened the car boot and picked up a bag. 'They're in here.' He handed the bag to Cassie. 'Could you bring them back to the office within the next week?'

'Sure. I can bring them next Thursday morning. Is that soon enough?'

'Perfect.' Jared leant over and kissed her on the cheek. 'See you soon. I'm glad you're happy.' Then he opened the car door and slid into the seat, leaving her cheek tingling and her senses reeling. Why had he done that? Just when she'd managed to convince herself that she had no feelings for him any more.

Why had he kissed her and ruined everything? Jared thought furiously as he drove off. The day had gone so well. Yes, it'd been awkward at first, Cassie had been a bit frosty with him, but she'd finally started to relax and they'd slipped into their old, chatty style of bantering, bouncing off each other. He'd really enjoyed her company, and felt that he could handle doing this. Then he'd gone and spoiled it all by kissing her. OK, it was only a peck, but the feel of his lips on her skin had seared through him, and it had been all he could do not to take her in his arms and kiss her on the lips. What the hell was the matter with him?

It was being with her again, it brought back memories. He'd forgotten how gorgeous she was, how funny, how crazy. How special. Well, he had to forget all over again because he'd had his chance and he'd turned it down. It wasn't right for him to walk into her life and mess it up again. Especially when he was planning on walking back out again; seeing as he couldn't seem to trust himself from now on, he'd better make sure he was never alone with her.

The sooner this wedding was over, and he could say goodbye to Cassie again, the better.

It was a peck on the cheek, no big deal, Cassie told herself. The shiver that had run all down her spine, the almost uncontrollable urge to wind her arms around his neck and snog him like mad, had stunned her for a moment. It rendered her unable to move, to speak, but he'd simply got into his car and driven off.

Obviously the kiss hadn't had the same traumatic effect on him that it had on her.

She took a deep breath. She was seriously over-reacting. People kissed each other on the cheek all the time. Jared was merely being polite, showing her that they'd now moved on to a friendly, professional level. That the past was forgotten.

But boy, did he still have an effect on her.

Ten

When she got into the office the next morning, Owen was waiting for her.

'This isn't good enough, Cassie. You need to redo it.' Owen thrust the 'Almost a Bride' column Cassie had sent over yesterday morning on the desk in front of her. She could tell by the way his chin was wobbling that he was angry.

'What's wrong with it?' she asked. She'd actually been quite pleased with it. She'd kept to the same chatty, personal tone of the previous column, with the odd mention of her 'monster-in-law' and other difficulties, but had deliberately kept Blake out of it, merely mentioning at the beginning that Blake had decided he didn't want to photograph her wedding so someone else from the company was doing it. It was a lively, interesting piece with plenty of personal interest, so Owen had no reason to complain. 'They will be interested in reading about the wedding dresses I tried on and helping me choose which one to buy.' They didn't need to know that she'd already chosen her dress – the voting option had been popular last week and she wanted to continue with it, so decided to ask the readers to vote for one of three dresses. 'Women understand what a nightmare it is trying to find the right dress. They'll- love to be involved in the decision.'

'They might have been if you'd started off that way. But you didn't,' Owen reminded her. 'So now they're interested in the triangle between you, Ian, and Blake. They voted for you to keep Blake as your photographer and to tell Ian. You've got rid of him.'

'The readers will soon forget about Blake,' she said. 'They'll be too busy wondering what my interfering monster-in-law does next and whether I'll manage to plan the wedding in time.'

Owen sighed. 'You've set this up now, Cassie, and the readers are gagging to find out what happens next with Paige and Blake. If you don't give them what they want they'll walk, and I can't afford to lose any more sales.'

'I'm not doing it.' Cassie folded her arms resolutely.

'Then I'll write the bloody column myself.'

What! He couldn't! 'You promised that you wouldn't alter my work again.'

'I won't alter your work. I'll take you off the column and I'll write it. It'll be *my* work. It's my bloody paper, I make the decisions.'

For a moment they locked gazes, then Owen sighed, pulled out the chair next to her and sat down. 'Look, Cassie, this was supposed to be a fictional column about a couple who were getting married. To get us a bit of female interest. You were the one who took it and made it personal.'

'I was messing around. Gary subbed the wrong file. You know that.'

'Everything you write in this office is copyright of the newspaper,' Owen reminded her. 'You shouldn't have been messing around. You should have been working. That's what you're paid to do.'

Silence swept over the office. She could feel everyone watching them, listening. Now she was telling the whole sodding office that her column was based on true facts. Damn. Damn. Damn.

'I think we'd better take this into my office, don't you?' Owen shoved the chair back, stood up, and marched over to his office.

Cassie shrugged her shoulders and raised her eyebrows so that anyone – make that *everyone* – who was watching would know that it was nothing to get het up about, and followed him into the office hoping that her cheeks weren't as red as they felt.

She came back out ten minutes later inwardly seething, having been forced to agree to continue with the column the way she'd been writing it, otherwise Owen 'Would write the bloody thing how he saw fit and she'd be covering flower and dog shows for the foreseeable future.'

Great. And she had an hour to write it or they wouldn't make the deadline for Saturday's paper. An hour to write something that included Jared – sorry, Blake – and didn't sound too much like her own life. Especially as she now knew that the man in question would probably be reading it. How did her life get so complicated?

A smile hovered over her lips. Well, she'd give him something to think about. She put her fingers on the keyboard and started to type.

Owen was delighted with it. 'That's better,' he said. 'I knew you'd come through.' He patted her on the shoulder. 'We've got another winner here, Cassie.'

Cassie smiled. She was pleased with herself. She just hoped Jared read it. That would show him that she was well and truly over him.

'He kissed you!' Sam gaped at her during lunchtime the next day. 'OMG, how did you feel? Do you still fancy him?'

'It was just a peck on the cheek,' Cassie told her, thankful that she'd waited until they'd sat down and put their lunch – cappuccino, chicken sandwich, and carrot cake for Sam, a mocha and salad wrap (less fattening than bread) for her – on the table, because Sam looked so shocked she would probably have dropped the tray. 'And no, I do not. Actually, I've decided, I don't want Jared photographing our wedding. I've got to talk Sylvia into choosing another photographer, so I need your help. I need to think of a convincing reason why I don't want to use Jared.'

'You sure you're over him? You were pretty devastated when he ditched you.'

89

Cassie felt herself blush as Sam scrutinised her face. 'Sam, watch my lips. I do not fancy Jared!' She declared forcibly. 'Yes, I was upset, I was a kid. It was eons ago. I realise now that it was for the best. I'm marrying Timothy. I love Timothy, not Jared.'

Sam took a forkful of her cake and chewed it slowly, as if considering it. Cassie tried not to drool as she watched her. Only the thought of her lovely, slim-line dress which fitted her like a glove gave her the strength to resist the urge to go and order herself a slice of carrot cake too.

'OK, I believe you. But I think you're right. You should get another photographer if you can.'

'What do you mean, if I can? Of course I'll be able to. Do you realise how many wedding photographers there are?'

'Good wedding photographers are booked up months, sometimes over a year, in advance. You might not be able to find another photographer who can do that date, especially one of the same calibre as I.D. Images. There's no point getting rid of this one before you have a suitable replacement.'

That made sense. 'I'll make some phone calls this afternoon when I'm back at the office,' Cassie told her. Surely someone among her network of contacts would know a wedding photographer. Then a thought occurred to her. 'When I find someone, what do I tell Timothy and his mother without making them suspicious?'

'How about I.D. Images have a brilliant reputation, but Jared's just joined the firm? Tell them you were a bit worried that he isn't experienced enough at wedding photography.'

'I knew you'd come up with something,' Cassie grinned. She leant over and spooned a corner of Sam's carrot cake.

'Hey, what about your wedding dress?' Sam reminded her.

'One teeny forkful won't hurt.' Cassie savoured the morsel of cake in her mouth for a moment before swallowing it. She hated this dieting lark. She couldn't wait until the wedding was over and she could get back to her normal size twelve figure.

'I've asked Emma and Amanda to join us tomorrow, with the girls. I need to make sure all the dresses match.' She and Sam had planned on choosing the maid of honour dress.

'We'd better start shopping early,' Sam told her. 'Meet you in Hutchins at ten.'

'Perfect. I'll phone Emma and Amanda tonight and let them know,' Cassie said.

Back at the office she made a succession of increasingly frantic calls to photographers – which she could quite truthfully tell Owen was research for her column – but they all proved fruitless. Everyone was booked. If she heard the astonished question 'June *this* year?' One more time, she'd scream down the phone. She had to admit, Sylvia had pulled a blinder by booking I.D. Images. She could find them a small-town photographer, of course, but what excuse could she give for dropping Jared in favour of such small fry? And she was quite sure that even if she initially managed to get Timothy on side, Sylvia would veto it and talk him out of it. It seemed she was stuck with Jared.

She dialled Sam's number and told her.

'Can't you swap to one of the other photographers in the firm?' Sam asked. 'Tell Sylvia that you wanted someone more experienced.'

'I can't, they're already booked for that day. That's why they've taken Jared on. I'm going to have to put up with him, I've got no choice.'

'So will you 'fess up to Timothy about your dark past?'

Cassie frowned at Sam's jesting tone. This was no laughing matter. 'I've thought about it but I can't. Not now. It will be too awkward and he'll wonder why I didn't tell him before.'

'Then you'd better make sure you're not alone with Jared again. We don't want a repeat of today – or worse, him giving you a proper snog,' Sam said firmly.

'As if!' Cassie retorted, indignantly. An unwanted image of Jared taking her in his arms and kissing her soundly on the lips, tracing a trail down her neck, her throat, like he used to do swept across her mind. She pushed it away. She was marrying Timothy. She wasn't going to waste any more time thinking about Jared. He was history.

She needed to get home to Timothy, wrap her arms around him, and remind herself how much they loved each other. Thank goodness he was home early tonight so they could finally spend some time together.

However, when she got home she found Sylvia seated on the sofa next to Timothy, sipping a small wine. A delicious aroma wafted out from the kitchen.

'Ah, Cassandra, we expected you home ages ago, didn't we, Timothy?' Sylvia said reproachfully as Cassie walked in. 'I've brought a casserole for us to eat, I cooked it earlier. I know you're too busy to cook in the evenings.' She put her glass down and gracefully got to her feet. 'You freshen up, dear, while I lay the table and dish up. Then you can tell us how your meeting with the photographer went.'

Timothy stood up and wrapped his arms around Cassie as Sylvia disappeared into the kitchen. 'Sorry, sweetheart, Mother arrived just after I got home. I know we planned to have the evening together, but she wanted to check we're happy with the photographer seeing as she booked him for us.' He gave Cassie a kiss on the cheek. 'You don't mind, do you?'

He really was sweet, Cassie thought, and it wasn't his fault his mother was such an interfering old busy-body.

'Of course not,' she reassured him.

Eleven

Jared took the paper he'd just bought out of his bag and turned to Cassie's column. He couldn't wait to read her interpretation of Wednesday's events.

Almost a Bride

Well, most of you voted that I tell Ian about Blake and I'm going to do just that this evening. I can't believe I got so worked up about Blake being the wedding photographer. It's no big deal. We had a look around the venue this week and it was all very relaxed. He even gave me a peck on the cheek as we said goodbye and I didn't feel a thing. I'm so over him.

She went on to describe her humorous attempts to find a wedding dress, and gave a selection of wedding dresses for the reader to vote for the one they liked best. It was all very light-hearted and amusing. And there was no doubt about it: Cassie was telling him that she had no feelings for him. She knew he had read her column last week and would probably read it this week, too. She wanted him to know that she was indifferent to him, that it didn't matter to her that he was photographing her wedding. Well, he got the message loud and clear. It didn't matter to him either. He could handle it. It was just another job as far as he was concerned. He'd got over Cassie a long time ago. He threw the newspaper in the bin and picked up his camera. He had another photography session to go to.

Amanda and Estelle were already in Hutchins when Cassie arrived, and Emma and Sophia arrived a few minutes later. So they all had a coffee – milkshake for the girls – while they waited for Sam.

'Have you decided on the colour scheme yet?' Emma asked, leaning across to quickly upright the milkshake Sophia had spilt before it spread all over the table.

'Yes, we thought sky blue for the bridesmaids' dresses and Timothy will wear a silk tie of the same shade,' Cassie replied. Blue was her favourite colour.

'Sky blue, that's an unusual choice,' Amanda remarked.

'It's a soft, pastel shade. It'll look pretty,' Emma said. 'Are you having blue in your bouquet as well?'

'Blue, ivory, and a touch of pale pink. I've got a picture of the one I want here.' Cassie rummaged in her handbag and took out a crumpled picture she'd cut out of a magazine. 'What do you think?'

'It's beautiful,' Emma agreed. 'Have you booked a florist yet?'

'Sylvia's organised one.' Just like she's organised everything else, including Jared to be their photographer. 'I'm going to see her on Thursday afternoon.'

'So what's left to do?' Asked Amanda.

'Let me see,' Cassie ticked them off one by one on her fingers. 'Wedding cake, table decorations, favours, buffet, evening entertainment. Horse and carriage.' She looked up.

'I didn't know you were having a horse and carriage,' Emma said. 'That'll be lovely. You're so lucky, Cassie.' Emma made no secret of the fact she thought Cassie had landed on her feet marrying Timothy. She and Simon had only been able to afford a small wedding.

'Well, I haven't booked it yet,' Cassie replied. 'It's on my to-do list.'

'Simon's friend's brother hires them out. Do you want me to find out the cost and see if they've got any available on your wedding date?' Emma offered.

'Please,' Cassie smiled. 'Now, have I covered everything? Is there anything I've forgotten?'

'Honeymoon?' Emma suggested.

'Timothy's dealing with that. He wants it to be a surprise.'

'Well, that sounds about it then,' declared Emma. 'All sorted.'

'I must say, you're very brave planning a wedding at such short notice.' Amanda took a pack of baby wipes out of her handbag and cleaned Estelle's banana milkshake-covered mouth. 'It took Daniel and I two years to plan our wedding, and I was still running frantically around in the weeks beforehand, trying to make sure everything went according to plan.'

Cassie remembered Amanda and Daniel's wedding. She hadn't been going out with Timothy long, and it was their first official engagement as a couple. It had taken her ages to decide what to wear. In fact, Timothy had picked up on her indecision and suggested she ask Sylvia to go shopping with her and help her choose. Gratefully, she'd done just that. The elegant, silver-grey, lace dress Sylvia had selected for her had been perfect for the society wedding, but unfortunately had set the precedent for Sylvia taking over under the guise of 'guiding her'. It had taken all her guile and patience to talk Sylvia out of coming along to help choose the bridesmaids' dresses. Cassie was determined to pick them herself, and although she hadn't got a clear picture in her mind, she'd know instantly when she'd spotted the dresses she wanted.

Sam came rushing over, long, blonde hair flying behind her. 'Sorry I'm late. My bloody car wouldn't start. It's a good job Paul was home.'

'Sam, you've met Amanda, Timothy's sister, haven't you?' Both Sam and Amanda had been at a dinner party Timothy and Cassie hosted last year. 'This is her daughter Estelle, my other flower girl.'

'Hiya,' Sam flashed Amanda a big smile, pulled out a chair, and sat down. 'How are you, Emma?' she asked, turning to Cassie's sister.

'I'm good,' Emma said, smiling. 'How about you and Paul? Are you tying the knot yet?'

'Happy as we are at the mo, but one day.' Sam looked over at Cassie. 'Still blue, is it?'

'Definitely,' Cassie told her. 'Do you want a coffee before we go?'

'No, I've delayed you all long enough. Let's go tackle those shops and find ourselves some bridesmaids' dresses.'

Estelle spotted a dress she liked in the first shop they went to. White with lots of frills, very girly. She headed for it instantly, clutched it, and refused to put it down.

'I want it. Please, Mummy,' she begged. 'I'll look like a princess in this.'

'It's up to Auntie Cassie, darling, it's her wedding,' Amanda told her.

Estelle turned her puppy dog eyes beseechingly at Cassie. 'Please, Auntie Cassie.'

Cassie felt like a total heel as she shook her head. 'Sorry, darling, but I want my bridesmaids to be dressed in blue. We'll get you a pretty dress, I promise.'

Estelle's face crumpled and she burst into tears. 'I don't like blue!' She wailed.

'I do,' said Sophia. 'Blue's my favourite colour.'

'That's not fair!' Estelle stamped her feet.

Cassie sighed as Amanda tried to console her daughter. This was going to be quite a day!

Estelle scowled every time she tried on a blue dress, constantly complaining that she wanted to wear a white dress, while Sophia loved every dress she tried on and didn't want to take it off. Cassie was beginning to wish she'd chosen older bridesmaids. Young ones might look cute but they sure were a handful.

Then Sam came to the rescue, picking out a gorgeous white dress with a blue sash and blue silk petals sewn into the hem. 'What about this?' she asked.

Both Estelle and Sophia immediately loved the dress. They squealed in delight and clapped their hands.

'They're gorgeous,' Cassie agreed. The blue was the exact shade that she wanted. True, she'd been planning the dresses to be completely blue, but the dresses really were pretty with lacy cap sleeves and lots of white net. And both girls loved them and looked wonderful in them.

'I need a dress for my maid of honour in the same shade of blue,' she told the sales assistant. 'Could you do that?'

'I certainly can.' The assistant walked off and returned a few minutes later with three long bridesmaids' dresses over her arm – the exact same shade of blue as the sashes and petals in the flower girl dresses.

They all sat down and waited while Sam tried on the dresses. She came out wearing each one in turn and parading around like a model, making them all giggle. With her blonde hair, blue eyes, pale skin, and English rose good looks, Sam looked lovely in any bright colour, but this delicate shade of blue really suited her. All three dresses were gorgeous, but the second one, a strapless dress with a sweetheart neckline and long A-line skirt, made her look stunning.

'That's the one,' Cassie nodded.

'Sammie looks like a princess,' Sophia squealed, clapping her hands in delight. 'Can I put my dress on again?'

'Good idea, then I can see how you all look together,' Cassie agreed.

So the two little girls went off with their mums to get changed again.

'Now we all look like princesses,' Estelle said as they stood each side of Sam.

It was true, they did. And such a contrast too, Estelle with her long, dark hair, and Sam and Sophie with blonde hair.

'The photos are going to be stunning,' Amanda said. 'Who's your photographer?'

'We're using I.D. Images,' Cassie told her.

'Wow! They're amazing. You're lucky to have got them at such short notice,' Emma said, clearly impressed. 'I would have thought they'd be booked up months ahead.'

'Timothy's mother knows one of the partners and heard they had a cancellation,' Cassie replied.

'That's just like Mum.' Amanda gave Cassie a knowing look. 'If she gets too much, politely put your foot down. It's your wedding. She drove me mad when I was planning mine.'

Cassie was surprised to learn that Amanda found her mother's irritating ways annoying too. 'Oh, she's OK. She means well,' she mumbled, not wanting to be running Sylvia down to her own daughter.

'She does, but she can be OTT sometimes, so politely rein her in if you have to,' Amanda said with a grin. 'I do!'

She's your mother, Cassie thought. Easier said than done when she's your almost mother-in-law. She knew Amanda was right though, she would have to start putting her foot down with Sylvia if she didn't back off once she and Timothy were married. Still, she'd deal with that when she had to.

The sales assistant was fussing around, checking the dresses. 'They all fit fine,' she said. 'There's usually a three-month wait for all our dresses, but I can rush these through in four weeks. You'll have to leave a deposit, of course,' she said to Cassie. 'It's lucky you didn't leave it any later or you'd have to make do with buying them off the peg.' She shuddered as if the thought was too horrible to contemplate.

'That only gives us two weeks before the wedding,' Amanda said. 'What if we need anything altered?'

'Unless anyone puts on or loses weight, we won't need any alterations. I've measured them exactly,' the assistant told her, then turned to Cassie again. 'If you do need alterations, we can rush them through but it will mean an additional expense, of course.'

'That won't be a problem,' Cassie assured her. 'Do you have a small sample of material that I could use to match accessories? My fiancé wants a tie in the same colour.'

'Yes, we keep a sample book for that very reason.' The assistant took a folder from under the counter and flipped through the pages. 'Here you are; I'll give you two. You might need one to match the flowers or other accessories.' She pulled two squares of blue silky material out of a clear folder and slipped them into a small paper bag. 'Our designers always supply us with sample squares. It's so important to match the colours, isn't it?'

'Thank you.' Cassie handed over the card Timothy had given her for the wedding account to pay the deposit and slipped the bag containing the colour samples into her handbag.

Next stop was the Tiara Palace, a quaint little shop down a narrow side street which specialised in custom-made tiaras. There were some amazing tiaras on display and it took a while to make a decision, but eventually Cassie ordered pretty silver tiara combs for the flower girls with tiny sparkling blue crystals, a matching tiara for Sam, and an exquisite peak diamante tiara for herself.

'Are you wearing a veil?' The assistant asked.

This was something Cassie hadn't made her mind up about yet. Sylvia was keen for her to, telling her it was traditional, but she wasn't sure.

'I haven't decided yet,' she said. 'Will this tiara be suitable both with and without a veil?'

'Yes, it can be worn either way,' the assistant assured her. 'If you can put down a deposit today I'll order these three for you. They'll be ready in a couple of weeks. Leave me your number and we'll phone you when they arrive.'

'You should do a feature on weddings for your newspaper, Cassie,' Emma said as they left the shop. 'You must have plenty of material seeing as you're planning your own wedding. I bet lots of women would be interested in a feature like that.'

Cassie frantically tried to think of what to reply when Sam cut in. 'Someone else is already covering that, aren't they, Cass?'

'Really? I'll have to read it. There might be some interesting tips in it,' Amanda said.

Great, now Amanda would be reading the column too so she had to make sure she didn't put anything in it that would connect it to her. Otherwise her secret would be up. Trust Sam to open her mouth.

'Sorry,' Sam mumbled, sidling up to Cassie as they went to tackle the shoe shops. 'I thought it might give you a bit of cover if she ever reads it. She'll think it's someone else.'

Better go for different coloured bridesmaids' dresses and alter the day's events a bit for the column, just to be on the safe side, Cassie decided.

Twelve

Timothy turned off his computer, slipped his files in his case, and reached for his mobile. He'd finally finished work for the day. He glanced at his watch. Three thirty. Cassie would still be wedding shopping. She'd said she wanted to get the bridesmaids' dresses today, so he wasn't expecting her home until the shops closed.

The wedding was coming together well now, thanks mainly to his mother. The venue and photographer she'd chosen for them were perfect. The whole day would be perfect, if only he could persuade Cassie to allow his mother to have more input. Cassie liked to please him but she could be stubborn at times. He'd soon smooth that out once they were married.

He'd thought hard about asking her to marry him. Beautiful, talented, and with a pleasant, calm personality, he was sure that she would be an asset to him. True, her hostess skills needed polishing up a bit – Cassie's idea of cooking was to grab something out of the freezer and put it in the microwave but his mother would help her with that, just like she was guiding her with the wedding. And yes, Cassie's dress sense was sometimes a little unusual, but she had such a sunny nature and was a delight to be with. All she needed was a bit of guidance, and his mother would do just that. She'd soon turn Cassie into the sort of wife he needed, someone with elegant dress sense, who could host dinner parties and be the ideal lawyer's wife. She would need to give up her job, of course, but he was confident that he could persuade her to freelance from home so she had more time to attend to his needs. Especially once they had a family. Two children would be ideal, hopefully a boy and girl.

His phone buzzed as a text message came through. 'Time for a coffee? Marco's? F x' Felicity. He was just about to text her. He smiled at the promise of spending a couple of hours in her company, knowing it would be at least six thirty before Cassie was home. 'Be there in twenty minutes' he texted back, then picked up his jacket and car keys.

'Did you get everything you wanted?' Timothy asked as Cassie staggered in loaded with bags later that evening. He'd only been home half an hour himself, just enough time to change out of his suit and into casual slacks and a T-shirt. He never wore jeans, he considered them too scruffy. He gave Cassie a peck on the cheek and took the bags off her. 'Am I allowed to look?'

'If you want to. It's only the shoes, stockings, and other bits and pieces. We've chosen the tiaras and dresses, but they won't be ready for a few weeks. You'll love them, they're gorgeous.' She followed him into the spare bedroom, which was now nicknamed the wedding room, and put the bags down on the bed. 'Look, this is the colour.' She opened her handbag and took out the bag containing the samples of material the assistant had given her. 'What do you think?'

'Perfect. That's the exact colour we agreed on. Well done. I'm sure I can get a tie made to match.'

She put one of the samples back in the bag and handed it to him. 'Perhaps you should keep it on you so you can sort it out.'

He out took his wallet and slipped the material inside, then put it back in his trouser pocket. 'I know it must have been a tiring day for you, but Felicity and Andrew have invited us over for drinks tonight. Of course I said I'd check with you first. Do you mind?' he asked, kissing her on the forehead.

Damn, all she wanted was to have a long soak in the bath, change into her pyjamas, and chill for the evening. She suppressed a sigh. Networking was important in Timothy's line of work and Felicity was a partner in the firm. 'Of course not. Do I have time for a quick bath to ease my aching bones?'

Timothy wrapped his arms around her and kissed her. She entwined her arms around his neck, returning the kiss. 'You do. I'll bring you a glass of wine, shall I?'

'That would be lovely.'

Timothy brought in the glass of wine just as she'd slipped into the foaming bath water. 'If we weren't going out for the evening I'd be tempted to join you,' he said, bending over to kiss her on the nape of her neck. He placed the glass down on the cabinet besides the bath. 'As it is, I'd better control myself and leave you in peace.'

Timothy was so loving and thoughtful, Cassie thought, as he closed the door behind him. She was so lucky to be with him. She loved him so much. Not in the same way she'd loved Jared. The thought slipped into her mind uninvited, and instead of banishing it away she let it linger so she could think about it. It was true, Timothy's touch didn't electrify her the same way as Jared's had. When he kissed her, tingles didn't run down her spine, she didn't long to drag him into bed, make wild love to him. She fancied him, of course she did, and enjoyed making love with him, but she didn't have the same hot desire she'd felt for Jared. Young love, she reminded herself, as she sank into the bubbles. When you were young it was all about hormones and desire. She'd grown up now; she was ready for a steadier, adult relationship with someone who was kind and caring, like Timothy. Jared was her first love, of course she would have fond memories of him, but he was her past. Timothy was her future.

'Cassandra, how lovely to see you again.' Felicity leant forward and air-kissed Cassie's cheeks. 'How are the wedding arrangements coming on? Timothy tells me you were shopping for bridesmaids' dresses today.'

'Yes, tiaras and shoes too. It's all sorted,' Cassie told her.

'Excellent. I must say I was a bit worried you'd have to settle for something less than you'd like at such short notice. Weddings are usually planned at least a year in advance. It's not like Timothy to be so impulsive. Not that I blame you for wanting to rush him down the aisle. He's quite a catch.' There was no mistaking the meaning in her saccharine-dripped words and false red-lipsticked smile. 'Do let me take your coats.'

What a nerve, insinuating that she was trying to get a ring on her finger before Timothy changed his mind. Forcing a smile on her face, Cassie slipped out of her jacket and handed it to her. 'It was Sylvia's idea to have the wedding this year, actually. She heard there was a cancellation at Hollington Castle and suggested we take it.' She met Felicity's gaze. 'I must admit, we didn't intend to get married so soon, but as Timothy pointed out it seemed too good an opportunity to miss.'

'Hollington Castle?' Felicity sounded impressed. 'How wonderful, it is a charming place. I don't blame you for snapping it up, my dear. Andrew and I got married at Wilconse Abbey. A traditional service, but very beautiful. The photographs were out of this world.'

'Yes, I remember. We've booked I.D. Images and I must say I'm very impressed with them,' Timothy told her as she helped him out of his jacket.

'I.D.? Oh yes, Imogen and Daniel do a lot of society weddings. You've got quite a scoop there. It should be a wonderful day. I'll have to make sure my outfit is up to the occasion.'

'As if you would wear anything that wasn't both elegant and fashionable,' Timothy teased, kissing her on the cheek. Felicity twinkled with delight, then swept off to the cloakroom with their coats.

Cassie forced herself to take a deep breath. This was going to be a difficult evening. She felt awkward with Felicity, she was always so snidey – although when Cassie mentioned it to Timothy he said she was imagining it. She'd prefer Felicity and Andrew not to come to the wedding, but obviously Timothy felt obliged to invite them as Felicity was his business partner.

Felicity floated back. 'Do come and meet the others.' She led the way into the lounge, where two other couples were sitting around the large glass table, which was covered with a beautiful white lace tablecloth and laid with expensive black tableware. In the middle was a black vase of red roses. It looked stunning.

'Timothy, you know Suzanne and Philip of course. And this is Martina and Adrian. Timothy, Adrian is the chairman of the company, dealing with the new business development.' She turned around and, with a flourish, announced: 'Everyone, this is my business partner Timothy and his fiancée, Cassandra. Cassandra works for the local newspaper.'

The way she said it made Cassie feel like the office junior instead of one of the features writers.

'Oh, a journalist, how interesting,' Martina said. 'You must tell me if you've interviewed anyone famous.'

Before Cassie could reply, Andrew walked in with his customary beam on his face, his arms open wide for a hug. 'Cassie, darling. Delighted to see you again.' Andrew was a very touchy-feely person. It gave Cassie the creeps a bit but she told herself not to be silly, he was just being friendly. She turned her cheek for his customary kiss and quickly slipped out of the bear hug that was almost a clinch. 'Hello, Andrew.'

'Timothy, delighted you could come,' Andrew shook Timothy's outstretched hand.

'Now, would you like a glass of wine? Red or white?'

'Red, please,' Timothy replied. He turned to Cassie. 'Would you like red too, Cassandra?'

He wanted her to have red, too, then. Timothy thought red wine was superior to white but Cassie found it a bit heavy and preferred rosé, not that she would dream of saying so. If they were at home rosé was permissible, but Timothy considered it cheap so she never asked for it when they were out.

'Yes, please,' she said with a smile. She didn't want to embarrass Timothy. She knew how important these social functions were to him, although they always made her feel awkward and gauche. She wondered if she'd ever get used to them. A sudden vision of years of attending dinner parties with the likes of Felicity and Andrew, ignoring the veiled put-downs, forcing herself to drink red wine and making small talk with people she had no connection with, flashed across her mind and a wave of panic engulfed her. Is this what she really wanted?

As evenings went, it wasn't too bad. Martina was very friendly and seemed genuinely interested in her work. Not something that Cassie was used to with Timothy's social network. His friends all tended to be in the legal field like him, or businessmen, and although they showed some interest when she mentioned she was a journalist, that soon waned when they found out that she worked for the small, local paper. Martina, however, had a barrage of questions she wanted to ask: had Cassie ever travelled abroad with her job, who she'd interviewed, the worst job she'd ever been on? Cassie felt herself warming to her, and although she was careful not to monopolise the conversation, they were soon chatting away like old friends.

'You made quite an impression on Martina,' Timothy told her, as they sat in the back of the taxi on the way home. 'Thank you for making the effort. We're hoping to be dealing with all the legal work for their new business, so tonight was very important.'

'I really liked her.' Cassie reached over for his hand but Timothy gave her a tight smile and moved it away. Stupid of her, she knew how he hated public displays of affection. They didn't go with his professional image. Back at home, he was only too pleased to show her his thanks.

Jared took a swig of his wine and looked around the room full of important and influential people. He hadn't wanted to attend Imogen and Daniel's dinner party, but the way Imogen had asked him made him feel that he couldn't refuse. He knew they were looking to expand their business, and meeting new clients was important to them. Important to him, too: he needed as much money as he could get. He had applied for a grant from the Wildlife Preservation Foundation to help with the costs, but it took six weeks for them to make a decision, so he couldn't afford to sit and wait hoping he'd get it. If he did, then he could extend his six weeks' planned expedition into three months.

'I hear you're the photographer for Timothy Campbell's wedding?'

The words jolted Jared out of his daydream. He gazed at the speaker, an immaculately-dressed woman with a heavily botoxed face that hardly moved as she spoke.

'Er, yes. Do you know him?'

'We dated for a while.' The woman took a swig from the glass of wine she was holding, her long, mascared eyelashes framing sharp blue eyes that studied him for a while. 'I hear his wife-to-be is a hack on the local newspaper. She must be very pretty to attract Timothy's attention. I never thought anyone would ever get him down the aisle. He was always the eternal bachelor.'

Judging by her bitter tone, Jared gathered that she would have liked to marry Timothy herself.

'Really? I've only met him once. He seems very ... successful.' Jared chose his words carefully.

'And what about the woman he's marrying? Is she beautiful?'

Cassie's face flashed across his mind, with her sparkling blue eyes, golden hair, and stunning figure.

'I gather that's a yes?' The woman raised her eyebrow.

'Yes, she is,' Jared acknowledged. 'They go very well together.'

'Well, she needs to be careful that her wedding isn't like that of Prince Charles and Princess Diana.'

'Sorry?' Jared stared at her, puzzled.

'There'll be three of them in it.' The woman finished her wine and tried to form her lips into a smile. They barely moved. 'Well, it's been nice talking to you.' She turned and swept away.

Three of them in it. The words swirled around Jared's mind. What did she mean? Was she insinuating that Timothy had a mistress? Or did she mean his mother? She seemed the interfering type, the sort of woman that thought no one was good enough for her son.

'I see you've met Margot?' Ingrid joined him.

'Is that her name? She was asking me about the Campbells.'

'Yes, she and Timothy had a thing for a while. Poor Margot, she thought he was going to propose, but he lost interest in her. Finished it saying she was too clingy.'

Jared shrugged. 'I guess we've all got a past.'

'True.' Ingrid studied him thoughtfully. 'I'm surprised you aren't taken yourself. I expected you to turn up with a beautiful woman on your arm.'

'I prefer to keep my relationships casual.'

'Really? Then there's hope for the women here who are gagging to meet you. Come along and I'll introduce you to everyone.'

Ingrid grasped him lightly by the arm and steered him over to a crowd of people talking in the corner of the room. He could feel the women's eyes on him assessing him, and fixed a broad smile on his face. A smile got you everywhere, his father always said. It cost nothing but made a lot of difference to how people viewed you. He'd always remembered that. So he joined the group and talked and smiled all evening, trying hard not to think about Cassie or what Margot had meant by the words, 'There'll be three in their marriage.'

It was none of his business. It was Cassie's choice who she married. Yet he couldn't help thinking that Timothy wasn't the right man for her: he was too uptight, too cold, and calculating. He wouldn't love her like he had done.

Well, he had walked away and now Timothy had picked up the pieces of Cassie and made her whole again. She probably thought that Timothy was a sensible, reliable partner. A safe option.

He hoped for her sake that she was right.

Thirteen

When Cassie checked her email in the office on Monday she was delighted to find one from Adele, the lady from the Discovering France exhibition, asking her to go on a press trip to write about wedding venues in the Dordogne region. The four-day trip was in three weeks' time and three of the hotels in the wedding company were providing accommodation for the party of journalists. Cassie almost whooped with delight. It had been ages since she'd been on a press trip. They didn't come in that often and when they did Owen usually shared them around, but this was a personal invitation. Of course she'd have to clear it with Owen, but she was sure he'd agree – it was tied in with her column and they could do a spread on wedding venues. He was in his office so she went to ask him right away.

'Sure. Go for it. Sounds perfect. You should get enough material for a few spreads linked to your column out of that,' Owen told her. 'When is it?'

'June 11th – three weeks' time,' she said. Two weeks before the wedding. She'd have to make sure she had everything pretty well wrapped up by then. She didn't think Timothy would mind, he had never objected to her going on a press trip before, although Sylvia wouldn't approve, she made it clear that she thought Cassie's place was at home looking after Timothy, as if Timothy couldn't cope without her for a few days. He'd barely notice, to be honest; he was a busy man and no doubt would take the opportunity to shut himself in his study and work until midnight without having to worry about neglecting her.

As she drove home she thought about the press trip to France. She wished now that she'd said Paige and Ian were getting married in France, that would shake everyone off the scent and she could use a lot of info from her press trip there. Maybe she could have them going on honeymoon to France? She wanted to write some stuff about the trip in the column, but how could she do that without making it sound too much like real life?

To her surprise, Timothy was home when she got in and the table was laid for two, candles burning, roses in bud vases, napkins tied with ribbons. The whole works.

'This looks lovely,' she smiled as he came forward to kiss her. 'Are we celebrating something?'

'I thought it was time we spent a bit of time together, and finalised some of our wedding plans,' he said. 'Don't worry, it's a low calorie meal. I know you're worrying about putting on weight for the wedding.'

I'm not, you and your mother are. 'Give me ten minutes to shower and change and I'll be with you.'

They spent an enjoyable evening going through the arrangements and ticking off all the things they had left to do. They also made a comprehensive list of the photographs they wanted, agreeing on engagement and pre-wedding shots as well as a mini booth for the guests.

'You can give the photographer this when you return the photo album on Thursday,' Timothy said. He always referred to Jared as 'the photographer', refusing to call him J.M.

She wasn't relishing the thought of seeing Jared again, but it would only take a few minutes to hand him the album and give him the details of the photos they wanted him to take. She could handle that.

'We still have the flowers, the cake, the reception, and the favours to sort out,' Timothy said. 'That's quite a list.' He looked at her. 'I think we might have to ask Mother to help.'

Oh heck, must we? Cassie stifled a groan. She had to admit that Timothy had a point. There was still a long list of things to do. What on earth had possessed them to bring the wedding forward!

Sylvia.

Timothy took out his diary and flicked through the pages. 'Do you realise that we have only five weekends before our wedding day? We really need to sort out as much as we can tonight.'

Cassie suddenly remembered that she hadn't told him about the trip to France yet. She quickly explained. 'A couple of wedding venues in The Dordogne want us to do a feature on them and they've asked especially for me. It's only for a few days. You don't mind, do you?'

'Not at all. It might come in useful. You could make a note of the table decorations, perhaps. It might be good to carry on with the French theme of the castle.' He opened his diary on June. 'So you're away when? Friday to Monday?'

'Thursday to Monday,' she told him. 'Are you sure you don't mind?'

'Of course not. Work's work. I'll miss you, obviously, but I'll be deep in the Winford case by then, so I'll be working all weekend.'

He made a note in his diary, then closed it. 'Now, what do you say we ask Mother to organise the table decorations and reception? She's so good at the kind of thing. That will leave you the wedding cake, flowers, favours, and bridesmaids' gifts to deal with. You should be able to do that in time.'

The nice bits, Cassie thought. Why not? Sylvia was good at organising.

'Of course, if she doesn't mind.'

'She'll be delighted. She loves to help, you know that. I'll phone her now' He took his phone out of his pocket and started to dial. Cassie picked up both their glasses and carried them into the kitchen to refill them.

As she opened the fridge to get the bottle of wine she could hear Timothy saying to Sylvia, 'Thank you, Mother. We'll sort out the present list tonight and Cassie will send it over.'

She hated the thought of doing a present list. It seemed so rude. She'd been brought up to believe that it's the thought that counts and you should be grateful for whatever anyone bought you. If it was left to her she wouldn't have a present list.

Or a big fancy do. Or Jared as her photographer.

111

Or even be getting married.

The thought slipped into her mind uninvited and she thrust it back out again. Of course she wanted to marry Timothy, it was just that things were happening so quickly. She poured the wine into her glass and took a big sip. Since she'd accepted Timothy's proposal on Valentine's Day, it felt like events were running away with her, and she wasn't in charge of her own life.

It's only natural to feel a bit nervous about the wedding. Everyone does, she reminded herself.

'Cassie, darling, have you poured that wine yet?'

'Coming!' She took another swig out of her glass, refilled it, then carried both drinks into the lounge.

'Cassie, is your column ready?' Gary called as soon as she walked in on Wednesday.

That column was the bane of her life. She'd been thinking about it this morning, wondering what to write about, and hadn't decided on anything yet. She cast her mind back to the weekend – she could write about choosing the bridesmaid dresses and give the readers the option of deciding which ones she should buy? She'd slip in a bit about Jared too, of course, just to keep Owen happy.

She ended up writing quite a lot about Jared. Once she started it just all seemed to spill out.

'This is brilliant,' Owen said when it finally landed on his desk. 'You're really getting the hang of this, aren't you?' He looked up at her questioningly. 'You are over this photographer guy, aren't you?'

'Of course I am! I wouldn't mention him if you didn't make me.' She paused. 'I'm trying to add a bit of drama to keep the reader hooked. Is it too much?'

Owen shook his head. 'No, it makes them wonder if she's still got the hots for him, which is a great selling point. They'll keep buying the paper to see if she gets married or runs off with the photographer.'

'Really?' Her words came out in a squeak. That was terrible. She didn't want Jared thinking that – she was trying to use her column to let him know she *wasn't* interested.

'Oh, don't worry, it's not overdone. Just enough to tease. You're making a fab job of this, Cassie. I might give you another column when you've finished with this one. I reckon you've got the knack for it.'

She grinned. Owen didn't give praise lightly.

'I just hope for your sake it is fiction, because if it isn't you shouldn't be marrying your lawyer.' He walked back into the office, leaving Cassie stunned.

Fourteen

Cassie wasn't the least bit bothered about seeing Jared again. The only reason she hadn't been able to sleep last night was because she had so much on her mind, what with all the wedding preparations, and the trip to France. It was nothing to do with having to see Jared again, nothing at all. She was only wearing this ultra-smart suit because she had to interview someone for the paper that afternoon.

'Ah, Miss Tyler. J.M. sends his apologies but he's tied up with another client. He'll be with you in a few minutes,' the receptionist said. 'Could I offer you a coffee while you're waiting?'

'No thank you. I'll just take a seat.' Cassie sat down and picked up one of the magazines on the table. A Sunday supplement to one of the major newspapers. As she flicked through the pages, her eyes rested on a photograph of a giraffe at a waterhole in the African sunset. It was a beautiful, evocative picture. She looked at the by-line underneath and saw that the photographer was Jared. He's good, she thought, and he obviously loves his job. Their break-up had hurt her terribly but looking at these photographs she saw that Jared had made the right decision. He was so gifted, if he had remained with her and they'd got married, he would never have realised his dream. Love can stifle you, she thought. It makes you compromise.

Like she was doing with Timothy: living in a city apartment when she'd really love a country cottage, working on the local newspaper when she longed to spread her wings and write for a travel magazine, getting married in few weeks when she'd really like to wait a bit longer. A lot longer. It all felt so rushed. As if she had no time to breathe.

'Cassie, so sorry to keep you waiting.' Jared was in front of her, casually dressed in faded denim and a white T-shirt, his dark hair slightly tousled as if he'd been running his fingers through it.

'These photos are fantastic. It must have taken you ages to get the right moment to take them,' she told him. She put the magazine back on the table and stood up, smoothing down her skirt.

'It did. You'll be amazed how patient I am now. I'll sit for hours waiting for the right photograph.' He grinned at her and her heart did a flip. He'd always had a melt-your-soul grin. Whenever he'd annoyed her, that soppy grin had always won her around.

He'd never been patient though, she remembered. He'd always been buzzing, so full of energy; everything had to be done *now*.

'I guess we've both changed,' she said, as she followed him into the side room. 'I've actually managed to get over my fear of heights. I went on a cable car in Switzerland, you know. OK, I felt a bit panicky, but I did it.' She'd been so proud of that. She'd been scared of heights as far back as she could remember, so when Timothy and the other members of their group had walked over to the cable car on their skiing trip last year, she'd been almost paralysed with fear. Not wanting to make a scene in front of everyone, she'd forced herself to get in and spent the entire trip clutching Timothy's hand, her eyes closed, praying silently. She'd been so relieved when they reached the top of the mountain. She'd done it. The next day, the trip hadn't seemed so bad. By the end of the holiday she could get in the cable car without shaking, and keep her eyes open for the mountain ascent, although she still dreaded it.

'I'm impressed.' His brown eyes twinkled with amusement. She knew he was probably remembering the episode when he'd tried to persuade her to climb up to Blackpool Tower, and she'd

116

stopped halfway, shaking so much he'd had to hold her hand and walk all the way back down again with her. Then she'd waited at the bottom while he'd gone back up and waved at her from the top.

'Take a seat,' he indicated the chair by the desk and sat down on the edge of the desk. 'Which album did you go for?'

'The embossed one, with a cream cover and heart inset.' Cassie took out the albums and pointed to the one they'd decided on. 'Can we have a pale blue heart, please? It's our wedding colour. And we'd like a pre-engagement shot at the restaurant where we got engaged. We thought it would be nice to build up a record of our engagement and the run-up to the wedding. Like a photographic diary. It was Timothy's idea, but I thought it was nice. We can recreate the scene, can't we? I can remember what I was wearing.'

'Certainly. What else did you have in mind?'

Cassie took out her notes. 'Perhaps you could come along for the wedding dress fitting? And the bridesmaids' one? Take a few shots of us all fooling around as we try on the dresses? And choosing the flowers, shopping with the mother of the bride, that sort of thing?'

'Of course. Pass me the list and I'll work out costings for you. Daniel has you on mates' rates as he is friendly with your "monster-in-law".'

Cassie flushed. 'You've been reading my column again?'

'Yes, and I got the message loud and clear.'

That's what she'd wanted, wasn't it? To let him know that she wasn't interested in him, yet now she felt like she'd been a bit ... mean. 'It's only journalism; nothing personal.'

As she went to hand him the notes, the papers slipped out of her hand. She bent down to get them at the same time as Jared did and their heads bumped together.

'Ouch!' She rubbed her head.

'Sorry, are you hurt?' He reached out and touched her forehead. 'It feels like you've got a bump.'

As he ran his fingers over the bump she felt her skin burn and an irresistible longing for him to run his fingers over her face, her neck, and her body, coursed through her. His eyes were gazing into hers just the way they used to, tenderly but laced with desire. Then his fingers were running down her cheeks, her neck, and she gasped, her eyes widening at the electrifying tingle that shot through her body. She saw his eyes suddenly darken with desire and then his head was bending towards her. She heard him murmur her name and felt his lips on hers, softly at first, then more intensely.

And, God help her, she was kissing him back.

I can't do this!

She pushed him away, grabbed her bag, and ran out, composing herself as she passed the reception desk.

'Goodbye, Miss Tyler,' the receptionist called.

She smiled and nodded, not trusting herself to speak, and walked through the doors, into the car park, over to the car. She didn't stop shaking until she was sitting in the driving seat.

What had possessed her to kiss him back like that?

'Damn!' Jared kicked the litter basket and sent it sprawling over the floor. Why had he done that?

He walked back around the desk and sat down in the leather chair, sinking his head into his hands. He'd promised himself he'd keep this professional. He needed this job. He couldn't afford to mess it up, but that's exactly what he'd gone and done. Cassie would cancel the contract with them after this. He doubted if losing the deposit would bother her or Timothy much – they were obviously very financially comfortable.

What if Cassie told Timothy about the kiss and he made a complaint about him? I.D.'s reputation was vitally important to them. He and Daniel might be friends from way back, but Daniel wouldn't risk losing business by keeping Jared on his books. Timothy seemed the sort of man who had lots of influential friends and would use them. He could ruin I.D.'s reputation in no time.

Cassie had kissed him back, he reminded himself. And with passion. She still loved him, he was sure of it. He could see it in her eyes, feel it when she was talking to him. She might not want to. It was obvious she wanted to go ahead with her plans to marry Timothy the twat, but that didn't change the fact that she still had feelings for him.

He loved her too. He didn't want to any more than Cassie wanted to love him. He had his life all sorted out, and loving Cassie – loving anyone – wasn't part of it. But he couldn't seem to control his feelings, the desire he felt for her. He'd probably never stopped loving Cassie, and now he'd met her again, those feelings had resurfaced.

He got up and picked up the rubbish, then buzzed Hannah, the receptionist, to bring him a coffee. He had an hour before his next client, an hour he had intended to spend going through paperwork, but now he had better use to get his head straight.

'Is everything all right, Jared?' Hannah asked as she put the coffee on his desk. 'Miss Tyler left in rather a hurry and she didn't seem quite herself.'

He shrugged. 'Pre-wedding nerves. You know what these brides are like. That's the reason I prefer to take shots of animals.'

'Daniel said you'll be going off on a shoot soon, to the Arctic.' Hannah's big blue eyes were fixed on his face and her voice was soft, seductive. Hell, was she trying to hit on him? That's the last thing he needed – his life was getting complicated enough. 'It must be a fascinating job.'

'Yes, it is. Thanks for the coffee, Hannah. I appreciate it.' He flicked open his notebook, hoping she'd take the hint that he was busy. He could feel her waiting and looked up, a fixed smile on his face. 'Was there anything else?'

She looked flustered. 'Er, no. I'll come back later for the cup. I can see that you're busy.'

'Thank you.'

As soon as she'd gone, he got up and walked over to the window. He had to phone Cassie. Apologise to her. Her mobile number would be in her records. He took out the file and was just looking through it when the intercom buzzed.

He pressed the button to answer.

'J.M., Mr Campbell is here,' Hannah informed him. 'Do you have time to see him?'

Damn! Had Cassie told him already? Was he coming to punch him? Not that it worried him: he was more than a match for Timothy Campbell, but it wouldn't go down well with Imogen and Daniel. They would be furious if he upset one of their clients. He shook his head. Violence wasn't Campbell's style, he was sure of it. He'd met men like him before. They liked control. He'd tell Jared exactly what he thought of him, then set out to destroy him professionally.

Well, he wasn't going to let him. He'd spent too long building up his career to stand by and let someone destroy it over a stupid kiss. He'd have to keep his head together, act like nothing happened. It was a minor incident. Acting innocent and tackling it full-on was his best course of action.

'Mr Campbell.' Jared smiled welcomingly and strode towards Timothy as he stepped in. He held out his hand. 'Good to see you again. What can I do for you? Were you meant to be meeting your fiancée here? I'm afraid she's just left.'

'Yes, I know. I telephoned to make sure she'd left before I came. I want this to be a surprise.'

So Timothy had spoken to Cassie. And she obviously hadn't said anything or he'd be fuming, not planning surprises.

Jared indicated the chair Cassie had been sitting on less half an hour ago. 'Take a seat and tell me what you have in mind.'

Timothy pulled out the chair and sat down. 'I'd like to book you for some honeymoon photographs, but I don't want Cassandra to know. The whole honeymoon is a surprise for her. She knows we're going on one, of course, but she doesn't know where.'

'And where are you going?'

Timothy named a very exclusive hotel in the Maldives, and paused to make sure this had the necessary effect. Jared assumed a suitably impressed expression on his face. 'We'll be staying for two weeks, and I'd like you to join us for three days at the tail end. I'd like some photos of us walking barefoot along the sand, having a romantic meal on the beach, you know, the sort of thing.'

Jared nodded. A week before he left for the Arctic. The timing couldn't be better – he would need to get away after spending three days taking photos of Cassie and Timothy on their honeymoon. He listened intently and made notes as Timothy ran through the arrangements, telling him the dates he wanted him there. 'I'll leave you to book your own flight and accommodation, and add it to the bill,' he said.

'No problem,' Jared agreed. I.D. would cover any financial outlay until Timothy paid the bill, which he knew had to be settled before the wedding.

'Well, thank you. As I said, this is confidential, so not a word to Cassandra. The only other person who knows is my mother, so if you need to ask anything and can't get hold of me, then contact her.' Timothy handed him a business card. 'Here's my number. I believe you already have my mother's number?'

'Thanks. Yes I do.' Jared slipped the card into Campbell's file. 'I'll be in touch when I've made my booking.'

He sat stunned for a while after Timothy had left, two thoughts fighting for first place in his mind: Cassie hadn't told Timothy about the kiss, so did that mean she felt the same as him? And how the hell was he going to handle photographing them on their honeymoon now that he realised he still loved Cassie?

Fifteen

'Earth to Cassie,' Craig said, teasing.

'What? Oh, sorry, Craig,' Cassie said, flustered. 'I was miles away.'

'So I see. Daydreaming about your wedding, are you? I know what you women are like when you're planning a wedding. It takes over your life.'

No, she'd been daydreaming about Jared's kiss; replaying it time and time again in her mind. But she couldn't tell Craig that. 'There's so much to do. Timothy reminded me last night that we've only got five weekends left.'

'And one of them you're away in France. Lucky bugger. You sure you want the job? There'll be no shortage of takers if it's too much for you.'

'It's fine, one weekend won't make much difference,' she said. It would do her good to get away, get her mind straight. Since meeting Jared again she'd been in turmoil. She had to get him out of her system. She'd be Timothy's wife soon.

'What were you saying to me, anyway?' she asked.

'I was reminding you that we're covering the Antique Toy Fair this afternoon. Have you seen the brochure? Is there anything in particular you think we should look at?'

Cassie picked up the brochure and turned her attention to the job in hand. She had to banish Jared from her thoughts once and for all. 'I love the Victorian dolls and the wooden toys,' she said. 'There's so much detail in them.' She was pleased to see that there were some listed in the brochure.

The Toy Fair was really interesting. Cassie found it fascinating looking at all the children's toys from years gone by, lead soldiers, teddies, Victorian dolls, spinning tops. She could spend hours here wandering around. Craig photographed quite a lot of the toys and they interviewed a few of the stall holders. Owen only wanted half a page, but Cassie made plenty of notes thinking that she might be able to sell a few features to magazines. It was a practice Owen frowned on, but didn't actually ban, so provided she kept it low-key he wouldn't complain.

She'd arranged to meet Sam for coffee after work. It was Sam's idea. She'd demanded to meet Cassie as soon as she knew she had met Jared again yesterday, and she obviously wanted all the news. Sam was already waiting at the table when Cassie walked in, and waved her over. 'I've just got here and it was so full I thought I'd nab a table first. You sit down and I'll get the drinks. You look bushed.'

'I am,' Cassie told her. 'I'd better have a black coffee, Sam. I don't want to risk having to have my wedding dress altered.'

'You sure? A skinny latté won't hurt and you look like you need a pick me up.'

Cassie hesitated. She was tempted, but this wedding was turning into enough of a disaster without her being too fat to fit into her wedding dress.

'Positive.'

'It's your call.'

What am I going to do? Cassie thought as Sam joined the queue for the coffees. It can't be possible that I still love Jared. Why do I keep responding to him like this? It's insane. I've got to get it under control before I ruin everything.

Timothy was a nice guy. Solid, dependable, kind. She would be stupid to throw that away for a fling with Jared. Not that he'd asked her to. But he wanted her, she could sense that. He wanted her as much as she wanted him. And it would be so easy to give in.

'OK, spill,' Sam said putting the coffees down on the table.

'Sorry?' Cassie feigned ignorance.

124

'Something's obviously bothering you, and I'm guessing it's Jared, as you had a meeting with him this morning.' She put sugar in her cup and whirled it around in the caramel liquid. Cassie was almost drooling as she watched her. Then Sam frowned and leant forward. 'Please don't tell me he kissed you again.'

Cassie flushed.

'OMG, he has!' Sam put down the spoon and stared at her, aghast. 'Tell me it was on the cheek again.'

Wordlessly, Cassie shook her head.

'You're not telling me he kissed you on the lips?'

Cassie nodded. 'Sam … I kissed him back.'

Sam looked at her in horror. 'I knew it! I knew you still have feelings for him. And it sounds like he still loves you too.'

'Of course he doesn't. And I don't love him either. I guess we're still attracted to each other but that's only natural, isn't it? They say you never completely forget your first love, and we went out for so long.'

'Cassie, you can't marry Timothy if you and Jared still have the hots for each other.'

'I don't. We don't. It was just one of those things. It just happened.' She pushed her hand through her hair. 'It won't happen again. It can't.'

Sam leant forward, fixed her gaze on her. 'Look, I haven't liked to say anything before because, well, it's none of my business … but do you think you and Timothy are really suited? He's so …'

Cassie stared at her. 'So what?'

She could see that Sam was choosing her words carefully. 'So … formal. You know, I don't think I've ever seen him laugh. Even when he smiles it's like a polite, staged smile. Does he ever kick off his shoes, let his guard down, or have a joke with you?'

Cassie was taken aback. She had no idea that Sam felt like this about Timothy. She'd never given any sign that she didn't like him. Timothy was great with people, he knew how to put them at ease, and he oozed confidence. He was cordial, reassuring, and impeccably mannered. Everyone liked him.

But she had a point. He never kicked off his shoes and had a joke with her. He never let his guard down. Even in their most intimate moments he was always in control. She had never seen him do anything remotely silly. He always behaved in an exemplary way.

Well, there was nothing wrong with that, was there? Timothy was a lawyer. He took his position seriously. He took life seriously. Look how he tolerated his interfering mother. And he was kind to Cassie: he never raised his voice or said angry, hurtful words to her.

He didn't need to. A look from him was enough. Sometimes, when she'd done something she knew he didn't particularly like, the disappointment in his eyes or disapproval in his tone made her feel really bad.

'Timothy's a practical person, but there's nothing wrong with that. He's loyal, trustworthy, and responsible.'

'And won't ditch you to travel the world chasing his dream, like Jared did.'

'No, he won't. But that's not why I'm marrying him. I love him,' she said hotly.

'Do you?' Sam asked softly. 'Does your heart quicken when you see him or hear his voice? Does your skin tingle when he touches you? Because if it does, I don't think you'd be kissing Jared.'

'I told you that was a mistake …'

'Look, I'm not getting at you or running Timothy down. I'm just trying to point out that you're getting married in four weeks' time, promising to love Timothy forever and you're still attracted to Jared. Admit it.'

Cassie swallowed. Sam was right: she was still attracted to Jared. She couldn't deny it. But that didn't mean she didn't love Timothy.

'I don't want to be attracted to him,' she snapped. 'I love Timothy and I want to marry him. I don't want Jared. I wish he wasn't my photographer. I wish I'd never seen him again.' Until Jared had turned up everything was fine. He had no right coming back into her life, stirring up old feelings and unsettling her like this.

126

'I'm going to make sure I'm never alone with him again,' she said determinedly. 'He doesn't want a relationship with me, he's off to the Arctic soon to take photographs of polar bears. And I don't want a relationship with him. Definitely not. I'm not going to let our past sabotage my future with Timothy.'

'Are you certain? You can't marry Timothy if you have any doubts at all, or it won't work.'

'I'm positive. Now can we just forget it?' She glared at Sam. 'You're supposed to be my best friend, my maid of honour, supporting me, not trying to make me cancel the wedding.'

'It's because I'm your best friend and support you that I'm talking to you like this,' Sam said. She shrugged. 'Well, if you're sure, let's get on with the wedding plans. Are we shopping again this weekend? Have you sorted out flowers and a cake yet?'

Cassie groaned. 'No, I haven't had time. It's hectic at work. And I'm away in a couple of weeks. I'm on a press trip to France.'

Sam whistled. 'Lucky you! How's Timothy feel about that?'

'He doesn't mind: he's due to work on a high-profile case soon, so will probably be working all over that weekend anyway. That's one of the nice things about being with Timothy. He never minds the hours I work. He's so busy with his own life.'

'Well, it sounds fab, tell me all about it,' Sam said.

The mood lightened as Cassie told her about going to the Discover France show, and how one of the companies had followed up her visit by asking her if the paper would do a feature on châteaux for hire for weddings and functions. 'It's all expenses paid, staying at three different hotels. And Owen's agreed that I can use some of the info for my column. Isn't that brilliant?'

Sam agreed that it was indeed brilliant. 'I'm *soo* jealous. It's been ages since Paul and I went away.'

'I know. I can't wait. It'll be good to get away from everything and do something completely different.' And to be miles away from Jared.

Sixteen

Sylvia didn't share Sam's opinion when she came around that evening to bring some samples of floral arrangements and see how preparations were getting on.

'You're going away two weeks before the wedding?' she repeated incredulously, staring at Cassie in undisguised dismay. 'Can't you get out of it? We still have so much to do.'

'My editor has asked me to go. It's my job.' There was no need to point out that if she said she couldn't go, then there would be plenty of others happy to step in and take her place. She needed this break.

'What do you think of this, Timothy?' Sylvia demanded.

Timothy handed her a glass of wine. 'As Cassie said, it's her job. I do agree, though, that there is still a lot to do for the wedding, so maybe we should tackle as much as we can before you go away, Cassie.' He handed a glass of wine to her. 'We can look through these floral arrangements for a start. And we still have to arrange the food and book the evening entertainment.'

'Would you like me to do that for you?' Sylvia asked. 'I seem to be the only one to have time to spare. And before you say it, I really don't mind.'

No, she doesn't mind, she loves it, wading in and taking over, showing Cassie how incompetent she was, Cassie thought resentfully. Her first instinct was to refuse and say she could manage everything, but she hesitated. It would make life so much easier to hand it all over to Sylvia. She knew that then they would have the perfect wedding, because Sylvia would make sure that nothing went wrong. She was pretty sure that if she did that, though, she would regret it later. This was her wedding, hers and Timothy's. Sylvia had already chosen the venue, the date, the photographer, and had a say in the guest list. She couldn't let her take over any more. Perhaps this is why she felt such a lack of enthusiasm, because none of it felt like her choice.

She had chosen the wedding and bridesmaids' dresses, the tiaras, and shoes, she reminded herself.

'What do you think, Cassie? It would make life easier for you, wouldn't it?' Timothy asked.

He was giving her the choice but Cassie sensed that he would like his mum to take over, too. He didn't trust Cassie to make the right decisions, to plan the perfect wedding for them. Well, what was there left to plan? The cake, flowers, entertainment, table setting, favours. That was it. They were all her chance to stamp a bit of Cassie on to the wedding day, to take control of at least some of her day. If it wasn't for Sylvia interfering and booking I.D. Images for the photography, she wouldn't be in this mess now.

'It would and I do appreciate the offer …'

Sylvia's face broke into a huge smile. 'Not at all.'

'But I'd like to do the rest myself. There isn't really a lot to do now and I want to contribute a little to the plans for my …' she looked at Timothy and smiled, '*our* special day.'

Sylvia could barely mask her disappointment. 'If you're sure that's what you want, dear?'

'It is, but thank you again. I appreciate what you've done so far.'

'It's lovely that you want to take over the rest of the wedding preparations, Cassie sweetheart,' Timothy said, kissing her lightly on the forehead. 'If you do feel that you need some help later on then I'm sure Mother will be only too happy to come on board, so don't feel that you can't ask. Now, I think we should have a quick look at the floral arrangement brochures Mother's brought, seeing as she's gone to so much trouble.'

He sat down on the sofa by Sylvia, took one of the brochures off her lap, and flicked it open. 'These look nice.'

I'm not going to be sweet-talked into letting her choose the flowers, Cassie thought stubbornly, as she took the brochure from Timothy's outstretched hand.

She had to admit that the flower arrangements were beautiful. Some of them were really stunning. They were mainly silk flowers though, and too elaborate for her liking.

'I wanted something simpler, and fresh flowers, not silk,' she said. 'Actually, I've got a picture of the sort of bouquet I wanted.' She opened her handbag and took the magazine cutting out of the pocket. 'See, the flowers are the exact blue of the bridesmaids' dresses, and the pale pink and white go so well with them.' She looked at Timothy. 'What do you think?'

'I think it's very pretty, and if that's what you want then of course, that's what you shall have. Are you thinking of the blue or white for buttonholes? I don't think the men will want to wear pink.' There was a teasing tone to his voice.

'I thought white, as you're wearing blue ties to match.'

'It is quite nice, in a simplistic way,' Sylvia stressed the word 'simplistic'. 'If you're sure this is really what you want, dear, then you need to sort out a florist quickly. They need plenty of notice, you know. And you'll have to arrange to pick them up either the evening before or the morning of the wedding; I would think in the morning. Fresh flowers wilt so quickly.'

'I know, but they look so lovely and smell so wonderful. There's a florist in town, I'll pop in on Monday and see if she can make them up for me. I thought a bouquet for me and Sam and posies for the flower girls. Plus buttonholes for Mum, Dad, yourself, Timothy, and the best man. That's about it, isn't it?'

'What about table decorations?' Sylvia reminded her. 'Are you intending to have fresh flowers for them, too?'

'I'd like to. I know they don't last, but I love the smell of fresh flowers.'

She could see that Sylvia disapproved but Timothy looked agreeable. 'Then that's all settled,' he nodded. 'Which leaves the wedding cake, favours, and entertainment.'

Sylvia whipped out another brochure from her bag. 'I brought along some literature on wedding cakes; I thought they might come in handy. And I've made a few enquiries, so I know these caterers can accommodate our date.'

'Can you leave them with us to look at?' Cassie asked in her best 'friendly' voice. 'I want to take my time choosing the cake.'

Sylvia pursed her lips. 'As you wish, but I promised to let them know our selection by Saturday so don't take too long deciding.'

'I won't,' Cassie promised, trying not to let the fact that Sylvia had said 'our' twice when referring to the wedding bother her.

'I brought some literature about entertainment, too.' Sylvia whisked some brochures out of her bag. 'It's so important to set the right tone, isn't it? Something classy.'

By the end of the evening the entertainment was decided; a string quartet and a solo performance by Alana Mayers, the famous vocalist. Cassie had suggested a rock band, but the look of horror on both Timothy and his mother's faces put paid to that.

It's your wedding, stick up for yourself, she told herself. She was out of her depth though, and afraid to fight her corner in case it turned out to be a disaster. She knew that many of Timothy's colleagues and friends would be there, and didn't want to let him down. He would be humiliated if anything went wrong. Never mind, I've chosen the dresses and am also choosing the flowers, table decorations, favours, and the cake, she reminded herself. It was Timothy's day too, it was only natural he wanted some input.

'How are you getting on with the Campbell's wedding?' Daniel asked, popping his head around the door just as Jared was about to leave.

'Fine, they want me to take some honeymoon photos too so I've got to go to the Maldives,' he grinned at Daniel. 'I bet you wish you'd taken on this job yourself now.'

'Completely booked all that month. Besides I know Sylvia personally, so I prefer someone else to deal with the photographs. Never mix friends and business and all that.' He perched on the end of the desk. 'Well, she's not exactly a friend but she's an important acquaintance and has very good connections. I hope you can keep her happy. She can be a bit difficult.'

'I'll do my best. To be honest, I've only seen her a couple of times. Most of my contact has been with the bride and groom-to-be.'

'Hmm, the bride-to-be is quite a beauty, isn't she? Not sure what she sees in Campbell, he's a bit stuffy. I guess his money helps.'

Jared fought back an angry retort, indignant on Cassie's behalf. She was just a client, Daniel would be suspicious if he overreacted. 'Who knows what people see in each other?' He shrugged. 'Each to their own, I guess.'

'How about you? No thoughts of settling down yet?' Daniel asked. 'Don't you ever want to put down roots? Have someone to come home to?'

Jared pushed away the image of Cassie waiting for him, arms open wide, lips poised to kiss. 'No way, I'm happy as I am. Footloose and fancy free.'

'Not even with the lovely Savannah?'

Definitely not with Savannah. She was good company for the occasional night out, but far too neurotic and high maintenance for anything permanent. He'd be living on edge all the time. 'It's just a casual thing. We just keep each other company when we're both in town,' he replied. 'She's on a modelling shoot in Cape Verde for a few days.'

'Great, that means you're free to come to the dinner party with us tonight?'

'What dinner party?'

'Lord Sundan's invited us. It'll be a good opportunity to network. There'll be lots of influential people there and Imogen wants to show you off. She's quite proud of the latest addition to our team.'

'Wants to match-make more like, knowing Imogen,' Jared said with a good-humoured grin. 'Go on then, it'll be a free meal and interesting company, but warn Imogen that I'm off the market.'

Daniel eased himself off the desk and slapped Jared on the back. 'You'll get smitten one day, you'll see, and then you'll be caught just like the rest of us.'

'Trapped, you mean.' Jared picked up his briefcase. 'Where and when?'

'Eight thirty, Royal Grande Hotel,' Daniel related the details. 'Smart dress – not your usual jeans and tatty jacket,' he called as Jared strode over to the door.

Jared gave a mock salute.

It was nearer nine when Jared strode into the hotel lounge. It had taken him a while to find his dinner suit, and then he'd realised his shirt needed ironing, but as he glanced around the room he was glad that he'd made the decision to wear it. All the men wore dinner jackets while the women wore a lavish selection of evening dresses and expensive jewellery. Thank goodness Daniel had warned him to dress smartly.

'Ah, there you are, Jared, come and meet Sir Hugh and Lady Miriam.' Isobel glided over to him, and grasped his arm, leading him through the throng to a join a middle-aged, aristocratic-looking couple.

Introductions were exchanged, and he was soon engaged in a conversation with Lady Miriam about the rainforest expedition he'd gone on last year. Champagne was being passed around. As he reached out to take a glass he noticed a familiar figure in the corner; his back was to him but he was sure it was Timothy Campbell. However, the lady he had his arm around and whose ear he was whispering into was definitely not Cassie.

Seventeen

'So what's next on the hit list?' Sam asked, pouring them both another glass of rosé. 'The way we're going we'll get it all sorted out in no time.'

Cassie studied her list. They'd decided on the favours – a gold chain bracelet for the women guests and a gold tie pin with diamond inset for the men.

'Presents for the bridesmaids, you and the best man. The flowers and the wedding cake.'

'I'm surprised monster-in-law hasn't booked you an appointment with a top florist and ordered a bespoke wedding cake to be made,' Sam said with a grin. She picked up the selection leaflet on the open box of dark chocolates on the coffee table and studied it carefully before selecting a strawberry cream.

Cassie rolled her eyes. 'Believe me, she wanted to. I don't know how I managed to stop her.' She reached out and selected a chocolate herself. She didn't bother to check the description, merely picking the nearest one. All chocolate was equal as far as she was concerned. She popped it into her mouth. Coffee cream. Delicious. 'Sylvia's only gone and booked us an appointment with Jared on Thursday evening for our engagement photographs. She said she checked Timothy's diary and saw that he was free. Of course, she didn't bother to check if I was. I'm just expected to fall in with her plans.'

Sam whistled. 'I forgot you were doing that. It's going to be a bit weird, isn't it? Recreating your engagement night while your ex films it.'

Cassie nodded. 'I could do without it, to be honest,' she confessed. 'Timothy's set on it, though. As far as I'm concerned, the less I see Jared the better.'

Sam studied her thoughtfully. 'Are you sure you haven't got feelings for him?'

'Of course not. It's just … like you said, awkward.' Cassie shrugged and helped herself to another chocolate. 'I guess it's no big deal, it'll only take a few minutes.'

'What will Timothy say if he comes home early and catches you scoffing chocolates and wine just weeks before your wedding?' Sam teased.

'He won't be home for ages yet, those dinner parties drag on a bit.' She'd been relieved that Timothy hadn't tried to persuade her to go with him that evening. He'd told her he was working late a couple of days ago, so she'd arranged for Sam to come around and help her with wedding arrangements, then he'd come home last night and informed her he'd completely forgotten about a dinner party invitation. She'd offered to cancel Sam and accompany him, but he must have sensed her heart wasn't in it and told her he'd go alone. 'It's only a few people from work, networking,' he said. 'You'll be bored stiff, darling. And I know you want to get the wedding sorted before you go on your press trip to France. Felicity and Andrew are going so I won't be a wallflower.' She'd readily agreed: she hated dinner parties. She always felt awkward with Timothy's friends; especially Felicity and Andrew. An evening with Sam feasting on chocolates and wine was much more her idea of fun.

She picked up another chocolate and bit into it. Turkish delight. She savoured it for a moment. 'I'll be too busy rushing around when I'm in France that I won't have time to eat, so I'll soon lose any extra weight. Now, let's take a look at some flowers.' She keyed in 'Wedding Flowers' on the internet search bar on her laptop. 'What do you think of these?' she asked, sliding the laptop over to Sam and pointing to a pretty posy of pale blue and ivory flowers. 'They're the same colour as the dresses.'

Sam peered over and nodded. 'They're lovely. But I thought you wanted pale pink, too? Didn't you show me a picture of the bouquet you liked?'

'I've got it here.' Cassie reached for the handbag besides her feet and rummaged through it, pulling out the crumpled picture. 'There we are, see, it's the same shade of blue.' She handed it to Sam. 'I thought if I was the only one who had pink in my bouquet then I'd stand out more as the bride.'

'Good thinking.' Sam carefully selected another chocolate and popped it into her mouth. 'Not that there'll be any doubt about that, as you'll be the one wearing the white dress.'

'I'll print it out so I can show the florists the sort of thing I'm after.' She sent the picture to the wireless printer in Owen's office. 'Let's have a look at wedding cakes.'

'I think you've left it a bit late if you want one specially made.' Sam licked her fingers and wiped them on her jeans. 'A lot of people have cupcakes now. Hey, that one's gorgeous.' She pointed to a pastel blue two-tier cake decorated with pearl piping and white sugar roses.

Cassie studied it thoughtfully. 'I just wonder if it's overdoing the blue.'

They flicked through more cake designs, with Cassie sending a few to the printer in Timothy's study. Then Sam noticed the time. 'I didn't realise it was that late. Paul's picking me up in five minutes.' She'd told Cassie when she arrived that Paul was dropping her off on the way to the gym, and picking her back up again on his way home, so she could have a couple of glasses of wine. She grabbed her jacket and bag. 'It's been fab. We must do this again.'

'Thanks for your help. At least I've got a few ideas to show the florists now.' Cassie walked to the door with Sam, reaching it just as Sam's phone buzzed to announce an incoming text. 'That'll be Paul. He said he'd text me when he arrived. Good luck with the florist.' Sam hugged her goodbye then was out of the door.

Cassie cleared away the wine and chocolates, throwing the empty chocolate box and wine bottles down the chute, then washed the glasses and put them away. That done, she padded down the hall barefoot and opened the door to Timothy's study to get the pictures of the cake designs. She rarely went in here, especially if Timothy wasn't in. It made her feel a bit of a snooper. Although Timothy had never asked her not to go in and always left the door unlocked, she knew he considered it his private territory and hated her to touch anything on his desk. Not that she would. She respected his privacy as he respected hers. Neither of them would dream of snooping at each other's text messages or email, or opening each other's post.

She made her way over to the printer and picked up the handful of pictures waiting for her. As she turned away her gaze caught something on the desk. A picture of Timothy and Felicity, both dressed up to the nines, holding a glass of wine. She guessed it was taken at one of the various dinners or networking events they went to, the ones Cassie always tried to avoid going to. They were smiling and looked relaxed together. She couldn't help thinking that someone like Felicity would make a more suitable partner for Timothy than her. Someone in the same career, who liked entertaining, putting on dinner parties, all the sort of things Cassie hated. She'd mentioned it to him once but he'd merely pulled her close and kissed her, telling her that he would be bored stiff with someone like Felicity and preferred someone warm and uncomplicated like herself.

She'd felt a bit miffed to be described as 'warm and uncomplicated'. Jared had always called her feisty and hot. 'You're so hot,' he'd murmured as he nibbled her ear, sprinkled kisses down her throat …

She pushed the thoughts away, put the photo back down on the desk, and returned to the lounge to study the pictures. She placed them all in a clear folder, folded it in half, and slipped it into the front pocket of her bag so she could easily find it to show the florists. She yawned and glanced at the clock. Timothy had told her he didn't know what time he'd be home so not to wait up for him. She loved the fact that their relationship was so trusting and non-clingy. Timothy gave her space to breathe, to be herself. She yawned again. Time for bed. It was pointless waiting up when she was so tired.

She quickly removed her makeup, washed, then slid into bed, her eyes closing almost the moment they touched the pillow.

It was some time before Timothy noticed Jared. When he did he merely acknowledged him with a brief nod, obviously not wanting to demean himself by socialising with him. Like he'd want to mix with a twat like that. Jared nodded briefly back, then turned away, and started talking to the person nearest to him. That'd show Campbell just how important he regarded him.

'Timothy!' Imogen made a beeline for him. 'And Felicity darling, how delightful to see you both.' She enveloped them in a hug then stepped back and looked around. 'Where are your other halves? I'd like to meet your fiancée, Timothy.'

'Cassie isn't really fond of dinner parties, so she's at home making wedding plans with her maid of honour.' Timothy glanced at Felicity. 'Andrew's away on a business trip and Felicity didn't want to miss your party, so we decided to keep each other company.'

'Not that I need Timothy to accompany me, I'm quite capable of attending events like this alone,' Felicity cut in. 'However, we thought it would be a good opportunity for us both to network.'

'Never miss an opportunity to network, that's my motto.' Imogen gave them both a little finger wave. 'Now, you must excuse me while I circulate.'

She swanned off around the room, leaving Timothy and Felicity to mingle. They didn't stay long. It was less than an hour later that Jared spotted them walking out of the door, hand in hand.

Eighteen

The next few days passed in a haze of phone calls and writing features. It was halfway through Wednesday morning when Cassie realised that her 'Almost a Bride' column was due that day. She decided to use some of the research she did the night before and write about choosing the flowers.

'How are you getting on with your column?' Owen was standing beside her.

She turned around. 'Just about to start it. It's flowers this week.'

'Don't forget to bring that photographer into it. The readers are clamouring for him.'

Cassie gritted her teeth. She wished she'd never started this. What had Jared – sorry, Blake – got to do with choosing the wedding flowers?

She spun back around to the computer and opened the file. As soon as her fingers hit the keyboard, it was as if her thoughts took over and she found herself writing how Timothy – sorry, Ian – had even suggested that Blake take photos of their honeymoon. It was as if the words wrote themselves. She read the column back when she'd finished and was amazed at what she'd written.

Almost a Bride

You'll never guess what's happened this week. I can hardly believe it myself. You'll never guess what Ian suggested AGAIN this week – that Blake accompanies us on our honeymoon to take some professional shots of us walking hand in hand along the beach, gazing at each other under the moon, etc, etc. Which, OK, yes, is a lovely thought but not when the photographer is my ex. How can I get all smoochy and romantic with Ian when Blake is recording every moment? Well, not every *moment but you get the picture.*

Andrea said that if I no longer have feelings for Blake then it shouldn't matter. I guess she's right. I should flaunt my happiness, let him see how much in love Blake and I are, and what a wonderful wedding and honeymoon we're having. Show him I don't care.

I still wish we had a different photographer though. Anyone but Blake.

The photos aren't my only problem. Monster-in-law has been interfering again. She came around the other night and completely took over, insisting on helping us choose the menu and entertainment for the reception – I just about stopped her from booking a violinist!

She's trying to take over it all. She wanted to arrange the wedding cake and flowers too, but I politely insisted I did it myself, and thankfully Ian backed me up.

Andrea came around last night and we had a fun evening looking for bridal flowers on the internet – while we tucked into wine and chocolate. I had to hide the evidence before Ian came home and gave me a lecture. Honestly, monster-in-law has got him almost as obsessed with my weight as she is. To be honest, my trousers felt a bit tight around my waist this morning, not surprising after the binge last night, and I was too scared to weigh myself. It's fine. I don't have another dress fitting for a couple of weeks, I can easily slim down.

Anyway, here's a few of the bouquets we liked. Which one do you think is best?

She'd put pictures of three bouquets at the bottom of the article. She read it again and shook her head. Owen wouldn't be satisfied with that. He'd want the readers to choose whether she should tackle Timothy about Blake taking photos of their honeymoon. She bit her lip. She'd started writing about all this, she couldn't back out now.

She switched it around so that she started with monster-in-law interfering again, and moved the first paragraph after that. Then she ended with *I still wish we had a different photographer though. Anyone but Blake.*

The three options were: should she tell Ian she doesn't want Blake to accompany them on honeymoon, have a word with Blake herself and ask him to back out, or decide to rub Blake's nose in it and show him how happy she was?

She nodded. Yes, Owen would go for that. It was amazing how easy it was to write about such personal stuff. She thought of some of the popular columns in the dailies and how the writers often wrote about their own family. She'd been amused at some of the incidents and had never really thought of it as a betrayal, but she was sure Timothy would.

Well, he'd never find out. She only had four more columns to write, then it would be all over.

'Fabulous news, darling.' Savannah floated into the restaurant on a cloud of very expensive perfume, bent over just low enough so that Jared could see her pert breasts down the top of her designer dress, and kissed him on the cheek. 'I'm off to France for a photoshoot next week and we're a photographer short so I've recommended you. Do say you can come. It will be so divine.'

Before Jared could rise from his seat, the waiter dashed over to pull her chair out and she sat down opposite him. She reached across the table to place her hand on his, smiling winningly. 'Sorry I'm late, darling, but I don't get to look this good without putting in a bit of an effort.'

She did look good. Stunning, in fact. 'No worries, I haven't been here long myself.' Liar; he'd been here over half an hour.

'What's this about France?' he asked. 'You've only just got back from Cape Verde.'

'It's a two-day photoshoot on the river for *Mademoiselle* magazine,' she explained. 'One of the photographers is ill, so I thought you might like to do it. It'll give us chance to spend some time together. What do you think? Are you free? Oh, do say you are!'

He was free. He had next weekend off. He was thinking of using it to drive to the country and take some wildlife photos. He'd had enough of taking celebrity and wedding shots and wanted to get back to what he liked taking photos of most: animals. He thought about Savannah's suggestion. While taking shots of Savannah parading around in different outfits wasn't the way he'd planned to spend the weekend, the Dordogne was a beautiful region and he might get some lovely nature shots there. Plus he'd get paid in the process, so more money for his Arctic fund. It was worth doing.

'When do we go?'

'Friday night and back Monday afternoon. Can you make it?'

He could. He wasn't due in work again until the Tuesday, and Savannah seemed eager for his company. It could be just what he needed to wipe Cassie from his mind. He'd hardly been able to think of anything but that kiss. The feel of her lips against his, the shiver that had coursed through his body when she'd responded, the overwhelming urge he'd felt to make love to her ...

'Jared?'

Savannah was staring at him, waiting for his reply. He shrugged. 'Sure. Why not? Tell me the details.'

'Would the lady like a drink, sir?' Jared raised an eyebrow questioningly at Savannah who smiled and answered in her 'little girl' voice.

'Mineral water, please.'

Of course, she'd be watching what she ate and drank if she was going on a photoshoot next week. A model's life wasn't as glamorous as most people thought. In fact, it was pretty boring. A restricted diet, early nights, constant worry about looks, weight, protecting their skin from the wind, and the sun. The money they earned was fantastic but what a price they had to pay. All the successful models he knew had been highly stressed and neurotic, beautiful to look at but far from easy company. Not like Cassie. She was beautiful *and* fun to be with.

Here he was again, thinking of her. Yes, he definitely needed to go away for a while.

Over a meal of chicken salad for Savannah and steak for him, they discussed the French trip. Savannah had no idea of the fee, but Jared was confident it would be a substantial one. She handed him a business card and told him to phone the number on it tomorrow. 'Madeleine is waiting for your call. I told her that I was pretty sure you'd be interested, but phone her before ten or she'll give the job to someone else.'

'OK.' He slipped the card into his wallet. 'Now, what do you fancy doing for the rest of the evening?'

Savannah leant forward so the neck of her dress once again revealed her bare breasts. 'How about we go back to yours?'

'Sounds good to me.' He beckoned the waiter over for the bill. It looked like this was one night he wouldn't be lying awake thinking of Cassie.

Nineteen

'I must say, I wish we'd had a bit longer to plan this wedding. Everything is such a rush.' Cassie stepped into the long, royal blue dress she'd worn for their engagement meal. 'I mean, it was very kind of Sylvia to save the cancellation at the castle for us, but ...'

'Yes, two months isn't long to plan a wedding.' Timothy buttoned up the crisp white shirt he'd worn that night and selected the royal blue tie that had accompanied it. He always liked to wear a tie that matched the colour of Cassie's dress. 'It was too good an opportunity to miss though, Cassandra.'

'I know.'

He came over and zipped up the back of her dress. 'You're not worrying about it all, are you?'

Cassie sat on the chair facing her dressing table mirror and opened her black velvet jewellery case. 'I am a bit,' she admitted as she took out a pair of sapphire and diamond studs. 'When we only got engaged on Valentine's Day, I thought we'd probably get married next year.'

'We can do it. It will take some organisation, of course, but Mother is very good at that, as you well know. Don't be reluctant to ask her to help. She'd be delighted.'

And completely take over.

He leant over and kissed the nape of her neck. 'Didn't you wear the diamond droplet earrings that night?' he asked.

He was right. 'Yes, of course. I forgot.' She put the studs back in the jewellery box and selected the diamond droplets.

'Forgot what you wore on such a special night? Really, darling.' Timothy's voice dripped with disapproval. She hated it when he spoke to her like that. It reminded her of Sylvia.

'A momentary lapse; my mind was on other things.' She took the gold back off the earring, slipped it into her right ear, and secured it. She selected the other earring and did the same with her left ear. Then she took out the matching diamond drop necklace – all Christmas presents from Timothy. 'Would you fasten this for me, please?'

'Do hurry, dear. We have to be at Alberto's in half an hour and you're nowhere near ready yet.' She could see the irritation on Timothy's face reflected in her dressing table mirror as he fastened the necklace. 'You wore your hair in a chignon, remember? That will take you a while to do.'

So she had. She was hoping he'd forgotten, so she could wear her hair down, that way she'd only need to give it a quick brush. 'Yes, I do. It won't take me long.'

Twenty-five minutes and a couple of attempts later her hair was finally secured up in a chignon. 'Sorry, I don't know why it wouldn't go right today,' she mumbled. Although she did know why. It was because Timothy was watching her, getting more and more impatient by the minute.

'The taxi's here. Are you ready?' Timothy glanced impatiently at his watch. Again.

'One sec.' Cassie grabbed her bag and white fur stole. 'Ready.'

She followed him to the door, hoping that Jared would be late. It would annoy Timothy if Jared arrived before he had time to set the scene exactly as he wanted.

He wasn't looking forward to this. It was weird seeing Cassie and Timothy together, and photographing their 'mock engagement' wasn't high on his list of fun things to do. That's why he'd agreed when Savannah had asked him to drop into the launch party for Midas Designs this evening, an event he'd usually run a mile from, as he found a lot of people in the fashion world to be self-obsessed and superficial. Tonight though, he'd be glad of having somewhere to go after the

148

engagement shoot; to have something take his mind off seeing Cassie all loved-up with Timothy.

They had just seated themselves at the table when Jared arrived, camera slung over his shoulder, looking roguishly handsome in a dashing light grey suit and pale blue shirt. The same blue as her bridesmaids' dresses, Cassie realised. It had been both their favourite colour, she remembered. She'd worn a dress that colour on their first date, at the local coffee shop, and Jared had turned up in a matching jumper. They'd both giggled and immediately felt at ease with each other. She couldn't believe she'd forgotten. That she'd chosen her and Jared's favourite colour for her wedding theme. What did that say about her?

What did it matter, it was only a colour.

'Hi. I was hoping you'd both be on time. I've a launch to go to after this.' Jared took his camera out of the case. 'I'll take a selection, shall I, then you can take your pick? Shall we start with recreating the proposal?'

'Sorry?' Cassie stared at him, bewildered. Was he serious? She'd thought Jared was going to take a couple of shots of them having a champagne toast, the table laid for the meal, perhaps, maybe exchanging a kiss. Not this.

'Mother suggested it and I agreed, it's a splendid idea.' Timothy slipped his hand in the inside pocket of his jacket and took out the red velvet box that Cassie's engagement ring had been in. He placed it on the table in front of her. 'Take your ring off, Cassandra, and place it in the box for a few moments, will you?'

She was stunned. Timothy and Sylvia had once again planned things between them without bothering to consult her. I can't do this. I can't have Timothy kneeling in front of me, proposing to me, with Jared watching and photographing it. That's seriously weird.

Even as the words whirled through her mind she was taking off her ring and placing it in the box. Then Timothy was down on one knee, holding out the ring, and Jared was flashing away. She could feel his eyes on her but she couldn't look at him.

'That's great, Hold it there. Let's see a smile, Cassie. This is a big moment for you. One of the happiest days of your life.'

She couldn't figure out if he was teasing her or being serious. She forced her red lipsticked lips into a big smile as she looked down at Timothy on one knee in front of her, hand outstretched holding the open box. The diamond sparkled in the flashlight of Jared's camera, but she barely noticed it. All she could think of was how horrified she'd felt the night Timothy had proposed, how trapped she'd felt into saying yes. Right now, she felt just as trapped.

'OK, Cassie. Hold your hand out so Timothy can slip the ring on your finger.'

She couldn't look at Jared; couldn't meet his eyes. She kept her gaze on Timothy, smiled at him, as she obliged. Then he was slipping the ring on her finger and kissing her and Jared was still snapping away.

How was she going to bear Jared photographing their wedding if she couldn't even stand this?

'That's great. Wonderful. Now how about a final shot of you both having a celebratory drink of champagne? That should wind it up nicely.'

The waiter opened the champagne, poured it into the glasses, they clinked glass in a toast to each other, then entwined wrists and sipped out of the glasses. It was exactly what they'd done on the night they got engaged. Except Jared was filming her and she couldn't stop thinking about her other engagement, hers and Jared's, when Jared had driven them to their favourite spot in the country, prepared a picnic hamper, and proposed to her in a field where there were only a few cows to witness it. He'd given her a ring with a tiny diamond in it that had taken up months of his part-time wages in the local café. They'd agreed they were too young to get married yet, but their engagement was a symbol of their love and commitment to each other. She was twenty. Two years later they split up.

That had to be the hardest thing he'd ever done. Cassie looked stunning and couldn't take her eyes off Timothy the twat all evening. It was obvious she loved him. *Or loved the lifestyle he*

150

could give her. As soon as the thought slid into his mind he shoved it away. Cassie wasn't that mercenary. No, she loved Timothy, that had been clear tonight. She'd had such a dreamy look on her face as he slipped the ring on her finger and her smile had almost stretched from ear to ear.

That kiss she had shared with Jared, the one that had taken them both by surprise, had meant nothing to her. Her body had merely reacted to him as if out of habit, and he'd assumed it meant she still had feelings for him. Tonight had shown him quite clearly that she hadn't. Cassie had moved on, and so had he. It was time he stopped taking a nostalgic trip down memory lane.

'I'll work on the photos and send them over to you sometime tomorrow,' he said as he put his camera in the case. 'Would you like me to email them over to you, then you can make your selection and email them back?'

Cassie looked relieved. He guessed she didn't want to spend time with him any more than he did with her. 'That will be perfect.' She tilted her face enquiringly towards Timothy, 'Would you like Ja – J.M. to email them to me or you?'

She almost slipped his name out then, which would have been awkward. Timothy didn't seem to notice.

'Best to give him your email address, my inbox is full enough as it is,' he replied. 'We can have a look at them together over the weekend.'

Cassie opened her bag and took out a business card. 'You can send them to my work email. I can access it at home,' she said, handing it to him.

'Thanks.' He slipped the card into his pocket then held out his hand first to Timothy and then to Cassie, taking care that he only shook hers lightly, that he didn't meet her gaze. He smiled at them both. 'I must dash now, the launch started half an hour ago and my girlfriend is expecting me.' He actually didn't class Savannah as his girlfriend but he wanted Cassie to know that he'd moved on, too. 'Enjoy the rest of your evening.'

He was glad of an excuse to get away. A night with Savannah and her media friends would take his mind off Cassie.

Twenty

The photographs had turned out lovely. Cassie had always been photogenic, but she looked absolutely stunning in these photos, Jared thought as he flicked through them all on the computer screen. He paused on a photo showing Cassie looking down at Timothy, who was on bended knee, holding out the ring and gazing up at her. She had a strange expression on her face. He enlarged the picture – she looked almost panicked. Perhaps it was because he was there. Was she afraid he would slip up, let Timothy know of their shared past?

He flicked through the other photos. She was smiling in them all, her eyes sparkling. He enlarged another shot, one of Timothy tenderly holding up Cassie's hand to show off the sparkling diamond on her finger. Cassie was looking down at him, a smile dancing on her lips, her eyes sparkling almost as much as the diamond ring. She obviously loved him. They looked so happy together. He should be pleased for her. He *was* pleased for her. She deserved happiness after the way he'd broken her heart.

He selected the best shots, enlarged them, and worked on them a bit, then took the business card Cassie had given him out of his pocket. Cassie Tyler, Features Writer, it said, with the name of the newspaper underneath, then her email address and the phone number of the newspaper offices. By giving him this, rather than her personal email, she was telling him that she wanted to keep things strictly business-like. That suited him just fine.

On a new email he typed in her email address and then 'Engagement Photos' in the subject bar. It seemed strange to be emailing her again after all these years. Best to play safe and address it to both her and Timothy, he decided, composing a brief email to say that he was attaching a selection of the photos for them to choose whatever they required, and email back the details to him. He signed it 'Best wishes, J.M.' and pressed send.

He wondered whether they would choose them together or if Cassie wouldn't be able to resist a sneak peek. The Cassie he knew wouldn't have. She'd have opened the file, had a good look, and carefully chosen the ones she thought were best beforehand. He'd lay a bet she'd do the same now, but she needn't worry: she looked good in all of them. She was a natural beauty, one of those women who looked just as good first thing in the morning when she'd just woken up as she did when she was all dressed up to go out. He'd always preferred the 'just woken up' Cassie, with the tousled hair and sleepy eyes, all warm and cuddly as she wrapped her arms around him and gave him a 'Good morning, I love you' kiss. He'd pull her close and they'd kiss, softly at first, then hungrier, skin touching skin – neither of them ever wore pyjamas. He wondered if she did now – hands caressing, their passion rising until they couldn't control it. The memories of the intensity of their lovemaking still had the same reaction as they always had. He shook his head and stood up. He needed a coffee. A black coffee. And if he kept thinking about Cassie that way he'd be in need of a cold shower.

Cassie was out following leads all morning but as soon as she returned after lunch she logged in to her email.

'Are you expecting a message from someone?' Beth asked. 'Another press trip away? Only this time I call dibs on it.'

Cassie grinned, knowing that Beth would hate to leave her beloved husband and two children behind to go on a press trip abroad. 'The photographer's sending me some photos over – we did a reconstruction of our engagement night so he could take some shots of it. Timothy – we – thought it would be nice to have a sort of photographic diary leading up to the wedding too.'

'It sounds a lovely idea. It must have been dead romantic to recreate such a special evening. I would have blubbed.' Beth was soft-hearted and cried at most things. A soppy text from her husband, or cute drawing by one of her kids would bring tears to her eyes.

Beth was right. It should have been romantic but it wasn't. It was awkward and forced. Cassie had felt uncomfortable all evening. That's one of the reasons she was so anxious to see the photos – she was hoping the smile she'd plastered on her face all evening didn't look as false as it felt.

There were loads of emails in her inbox, most of them about her 'Almost a Bride' column. It was getting more popular every week. Owen had remarked that if the emails carried on like this they would crash the server, but she knew he was delighted about it. Sales had now trebled and were rising each week. She was proud of the success of her column, even though she was still constantly worried that someone Timothy or Sylvia knew might read it.

'Have the photos arrived?' Beth asked.

'I don't know yet.' Cassie skimmed through the emails, then nodded as she saw J.M@IDimages.com in the subject bar. Jared. 'Got them.'

'Can I see them?' Beth pulled her chair closer.

She felt ridiculously apprehensive as she opened the email. It was addressed to both of them, polite and to the point. What had she expected? A love letter?

'Hang on while I download them.' Cassie clicked on the attachments. A few seconds later, the first photo appeared on the screen. She stared at the picture of herself gazing lovingly at Timothy, who was bending one knee and holding out the engagement ring. How could she look so happy and in love when she'd felt so uncomfortable? Who said photos never lie?

'It's gorgeous. Oh, look at you both. It's so obvious you adore each other,' Beth gushed. 'Let's see the others.'

Cassie flicked through them all one by one, with Beth 'ooing' and 'ahhing' as she looked at them. She had to admit that Jared had done a fantastic job. She could see that the images had been enhanced, but it was so skilfully done that they looked perfectly natural. Timothy looked dashing and she looked more gorgeous than she'd ever thought possible, even if she said it herself. Sylvia had been right to book him. The wedding photos would be stunning.

Some of the others heard their comments and came over to have a look, too.

'You're so lucky, Cassie. My Harry didn't even get down on his knee the first time he proposed, and if he had there's no way he'd do it again just for a photo,' one of the women said.

She's right. She was lucky, Cassie acknowledged, and if seeing Jared didn't mess with her head so much she'd be really looking forward to the wedding. Thank goodness she didn't need to see him again until the week before the wedding, when he would be taking pictures of the dress fittings.

Timothy was pleased with the photographs when she showed them him on her laptop that evening.

'Very professional. There's a certain sophistication about them, yet they look natural and unaffected. I knew I could trust Mother's judgement,' he said approvingly.

'How many would you like and which do you like best?' she asked. She thought three were enough and had already selected her favourites.

Timothy flicked through them all again, pursing his lips thoughtfully. 'They're all extremely good, I'd say four, recording the event chronically.' He clicked on a picture of him getting down on one knee, then one of him slipping the ring on her finger, one of them kissing, and finally toasting their engagement. 'I'd choose these four. Do you agree?'

They weren't the ones she'd chosen. They were nice but they looked a bit ... polished. 'I preferred the more natural ones,' she admitted. She flicked back through the photos. 'See, this one here. It's almost the same as the one you chose but our smiles seem more relaxed.' Well, her smile did, anyway. 'And this one, we're turning towards each other slightly as we do the toast. I agree about the other two, though.'

'Let's compromise. I'll concede this one.' He pointed to one of the pictures she'd chosen. 'Agreed.'

'Agreed. I'll email J.M. tomorrow and let him know our selection.'

'Thank you, sweetheart.' Timothy kissed her on the forehead. 'That's another thing to tick off the list. I really think we're getting there.'

'We are. I'll nail down the flowers and wedding cake next week,' she promised him 'I'll have it all sorted out before I go on my press trip.'

It was all coming into place, she thought happily as she lay in bed that night listening to Timothy snoring. She could do this. This time next month she'd be Mrs Campbell and would never have to see Jared again. She'd look back on this as a blip.

Twenty-one

It had got to be a habit now. Every Saturday morning on the way to work, Jared bought a copy of the newspaper Cassie worked for, and as soon as he'd picked up a cup of coffee he took it into his office, opened it, and read her column. He was looking for any mention of himself, of course, but he enjoyed reading it. Cassie had an easy, humorous writing style and he could see why the column was so popular. He settled in his chair, took a sip of his coffee, and turned to the Femail supplement.

Almost a Bride

It gets worse and worse. I don't know where to even start this week. First, monster-in-law arranged for Blake to recreate our engagement shots without even clearing it with us first. She checked Ian's diary to make sure he was free. What a cheek! I know we talked about having some engagement shots done, but no one asked her to sort it out for us, the woman just takes over. It was awful, I can tell you. We dressed up in the same clothes as on our engagement night, went to the same restaurant, and Ian actually got down on one knee and proposed again while Blake clicked away. I don't know how I got through it. It felt so wrong for my ex to be photographing such an intimate moment. Mind you, it was a good opportunity to show him how in love Ian and I both are and how I am so over Blake dumping me. It

159

was worth the awkwardness to do that. And yes, OK, for a teeny nanosecond I couldn't help thinking how different it was when Blake proposed to me. Then I pushed the thought away. Blake is history.

Then monster-in-law came around AGAIN to talk about the wedding arrangements and spent most of the evening lecturing me on watching my weight. Her eyes almost popped out of her head when she saw me have a second glass of wine. Honestly, I was so stressed by the time she left I had to tuck in to my secret chocolate stash. The woman is a control freak. She even tried to talk me into getting a wedding planner. I don't need one. I could manage fine if I hadn't been pushed into this elaborate wedding at such short notice.

I'm getting there, anyway. The bridesmaids' dresses and tiaras are all chosen now. And they're gorgeous. Maisie and Jemma were both throwing a right strop because they liked different dresses, but Andrea came to the rescue and found one the two girls adored – thank God! – and in the colour I wanted, too.

I've got to go away for few days for work soon. Of course monster-in-law disapproves but has seized upon the opportunity to take over more of the wedding preparations. We have now decided that I'm in charge of the flowers and wedding cake and monster-in-law is doing the rest. Honestly I don't know why I don't hand it all to her, and just turn up on the day.

I keep telling myself it will all be fine. And it would be if I didn't have monster-in-law breathing down my neck.

And Blake wasn't my photographer.

I'm going to check out cakes and flowers this week. I've done my research and here's a few wedding cakes I like. Which would you choose?

As usual, there were three options to choose from.

Jared read the article over again. She hadn't said much about him, but she had suggested that she still found it difficult with him being her photographer.

He opened his email, logged on to the newspaper website, and checked out the comments for her column. There were hundreds, most of them telling her to ditch Ian and give Blake another chance. 'It's obvious you still love him,' one of them said. 'Ian is a mummy's boy,' said another.

Cassie had certainly got people talking. Did he agree with their advice?

He had to admit that until Thursday night he was convinced Timothy was the wrong man for Cassie. But they'd seemed so happy together, so in love, when he'd taken the engagement shots.

He tossed the paper onto his desk. Cassie had moved on, and so had he. He couldn't wait for this job to be over, for her to get married, then he wouldn't have to see her again and could finally get her out of his mind for good.

Cassie and Sam spent the afternoon shopping for shoes, bridesmaids' gifts, and other odds and ends.

'I saw your column,' Sam said, as they stopped for a break – coffee for her and fruit tea for Cassie, who was feeling a bit guilty about the bar of chocolate she'd sneakily eaten after Sylvia had gone last night.

'So?' Cassie challenged her.

'It's good. Really. I don't know how you put up with Sylvia. And,' she leant forward and whispered, 'come on, 'fess up – how did you feel redoing the whole proposal thing so Jared could take photos?'

'It was excruciating.' Cassie sighed. 'I couldn't wait for it to be over, to be honest.' She met Sam's gaze. 'I couldn't help remembering when Jared had proposed to me. I know we were little more than kids, that we weren't planning on getting married for ages … but it brings it all back. I wish Sylvia had chosen anyone but him to photograph our wedding.'

'What are you going to do? Can you handle it?'

'I have to. I'll be fine once the wedding is over. It's just seeing him again, it drags up all the old memories.' She finished her drink. 'Come on, we've still got the flower girls' gifts and our shoes to get. I'm away on that press trip next weekend so I've got to get them sorted today.'

'What are you thinking of getting them? Jewellery?'

'I don't know. A cross or a bracelet is traditional but I wanted to get something a bit different.'

'How about a bride bear?' Sam suggested. 'There's a fantastic store in the precinct called Choose a Bear with lots of bears and assorted outfits to choose from. I'm pretty sure I've seen a wedding dress among them.'

'That's great. The girls will love that.' Cassie smiled at her. 'I knew you'd come up with something, Sam.'

Cassie was delighted with the selection of bears and outfits in the shop. She and Sam walked around the aisles 'ooing' and 'aahing' at all the gorgeous bears, ranging from tiny ones that fit in your hand to big ones the size of a toddler.

'Oh, look,' squealed Sam, running over to a big, golden-furred teddy bear standing upright against the wall. 'You could dress this one up as a bride and that one,' she pointed to a darker furred bear that looked decidedly male, 'can be the groom. That would be soo cute! Go on, Cas, you know you want to.'

Cassie couldn't help grinning as she watched Sam fishing through the outfits for a wedding dress, then holding it up against the golden teddy. Yes, it did look cute, and she was pretty sure that if it was Sam's wedding she wouldn't be able to resist buying the huge teddies and dressing them up as the bride and groom. Paul would probably find it funny too; knowing them, they'd even include the bears in their wedding photos. She was pretty sure that Timothy wouldn't find it amusing though, and Sylvia definitely wouldn't. She did like the idea of small bears for Emma and Sophia, and was sure the little girls would love them.

Emma took out her camera and snapped the two bears. 'I've got to show Paul these.'

Smaller versions of both bears lined up on the shelf caught Cassie's eye. She picked up a bear for a closer look. Its face was so cute, with beady brown eyes and a little black nose. She ran her hands over the soft fur. Two of these would be just right.

'I can't tempt you to have the big ones?' Sam asked as she joined her.

'No, but these are ideal. Do you think I should get them both the same colour bear or two different ones?'

Sam scratched her cheek thoughtfully. 'It's a tough one, because if you get them different ones they might argue over who wants which one, and if you get them the same they might get them mixed up and then argue which bear is whose.'

Which is exactly what Cassie was thinking. Then she noticed that some of the bears had different coloured ribbon around their neck. That was the answer! She was holding a bear with white ribbon, so she reached up and took a bear with blue ribbon down from the shelf. 'What do you think?' she asked Sam.

'Perfect!'

Cassie popped the two bears into a basket then wandered over to the clothes section. There were several designs of wedding dresses hanging on tiny white hangers, all complete with veils.

'I can't believe the cuteness.' Sam took a floaty dress with short, puffed sleeves off the hanger. 'Look at this. Isn't it divine?'

It took them several minutes and lots of 'oohs' and 'aahs' to decide on the dresses they wanted, select two veils, and take them all the till.

'Gorgeous, aren't they? Are you buying them for a bridesmaid gift?' The cashier asked as she scanned them.

'Yes, I'm getting married in a few weeks,' Cassie told her, taking the wedding cash card out of her purse and handing it over to pay.

'Congratulations. What an exciting time for you. Would you like them packed separately?'

'Yes, please.' Cassie keyed her pin into the card machine.

A few minutes later they left the shop, holding a teddy in a bag each. 'You're going to have such fun dressing up these,' Sam said. 'I'm beginning to feel dead jealous of you.'

As they walked to the car park it suddenly struck Cassie that Sam was far more excited about her wedding than she was.

I should be brimming with excitement, like Sam, she thought. I should be counting the days, making lists, planning all the lovely things I'm going to buy. Yet she couldn't summon up any enthusiasm at all. It was as if she was on a conveyor belt that was speeding her towards her wedding day, and she couldn't get off. The only thing she felt was panic.

Twenty-two

Cassie was on earlies the next week, so she spent the afternoons checking out florists and wedding cake makers. Finally, she found a very helpful florist called Daphne who seemed to know exactly what she wanted, and what's more, was free for their wedding date. 'I can bring the flowers to you on the morning of the wedding, if you wish,' she suggested. 'Then I can go straight to the château and do the table decorations.'

'That would be wonderful, thank you.' Cassie was relieved. Another task crossed off. 'I don't suppose you know anyone who could make a wedding cake for that day, do you?' If she didn't find someone soon, she'd have to opt for a traditional, white three-tier cake and she really wanted something different; something that would show Sylvia and Timothy that she had taste.

'Tilly and Mark Walters are what you need. They run the little cake shop in the village with a "design your own" cake service. They're very good.' She mentioned a couple of magazines they'd been featured in. 'If you tell them what you want I'm sure they could do it.'

'Do you think they could make one for three weeks' time?' Cassie asked anxiously. She was beginning to realise now why people planned weddings a year or so ahead.

'I don't think that would be a problem at all. Tilly and Mark are amazing, but are still a fairly new business so they're not besieged by orders yet.' Daphne assured her. 'Tell them Daphne sent you and I'm sure they'll try to fit you in.'

'I will. Thank you,' Cassie said gratefully. Tilly and Mark sounded ideal.

She followed Daphne's directions to the cake shop and introduced herself to the very pleasant couple, who both radiated smiles and bonhomie. Tilly and Mark were obviously happily married – they finished each other's sentences and constantly smiled and nodded at each other in agreement. They looked so much in love that Cassie felt a pang of regret that she and Timothy would never be like that. Yes, they loved each other but it was more of an adult, reserved kind of love. They never held hands or looked into each other's eyes like Tilly and Mark did. In fact, they only time they ever had close physical contact was when they made love.

Whereas when she was with Jared they had barely been able to keep their hands off each other, always touching, stroking, kissing …

She shook the memories from her mind. So what? They had been young and in love. She was older, more mature now and while Timothy wasn't a touchy-feely kind of guy, he loved her and would always be there for her. He wouldn't run out on her like Jared did.

'So how many tiers would you like?' Tilly was looking at her as if she'd already asked her the question once and been waiting for an answer. Maybe she had.

'Four please, octagonal, and could you trim them with pearl icing the same shade of blue as the bridesmaids' dresses, do you think?' She opened her bag and searched for the piece of blue fabric which she'd slipped into a small plastic bag to stop it getting grubby, along with a few other pictures of things she liked. She fished it out of the bag and took out the material.

'May I?' Tilly carefully took it off her and laid it out on her palm. 'Isn't it a lovely colour, Mark?'

He leant over and stroked the silky material. 'Beautiful. We could use this colour icing for the edging, and also make some sugar flowers for decoration, if you'd like.'

'Could you make a posy like this as the centrepiece?' Cassie asked, pulling the bouquet cutting out of the plastic file.

This time Mark was the one who took it off her. 'How exquisite. This is your bouquet, yes?'

'Yes. I don't want a lot of pink in it, and not too bright either. I'd like the colours delicate as in the picture.'

'I understand. No problem. We could do a small posy of this colour on every tier, in the corners, perhaps?' He glanced at her. 'Would you mind if I copy this picture? I have a photocopier in the flat if you could wait while I nip up.'

'Of course.'

Mark disappeared with the picture, leaving Tilly and Cassie to chat about her wedding plans. To Cassie's relief, the short notice was no problem, and Tilly even offered to personally deliver the cake to the castle on the day of the wedding. Mark returned with the picture, then cut a small sample off the blue material to make sure he matched the icing. Cassie left a deposit and her phone number, and it was all settled.

That was it, all sorted, Cassie thought as she walked over to her car. Every box was ticked with almost three weeks still to go. Planning a wedding wasn't so difficult after all.

'How's your column coming on, Cassie?' Owen asked when she walked into the newsroom.

She sighed. This column was getting to be a bit of a bugbear. 'Just about to write it,' she told him.

She'd decided to write about choosing the wedding cake this week, fruit or plain, different designs. Of course she'd have to bring Blake into it again, Owen always insisted on that. She sat down at the computer and opened a new document. Just write, she thought, then she could edit afterwards.

Almost a Bride

Three weeks to go and counting. There seems to be so many things to do that I almost wished we'd decided for a beach wedding abroad – just like Blake and I were planning to do all those years ago. I am not going to think of Blake. We are over, dead in the water. I'm marrying Ian and he's a wonderful man. Worth two of Blake. A wedding abroad would have been far easier though. All we'd have to do is choose our outfits and the rest would be done for us. Maybe I should have gone along with monster-in-law's suggestion of bringing in a wedding planner, then I could have sat back and left her to it. It didn't seem right thought, someone else planning my – our – wedding although TBH we have had someone else planning it, Ian's mother! If she had her way she'd have chosen the cake and flowers too but I resisted, although I could see that Ian wanted her to. None of them trust me to get it right. I mean. How difficult can it be?

She paused. Owen liked the readers to have a choice so they could vote: encouraging readers to participate increased sales, he said. What could she get them to vote on? She gnawed her lip for a moment. Ah, the cake! They could decide what flavour and style to go for.

It wasn't difficult at all, actually. I found a lovely florist and a cute cake shop in a little village. So the flowers and cake are now ordered. Thank goodness. I've decided on four tiers, which won't please monster-in-law. She said we should have three tiers, one to cut up on the day, one to cut up on our anniversary, and one for the christening of our first baby. I don't think I want to keep the cake that long, surely it'll be stale? I mean, I'm not intending to have kids for years yet although I know she thinks we should have them ASAP, preferably conceived on our wedding night. She's so eager to be a gran, not that she'll let the kids call her gran – it will be Grandmother. I don't know what Ian thinks, we haven't actually discussed having children. My best friend Andrea is aghast at this, and says it's too important a subject not to discuss, but actually I think it's too important to discuss before the wedding. I mean, what if Ian wants a family right away? There's no way I'm going to agree to that. Or what if he doesn't want one at all? I'd rather leave topics like that until we have to discuss them, why go looking for an argument? Not that we argue, Ian doesn't believe in arguing, but the long silences and clipped replies of 'yes' or 'no' can be rather hard going.

Anyway, back to the cake. Monster-in-law said that fruit cake is traditional for weddings but I hate fruit cake. I'd like a chocolate cake. Or at least one layer of chocolate. What do you think?

Here's a few wedding cake designs the lovely bakers make. Which one would you choose?

Cassie pasted three wedding cake photos in the document and read it through again. There, that sounded OK. She might as well send it over for subbing now: she was due to go home in half an hour.

She looked over at Owen's office. The door was open as usual and he was sitting at his desk. 'I've sent it to sub,' she called.

He put up his thumb and grinned.

He wasn't grinning when he called her into the office the next morning. 'Look, Cassie, you need to up the stakes with this column a bit. We need more reader interest, more conflict. You need to add another meeting with that photographer. Let Paige doubt her decision to marry Timothy. The readers like that.'

Damn the photographer. She wished she'd never written that mock column. It had turned into a monster she couldn't get away from. 'Look, he's a photographer. There's no need for me to see him every week. The readers won't buy it if I keep bumping into him. Surely they want to know more about the wedding plans? That's what the column is all about.' She paused for breath. 'Anyway, I have mentioned him.'

'Not enough,' Owen shook his head. 'You've set the precedent now, there's no going back. You've got to build up the tension. The readers want a "will she or won't she?". They want to be kept guessing as to whether the wedding will go ahead.'

Cassie stared at him, horrified. He's insisted on her upping the attraction between her and Blake every week but she'd no idea he was planning this angle. 'You've got to be kidding.' She

169

knew he was right. Her email box was full of messages asking the same thing, and wanting to read more about Paige and Blake. What had she started? 'Just tweak it a bit. Bring in another meeting with Blake. Maybe she can run into him at a coffee shop or something. And Cassie …'

'What?'

'It's a newspaper column, not a diary. You need to distance yourself from it a bit, stop comparing it to yourself and that bloody photographer ex of yours. Give the public what they want. Make things up.'

Cassie sighed and went back to her computer. Half an hour later she sent over the new column featuring Paige having to visit Blake, because she and Ian had changed the wedding album design, and leaving the studio wondering what her wedding to Blake might have been like and whether she was doing the right thing marrying Ian. A completely fictional account. Apart from the last bit. She'd found herself wondering what her and Jared's wedding would have been like quite a lot lately. It wouldn't have been so stressful, she was sure. And she'd have been a lot more excited about it. Excitement was something lacking from her and Timothy's wedding preparations. And that unsettled her more than she cared to admit.

Jared pulled up outside the little newsagents, turned off the engine, and got out of the car. He stepped inside and looked around for Cassie's newspaper, eager to read her column and find out if he was mentioned again. He devoured her words over and over again, a smile playing on his lips as he spotted the subtle digs at him, letting him know that she was so over him.

He never mentioned the column when he saw her, not since the first time. He didn't know if she thought he still read it, but he guessed she did. It was unspoken between them; something they both ignored, like the frisson that ran through them when they both touched. He knew Cassie was still attracted to him. It was in her eyes, her posture, and he was still attracted to her. He also knew that neither of them would do anything about it, they would continue along the paths they'd chosen for themselves. She would marry Timothy and become a lawyer's wife, probably give up work, have a couple of kids. He felt a wrench in his gut at the thought of Cassie and Timothy's kids. Would they have her blue eyes and golden hair? Timothy's smooth, sculptured good looks? They'd never be short of money, that's for sure, would probably be sent to public school, their careers mapped out in front of them as soon as they were born.

He wondered what their children would have been like, his and Cassie's. An image of a little girl with his dark hair and Cassie's twinkling eyes flashed across his mind. He thrust it away and picked up the newspaper. Their time had gone.

It was midday before he had a chance to read her column. He smiled as he read it. She had such a fluid, chatty style, he could imagine the scenarios she recounted – Sylvia with her pursed lips and tight face trying to take control over everything, Timothy the twat trying to keep the peace with his mother and Cassie determined to do things her way. He wondered how long it would be before twat and monster-in-law wore her down and turned her into a Trophy Wife.

Then he saw it, the bit about him at the end. He'd been wondering what she'd put, as she hadn't seen him this week, but had guessed her boss wanted her to keep up the tempo so she'd had to make something up. The column was getting a lot of hits. He read the last paragraph a few times. Was there any truth in it, he wondered. Was Cassie asking herself what her wedding to him would have been like? Because he was sure as hell asking himself the same question.

Twenty-three

'Dresses.'

'Sorted,' Cassie said. She'd had another fitting the weekend and miraculously, the dress still fitted. A bit snugger than last time, yes, but she'd soon lose that extra couple of pounds now she was cutting out chocolates and wine.

Well, trying to anyway and so far she'd managed two whole days.

'Flowers.'

'Sorted.'

'Horse and carriage?'

'Emma's got it all sorted.' Timothy and Sylvia didn't know that she was turning up at the castle in a horse and carriage. It was her little surprise. She'd given them the impression she'd booked a limo.

Sam read out the list of the wedding preparations and ticked them off one by one. 'I actually think we're done.' She sounded surprised. 'We're all ready for your wedding.'

'Which is a relief as I'm flying out tomorrow.' Cassie gave her a worried look. 'Are you sure we haven't forgotten anything?'

'We've ticked it all off. Three weeks to go and you're ready to roll,' Sam grinned. 'So you can go and relax. You lucky thing.'

'It's work,' Cassie said defensively. 'Owen will be expecting me to write loads of articles about this, and to bring in some advertising revenue.'

'I know it's work, but lucky you to be able to do it in France.' Sam slipped the notebook in her bag and took a sip of her coffee. 'Seriously, Cassie, it will do you good to get away. Take your mind off the wedding.' She paused. 'And Jared.'

Cassie raised her head in indignation. 'Who says I'm thinking about Jared?' she demanded.

'Your column says it. You mention him every week.'

'That's because I have to, Owen insists on it. He drives me mad with that perishing column. Thank goodness I don't have to write it for much longer.' She stirred a sweetener into her black coffee and gazed earnestly at Sam. 'You don't really think I've still got feelings for him, do you?'

Sam studied her thoughtfully. 'Haven't you? Even if it's only a little smidgen of a feeling?'

'Absolutely not,' Cassie said emphatically. 'Now can we please stop talking about him? I'm getting married in just over two weeks and the last thing I want to do is talk about my ex.'

Sam still looked thoughtful but changed the subject to the forthcoming trip, making Cassie promise to take loads of photos and bring her a souvenir back.

'I must go now.' Cassie pushed her chair back and rose from the table. 'I haven't packed yet and Timothy wants to take me out for a meal tonight. We've barely seen each other all week.'

'That's normal for you two. I've never known a couple to spend so much time apart.' Sam rose too and gave Cassie a hug. 'Have fun. Message me and let me know how you get on.'

'I will.' Cassie grabbed her bag and with a final wave to her friend, hurried out of the coffee shop. She'd already been longer than she planned and didn't want to keep Timothy waiting.

It would be a relief to get away for a few days. She needed some space to clear her head. The wedding was practically upon her and all she could think about was Jared. And it was all the fault of Owen and his bloody 'Almost a Bride' column. Writing about Jared – Blake – meant he was never out of her mind. She was constantly comparing how much she and Jared had been in love, how excitedly they'd planned the future, with the almost distant relationship she had with Timothy. Sam was right, they were both so busy working that they hardly seemed to spend any time together, although Timothy always made sure that they had their two nights of sex a week, usually Saturday and Wednesday night. Regular as clockwork. Timothy had discussed this with her when she'd first moved in, telling her it was important that they made time for each other in their busy schedule. So Saturday nights and Wednesday nights they always spent the last hour together drinking a glass of wine and catching up, then off to bed for sex. Not that she was complaining, the sex was OK. Pretty good, in fact. Timothy was an accomplished lover, but it was all so ... mechanical. Sometimes she wished he'd be spontaneous, sweep in on a Monday or Tuesday night, pick her up, and carry her off to bed.

Like Jared used to.

Jared, who was so spontaneous he ditched her to go off and take photos the other side of the world. At least with Timothy she could rely on him.

She shrugged. She was done with thinking about Jared. She was going to concentrate on Timothy and their marriage. Starting right now.

To her surprise Timothy was home, showered and changed when she got in.

'I'm not late, am I?' she asked. 'I thought the table was booked for eight?' Timothy had insisted on them having a meal together the night before she went away. She knew what would be for dessert – it was Wednesday night – and wondered if he'd change his routine if she was going away on a Friday. And would he leave it until Wednesday for them to make love next week or insist on doing it Monday when she returned seeing as he'd missed his Saturday night session?

'It is and no, you're not.' He curled his arm around her neck and pulled her into his body, kissing her forehead. 'I wanted to make sure I finished early so we could enjoy the evening. Why don't you go and freshen up while I make you a coffee?'

'That would be lovely.' She snuggled into him, breathing in his warmth. It was unusual for Timothy to be so demonstrative.

'Black?'

'Please, no sugar.'

He kissed her on the cheek then released her and went into the kitchen. A few seconds later she heard him whistling as he filled up the kettle. He sounded in a good mood. She guessed that the case had gone well. She'd ask him about it over dinner, but right now she needed to get showered and changed. She hurried into the bedroom, placed her bags on the floor, opened the wardrobe door, and took out her crimson dress. She'd been thinking what to wear on the way home and decided on this one. With its spaghetti straps and fitted bodice which then fell into fine pleats that sashayed sensually when she walked, it was one of Timothy's favourites. She wanted to make sure that tonight was really special.

Timothy obviously had the same idea. He'd booked them an intimate table in a secluded corner of the restaurant and was very attentive all evening, even showing an interest in her trip – something he rarely did.

'Owen is hoping I'll sell some advertising space as well as get material for a few features,' she told him as she tucked into her pâté starter.

'I'm guessing that's holiday features?' Timothy sounded genuinely interested.

'Yes, and weddings.' The words were out before she could stop them. She'd deliberately avoided mentioning that the paper was running a wedding section, as she didn't want Timothy to get curious and read it. She had two more articles to do and then it would all be over. Thank goodness, the strain of anyone she or Timothy knew reading it and putting two and two together was telling on her. Although, she had to admit that she was delighted with the reaction to her column. Owen said circulation figures were going through the roof, and there was a constant stream of emails about her column every week. In fact, Owen was talking about giving her more features in the weekend supplement. None of this she could tell Timothy, however.

'Weddings?' Timothy repeated curiously.

'Yes, some of the châteaux I'll be visiting are wedding venues so Owen's hoping I can talk them into buying advertising space if we run a feature on a few of them.' That was basically true.

'I thought you just reported on local news. I didn't realise you did features too.' Timothy wiped his mouth with the napkin. 'I really should take more interest in your work.'

Nooo! Her mind screamed. Not now! Oh, the unfairness of it. The times she wished he would talk to her about her work, read her columns now and again instead of dismissing it as irrelevant. And now, the very time she didn't want to discuss it, he'd decided to bring up the subject. It's just because you're going away for a few days, so he's making an effort, she reminded herself. She smiled sweetly and placed her hand on his. 'You're far too busy winning important court cases. I take it the one you've been working on has finished? Did you win?'

His face broke into a wide grin. Actually, it was more of a smirk. 'I did. What's more, I wiped the floor with Denver. If I say it myself, it was the best closing speech I've ever given.' The danger had passed as he spent the rest of the evening telling her about his part in the court case, how the judge had praised him, how annoyed Denver had been, and how delighted Felicity had been that he'd won such a high-profile case that was bound to bring them in more important clients. 'We may have to take on another partner if we keep expanding as we're doing,' he said proudly.

'That's excellent.' She nodded approvingly. 'I'm so proud of you.'

'If we do expand it will mean you won't have to go out to work, sweetheart. You could freelance from home. Just think, no more going out on cold winter mornings, no more long days in the office. We can move to a bigger house and you can have your own office there.'

She stared at him in dismay, not knowing what to say. She loved the hustle and bustle of working in the newspaper office, the company of the other journalists, working to tight deadlines, everything. She wasn't sure she wanted to swap all that to work at home.

He's just trying to make your life easier. Don't get worked up about it tonight. You can argue your corner when the time comes.

His next words completely floored her. 'That will give you more free time to look after the house and organise our dinner parties.'

What? They'd never discussed this. Whenever Sylvia suggested that she give up work to be Timothy's full-time wife after they got married, Timothy had given her the impression that he didn't think the same. Now he was landing this on her.

She swallowed. She wasn't arguing about it now. Not the night before she went away. She'd discuss it with him later. After all, it might never happen. Timothy was talking about *if* the firm expanded.

She took a gulp of her wine. 'It's good to hear that your business is doing so well,' she said diplomatically. 'At least I know you won't be lonely while I'm away.'

'No time for that, I've a big case to get ready for.' He reached out for her hand, picked it up, and kissed the back of it. 'I'll miss you terribly, though.'

She flashed him a big smile. 'And I'll miss you too.'

She put the conversation of her giving up work out of her mind and they spent the rest of the evening chatting pleasantly.

Later though, after they'd made love and Timothy lay snoring by her side, she thought back to the conversation and felt a wave of panic. What was she getting into? She would soon be Timothy's wife and it was clear that his expectations of her future life weren't quite what she expected.

I'll talk to him when I come back from France, she resolved. Make him understand how important my job is to me. It'll all be fine.

But it was a long time before she got to sleep that night.

Twenty-four

The wedding company had booked Cassie's seat on the plane, economy class of course, but that was fine by her. She sat by a man who introduced himself as Steve, a journalist on a travel magazine. They spent the hour and half flight to Bergerac Airport exchanging anecdotes about the various articles they'd written and people they'd met. Steve's anecdotes were far more exciting than Cassie's.

'I've always wanted to travel the world and write articles about the places I go to,' Cassie told him. 'Nowhere too exotic though, I don't like to take risks. Europe and the neighbouring countries are about as far as I'd like to go.'

'Well, why don't you?' Steve asked her. 'There's plenty of magazines looking for a constant supply of travel articles. You'll have to take the plunge and freelance though, I shouldn't think there's a lot of scope for them in your local newspaper and your boss probably won't be happy at you freelancing for other mags.'

'He'd be cool about the odd one, but not on a regular basis,' Cassie replied. 'I like working on the paper. There's a lot of variety, and it's a regular wage, but I'll definitely think about freelancing.' Maybe Timothy's idea of her freelancing from home once they got married wasn't such a bad one after all. It would give her the opportunity to spread her writing wings a bit and aim for some of the commercial magazines. Of course, it would mean she'd be away from home more often but she doubted Timothy would mind. He was always so busy, she was sure he'd appreciate having the house to himself for a few days. Then she remembered Timothy's worrying remarks last night. He was obviously expecting her to be some sort of trophy wife when they got married. Well, I'm not going to, she decided. Sylvia can do the entertaining for him, she enjoys that kind of thing. In fact, the more she thought about it the more she thought that would be the perfect solution. Then Sylvia would feel useful and might stop interfering in Timothy and Cassie's life. Result all around.

Gwen, the manager of Dream Weddings, was waiting to greet them as soon as they came through customs.

'Welcome, everyone. I hope you've all had a good journey.' She smiled at the chorus of 'yes'. 'There's a minibus waiting for us outside to take us to our first venue, Le Château Tranquil. It's a beautiful château set in the countryside and you'll be staying the night there.'

Once on board, Gwen explained that she would be with them for the four days they were in France, as would the bus driver, Jean, and they were to ask as many questions as they wanted. The other journalists were a friendly crowd and Cassie found herself seated next to Leah, a features writer from *Beautiful Brides* who was planning on doing a four-page spread on wedding venues in the Dordogne area. Leah, a tall, dark-haired woman with a guffawing laugh, was hilariously funny, telling Cassie some of the horror stories would-be brides sent in to them. 'If there's one thing writing for this mag shows you, it's that people get really worked up over weddings,' she said with a grin. 'It's as if the day takes over everything. The brides get so blinkered they can't see anything beyond having the perfect day where they get to be princess, and they don't care how much it costs. When I get married I'm not going to get obsessive. I'm going to keep it relaxed and low-key.'

'That's what I intended to do but I got ambushed.' The reply was out of Cassie's mouth before she realised.

Leah jumped on it. 'Intended? Are you married then? Or going to be?'

Cassie hesitated, not wanting Leah to link her to the 'Almost a Bride' column. 'Not married yet,' she smiled, 'But we are planning to, and I can't believe how carried away everyone gets with the preparations. Personally, I don't care where we get married or how much my dress costs as long as I'm marrying the man I love.'

Was she marrying the man she loved, though? Thankfully, before she had time to explore the thought, Leah started telling her an amusing story about one bride-to-be's effort to find the perfect dress, finally deciding on a huge white meringue she could barely walk in. 'Honestly, the hoops under the dress were so wide she got stuck in the doorway when she went to the loo. Everyone pushed and pulled but they couldn't budge her. They had to call the fire brigade in the end and the dress had to be cut so they could free her. She was really upset. It's a good job they'd already had the wedding ceremony, otherwise I'm sure she would have called it off.'

'How embarrassing!' Cassie said sympathetically, although she couldn't help giggling at the image of everyone trying to free the poor bride. Fancy having a dress so wide she couldn't get through the doorway, and to be stuck in the toilet of all places? She bet the bride was mortified.

'Then there was the bride who wanted a red wedding: everything had to be red, including her hair.' Leah's wedding anecdotes kept Cassie chuckling for the rest of the journey.

It was just over an hour's drive to the château, which nestled in a pretty valley surrounded by quaint villages. As they all stepped out of the coach, they were greeted by Chloé, the manager, who had arranged for coffee and pâtisseries to be laid out in the reception area, a welcome treat after the long trip.

'Mesdames et messieurs, bienvenue à Château Tranquil. I am Chloé Martineau, the manager. Please do be seated and avail yourself of the refreshments. The porters will take your luggage to your rooms while I tell you a little about the château.'
'If all the châteaux are like this I'm going to enjoy this trip,' Leah whispered.

Cassie smiled, she'd been right to get away. This was just what she needed. A break from Sylvia and the wedding plans, time to be herself, to get things into perspective. And, best of all, a break from Jared.

Jared zipped up his case and glanced at his watch. He had half an hour to get to the airport. Part of him wished he wasn't going now. Most men would probably think he was mad, but spending the next three days filming Savannah and the other models in their beachwear didn't appeal to him at all. Neither did going to the South of France. The only reason he'd accepted the job was the very generous fee. He knew that some photographers wouldn't sacrifice their art for money but he looked on jobs like this as a means to an end. If taking photos of celebrity weddings and models frolicking on the beach paid for a few weeks filming wildlife then it was a sacrifice he was willing to make.

And it would do him good to get away and get Cassie out of his head.

As the wedding approached, he found himself thinking about her more often. He told himself that he could be professional on the wedding day and the honeymoon, that she meant nothing to him, but she was constantly on his mind. Everyone said that your first love was the one you never forgot, what chance did he have of forgetting Cassie when he was constantly in such close contact with her?

At least now he wouldn't have to see her until her wedding day, when Cassie would be Mrs Campbell and it would all be over. Yes, there were still the few days he had to join them on honeymoon but then he'd be off the Arctic and would never see Cassie again. As far as he was concerned it couldn't come soon enough.

A beep outside announced the arrival of his taxi. He was meeting Savannah and the rest of the modelling team at the airport. He grabbed his bag and set off.

Twenty-five

The château was wonderful, Cassie thought, as she turned back the covers of her bed that evening and climbed in. Climbed being the right word, the bed was so high she had to stand on tiptoe and almost haul herself onto it. Once there, she wriggled into the middle of the thick, marshmallow soft mattress and leant back against the plumped-up feather pillows. Chloé had told them they were all staying in the guest bedrooms, so they could see for themselves the quality of the rooms. Cassie's room was decorated in a cream and violet tiny floral pattern with rustic wooden furniture, so pretty and quaint that she'd immediately taken several pictures of it.

Chloé had given them a detailed tour of the château that afternoon, pointing out things they might want to photograph or mention in their articles. The two honeymoon suites – the château could accommodate two weddings at the same time – were spectacular with gorgeous four poster beds, Jacuzzis, mini bars, and patio windows leading on to a private balcony overlooking the lake.

The immaculate gardens were exquisite, with a small chapel beside the lake where the ceremony took place. The reception was either held outside in a private lawn area laid with white round tables and chairs, decorated with white covers and coloured bows, or, if preferred, in the luxurious reception hall with seating for two hundred guests and a large dance floor.

There were a couple of little gîtes in the grounds if the newly married couple wanted seclusion from their guests, and enough rooms to cater for fifty guests. Cassie took lots of photos and made numerous notes, wanting to have plenty of material for articles.

She flicked open her phone and Skyped Timothy, but he was busy so they only talked for a few minutes, then she Skyped Sam, who begged her to show her the room and almost squealed in delight when Cassie told her all about the reasonably-priced wedding packages.

'That's what I want when Paul and I get married,' she said. 'A wedding in a French château sounds so romantic.'

'I've another three venues to see yet,' Cassie told her.

'You're so lucky, why didn't I become a features writer? Then I'd be able to have all freebie holidays abroad, too.'

'Hmm, well it's not always so exciting, most of the time I'm covering court cases and dog shows,' Cassie reminded her. She did love the variety of her job, and the fact that every day was never the same, but the idea of working for a travel magazine was still niggling in the back of her mind. Perhaps she should seize her dream, like Jared had done.

For the first time she realised that Jared might have done the right thing by finishing with her. Their relationship would never have worked if he was hankering after something else. In time he would have resented Cassie for stopping him doing what he wanted to do with his life, for clipping his wings.

It was a sobering thought. She'd been so wrapped up in her own hurt and distress that she had never stepped back to ask herself if it had been a difficult decision for Jared. Now she remembered the pain on his face when he'd told her he thought they should finish, set each other free.

'We're too young. I'm too young. There are things I want to do.' He'd pleaded with her, begged her to understand, for them to remain friends, but all she'd understood was that she loved him and her heart was breaking.

For a long time she'd been too hurt, too numb, too busy coping with the pain of getting through each day without Jared to think about what she wanted from life.

She could see now that he was right, they had been too young. As she snuggled down onto the soft mattress and wrapped the cool, cotton duvet around her she realised that Jared had done a very brave thing. He'd walked away from their relationship because he knew that he wasn't ready to settle down, that it wasn't right for him. He'd probably saved them both from a lot of future heartache.

Was she heading for more heartache? Was she doing the right thing now by marrying Timothy? Did she really want to spend the rest of her life with him? And if she didn't, could she be brave enough to call it off?

Twenty-six

The next day they all climbed into the minibus again to visit a stunning château on top of a hill, overlooking a medieval village. The facilities were amazing. 'It's almost like a fairy-tale castle,' Leah said as they took some shots of the round tower in the centre of the château. Cassie knew Sam would adore this. She was such a romantic. She wouldn't mind betting that once Sam saw these pictures she'd be working on Paul to get him to propose!

They drove on to visit a 14th century château later that afternoon, with its own chapel in the grounds. Gwen told them the history of the places they visited, handed out promotional materials, and happily answered any questions they had.

They all gathered in the dining room of the hotel for dinner and spent a lovely evening chatting. Cassie sat next to Leah and asked her more about her travel writing. As Leah related the countries she'd been to, Cassie realised more and more that it was what she wanted to do.

What about Timothy? The question niggled at her mind.

Getting married shouldn't stop you having a career. Timothy will still carrying on working as usual, she reminded herself. He's never complained if you've been away from home before.

She'd only been away a couple of times, though, and she wasn't his wife now. She couldn't get Timothy's conversation during their last meal together out of her head. Even if he went along with her idea that Sylvia should take over the entertaining, would he still expect Cassie to be more of a 'corporate wife'?

Well, if he did, tough. She still had her own life. This was the 21st century, for goodness' sake!

'Look, if you'd really like to do more travel writing we could swap emails and I'll let you know when another trip comes up,' Leah told her. 'You might be able to clear it with your boss and come along.'

'That would be fantastic. Thank you.' Cassie opened her purse and took out a business card.

'It'd be good to go on another trip together,' Leah said with a grin.

It certainly would, Cassie thought. Leah was great company.

The next day they travelled on to the last two châteaux, down in the Champagne region of the Dordogne. The first looked over the Dordogne River and had been restored beautifully, while still keeping some of its traditional features. The final château, where they would be spending the rest of the day and the night, was a medieval château in the heart of the Champagne region.

'It's breath-taking,' Leah gasped, taking shots of everything in sight.

Cassie agreed, it really was wonderful. There was certainly enough material for a few features. She'd take some notes about champagne making, and Owen might even let her write a feature about that. Or maybe she could sell a feature to a magazine. This trip had certainly been worthwhile.

As she snapped some shots of the château she couldn't help comparing it with Hollington Castle where she and Timothy were holding their wedding. The castle was beautiful, but part of her wished they were coming here instead, getting married in the picturesque little chapel overlooking the river, then after the wedding they could retreat to their own private accommodation in the converted barn. She imagined spending a week exploring the French countryside. It would be so relaxing and intimate. She and Timothy rarely managed to spend more than a couple of hours in each other's company. She sometimes felt that she didn't really know him. She was looking forward to spending some time together on their honeymoon. Timothy would no doubt have booked somewhere exotic, far more exclusive than this little French town. It would be lovely, she was sure of that. She sighed. If only Jared wasn't coming along for a few days. How was she supposed to deal with that?

'You look a bit wistful.'

Leah's words brought her out of her daydream. 'Oh, I was just thinking how much my friend Sam would love this. She wants a huge wedding when she gets married. She'd feel like a princess at this château.'

'That's what most brides are like,' Leah replied. 'They want to be a princess for the day. To feel beautiful, cosseted, pampered, and desired. That everyone is looking at them.'

I don't. I just want to know that I'm marrying someone I love; who loves me. And she was, wasn't she? She loved Timothy and he loved her. Not a wild, raging love that made your heart quicken and pulse race, but a quieter, adult love that was secure and reliable.

'Hey, look, someone's doing a photoshoot here,' Leah said. 'I wonder what magazine that's for.'

Cassie followed her gaze over the river and saw a young woman rowing a boat. She had long, dark hair and was wearing a tiny white bikini that showed off her tanned skin. Several other women were standing on the beach, all dressed in bikinis, and a man was taking photos of them, watched by a crowd of people who shouted out now and again. She could tell by the women's poses that Leah was right, they were models. Then the woman in the boat reached the shore and stepped out. There was something familiar about her.

Cassie shielded her eyes and squinted, but it was no good. She couldn't see her face clearly.

'What a glamorous job, hey?' Leah said.

Cassie shook her head. 'I don't envy the models. They rise and fall on their looks. I'd hate to live like that, having to watch what I eat, making sure I look my best all the time. I couldn't stand the strain. It'd be like getting married every day of your life!'

Leah shot her a questioning look. 'How far away is your wedding? You don't strike me as a very happy bride-to-be. Most of the ones I meet can't stop talking about their wedding, and the preparations, but you hardly mention it. And when you do it's as if you find it a real strain.'

Did she? She forced a smile on her face. 'Oh, take no notice of me. Of course I'm looking forward to it. I'm just not a "dressing up and planning" sort of girl. I'm a "running away and having a beach wedding" sort.'

'Then why don't you do that?'

'Because my fiancé has got quite an important job and his mother wants us to have a big society do,' she confessed.

'Oh dear, tough luck. I've met mother-in-laws like that.' Leah touched her arm sympathetically. 'Just remember that it's *your* wedding as well.'

Cassie stared at the model party. The photographer had his back to her but there was something disturbingly familiar about his stance, the way he held his camera, his thick, dark hair.

It couldn't be.

Of course it wasn't him. Jared wasn't the only photographer in the world who had dark hair and adopted that particular stance when he was taking photographs. Besides, why would he be in France? She shook her head, she'd been thinking about him far too much she was imagining him everywhere.

It was Jared. He walked into the dining room later that evening, his model girlfriend – the one he'd been dining with at the restaurant that night a few weeks ago – hanging off his arm. He looked devastatingly handsome in a superbly tailored black suit. His girlfriend looked stunning in a long, electric blue dress that fitted her like a corset. So Jared's photography skills now extended to beauty shots for magazines, too. She guessed he'd do anything to fund his trip.

She saw his eyes rest on her for a moment and hold her gaze, then he nodded and turned away, guiding his girlfriend by the elbow to an intimate table in the corner.

'You know that hunk?' Leah asked.

Nothing missed her sharp eyes. 'Yes, I've met him a couple of times.' When did her life get so complicated? She hadn't told Leah she was planning her wedding so now she couldn't tell her Jared was photographing it. And all because of that perishing 'Almost a Bride' column. She wished Owen had never asked her to write it.

Well, if she hadn't she wouldn't be here would she? And she wouldn't have missed this for the world.

'He can't take his eyes off you,' Leah said as they tucked in to their main course.

'Who?' Cassie looked up, startled.

'That photographer. He's been staring at you all evening. If I was his girlfriend I'd have chucked my glass of wine over his face by now.'

Cassie chuckled as a sudden memory flooded into her mind. It was Jared's birthday and she'd spent most of the day cooking a special meal for them both. She desperately wanted everything to be right. She'd lit candles, plumped up the cushions, laid the table and was carrying the meal – steak and stilton with French fries and petit pois, over to the table when she'd tripped and the whole lot had landed in Jared's lap instead. She'd burst into tears and he'd burst out laughing. He'd dried her tears, helped her clear up, then they'd shared her meal and a huge bag of popcorn as they'd watched a DVD together. Jared had been so easy-going then. She wondered if he was still as easy-going today.

Leah was staring at her curiously, so she quickly explained. 'Sorry, your comment reminded me of a time when I did chuck a meal over a boyfriend – by accident, of course.' She briefly related what had happened without mentioning that Jared was the boyfriend in question. Soon everyone else on the table joined in with anecdotes of dining disasters and Leah's attention was turned away from Jared, thank goodness.

Jared was stunned when he saw that Cassie was here. It was the last place he expected to see her. He wouldn't have thought that a small local paper would have the funds to pay for a trip to

France. Unless the hotel had paid, of course. Perhaps she'd joined a press trip.

She looked drop dead gorgeous, as usual, and perfectly at ease, chatting and laughing to the crowd seated around her table. He tried not to stare at her but he couldn't help it. His eyes were drawn to her like nails to a magnet and he had to keep forcing himself to look away. He could see that Savannah was getting annoyed. She didn't expect commitment from him, but she did expect his exclusive attention when he was with her. Beautiful models like Savannah didn't take kindly to being ignored.

'What is it with you and that woman?' she snapped, managing to make the word 'woman' sound derogatory. 'And what's she doing here?'

'She's a journalist so I'm guessing she's on a press trip.' He forced his gaze away from Cassie and rested it on Savannah. 'Sorry, babe. I was just surprised to see her.'

'She seems to pop up wherever we go,' Savannah said sullenly. 'I know you're photographing her wedding but you don't have to be friendly to her. She's just a client.'

'I know, but her husband-to-be is a very influential client and Daniel and Imogen want me to keep him happy. They're hoping he'll recommend us to his illustrious and very rich friends. I'll have to pop over and say hello to her in a few minutes, it's only polite. Come with me, I'll introduce you.'

'No thanks.' She pushed back her chair and grabbed her bag hanging on the back of it. 'I'm going to the little girls' room so if you must talk to her, do it now then you can give me your undivided attention when I come back.'

'Sure.' He went to get up but Cassie had disappeared, as had most of the crowd she'd been seated with. He'd catch up with her later, he decided.

When Savannah came back she looked even more sullen. 'Your client was in the loos, too,' she said. 'Giggling like a schoolgirl with a bunch of other women.' She pouted. 'I guess that means you didn't get a chance to speak to her, so are going to carry on staring at her all evening.'

Jared shook his head. 'Of course not. Now tell me what we'll be doing for tomorrow's shoot.' He deliberately sat with his back to Cassie's table so that when she and her friends returned he couldn't stare at her, but his senses were on alert all through the meal, listening for her voice, her laughter.

Cassie's entire body was aware of Jared's presence. It took all her willpower to ignore him and concentrate on talking to the people around her. She couldn't believe he was staying in the same hotel, but she wasn't going to let him spoil this trip for her. If she bumped into him she'd say be polite, and say hello, but she definitely wasn't going out of her way to talk to him. Judging by the daggers the woman he was with kept giving Cassie, she wasn't very pleased to see her either.

Don't worry, love, he's all yours, Cassie thought, turning away to talk to Ben, a journalist from *Travel the World* magazine. He was travelling around France for a week for a 'See France in a Week' article for the magazine, and was only stopping in the Dordogne for a day.

'Have you written any other similar features?' Cassie asked him.

'Sure, I've done a week in Spain, a week in Italy, a week in Greece, and a week in Portugal. It's a regular feature the editor's running for a while. It's very popular and we get a lot of reader feedback.'

'It sounds fascinating. I'd love to write features like that. I wonder if I can persuade Owen, my editor, to let me do a few features on weddings abroad. Weddings in Spain, weddings in Greece ...' She picked up her glass and took a sip of wine. 'Especially if I'm wined and dined like this. I feel very spoilt.'

'Which magazine do you work for?' Ben asked.

'Oh, just the local newspaper – we're doing a special wedding feature this month, that is why I'm here. It's not something Owen normally does, so I doubt if I'll get him to agree to other trips, much as I'd enjoy it.'

'If not, I'm sure plenty of other magazines would pick up the idea,' Ben told her. He took his wallet out of his pocket and handed her his card. 'If you're ever looking for a job, email me. I've a few contacts, I might be able to help.'

'Thank you.' Cassie took the card and slipped it into her handbag. If she did decide to freelance after the wedding she might take Ben up on his kind offer.

Out of the corner of her eye she was aware that Jared had glanced over at her. She would have to speak to him at some point – it would be rude not to. Not now though, with everyone around. She wanted to get him on his own and ask him not to mention that her wedding was only a few weeks away. If Leah found out she might read her column, and realise that Cassie was writing about her own life. She couldn't risk that.

After dinner, there was entertainment in the lounge, as an example of the sort of things included in the wedding package. Cassie, Leah, and several other members of their table drifted in and sat down, listening to the music for a while. Before long, a few people got up to dance, including Jared and Savannah; she immediately steered Jared to the middle of the dance floor, and started to dance seductively, obviously hoping people would be watching her. Jared looked slightly embarrassed, Cassie noticed. She tore her gaze away from them and turned to Leah.

'Something tells me that one likes to be the centre of attention,' Leah said with a grin. 'She's gorgeous though, and the way she moves her body … Just look at the guys drooling over her.'

She was right, Ben and the other men were staring at Savannah transfixed.

'The group's brill. Are you brave enough to get up and dance? We can hide away in the corner so we don't have to try and compete with Miss Universe.'

'Sure.' It had been ages since she'd let her hair down and had a dance. She followed Leah onto the dance floor and they were soon jigging away to a jazz number. Some of the other journalists joined them, including Ben, who entertained them by performing a spectacular breakdance. They all clapped and cheered him on. He grinned sheepishly when he'd finished.

'How did you learn to dance like that?' Cassie asked him.

'A remnant of my misspent youth,' he said with a grin.

Then the music changed. It took her just two heartbeats to recognise the song. *Sunshine Girl*. Their song. Hers and Jared's.

She couldn't dance to this. Cassie turned to make her way back to the table when she felt a hand on her arm. A hand that sent a familiar sizzling tingle all the way up it, right to the hairs on the back of her neck.

'Fancy a dance?'

Before she could reply she was enclosed in his arms, swaying to the music. As his arms tightened around her she couldn't resist the temptation to nestle into them and the years seemed to fade away. All that mattered was her and Jared in each other's arms. She was dimly aware that the music had changed, another song was playing, but still they were in each other's arms, swaying slowly, enclosed in their own private bubble, and she had to admit that she didn't want it to end. She wanted to stay in Jared's arms forever.

'Excuse me, but I'd like to dance with my man.'

A hand grabbed her arm and pulled it off Jared's shoulder, jerking her out of her daydream, and Jared's model girlfriend forced herself between them. It was as if she'd been doused with cold water. What the hell was she thinking, cosying up to him like that? Cassie immediately stepped back from Jared, feeling her cheeks burn. Everyone must be staring at them. She wanted to turn and run, lock herself in her room and stay there until Jared had gone, but she forced herself to pull herself together and meet Savannah's angry gaze. They were only dancing, after all.

But way too close.

'Of course. Be my guest,' she said coolly and turned away.

'Take it easy, Savannah. I told you, Cassie and I are old friends. I'm photographing her wedding,' she heard Jared say as she stumbled across the dance floor to the French doors.

She couldn't face Leah and the others at the table yet. She had to get some fresh air, bring herself back to her senses and cool her burning cheeks. She stepped through the open doors and into the cool evening air. It was a beautiful night; the inky dark sky was splattered with tiny twinkling stars, and a slight breeze blew through the colourful flowerbeds around the immaculate lawn. She crossed her arms, hugging herself, and walked slowly over to the fountain, her mind in turmoil. How could she still respond to Jared like that? She'd thought she was over him, that her feelings for him were dead and buried, yet here she was practically snogging him in public. She gave an involuntary shiver.

'I guess I should apologise.'

She spun around at the sound of Jared's voice behind her. He looked incredibly sexy with his sleeves rolled up and pale blue shirt open at the neck. 'What are you playing at?' she asked furiously, lashing out at him, but in truth she was angry with herself more. How could she act like that when she was getting married in two weeks?

'I'm sorry. It's just, well, that was our song and I couldn't help myself. Before I knew what I was doing I was walking over to you, dancing with you.'

'What the hell are you doing here, anyway?' she demanded. 'Everywhere I turn you're there. It's like you're stalking me.'

'Savannah's modelling agency needed another photographer, so she asked me to come along. I wasn't doing anything else and the money's good.' He shrugged. 'How was I supposed to know you'd be here? What are you doing here?'

'I'm on a press trip, covering wedding venues.'

'Another one for your column?'

She had to get away from him, he was standing too close. She could feel his breath on her face, smell his heady male scent, and her hands were aching to reach out and touch him. She stepped back, anxious to put some distance between them.

'Look, I'm going home tomorrow. Let's keep away from each other until then. Your girlfriend is already furious with you and I don't want anything getting back to Timothy.'

'She isn't my girlfriend. Not really. We hang about together when we're both in the same location, but it's nothing serious.'

'Well, Timothy is my fiancé and …'

'And you don't love him.' Jared reached out and gently touched her cheek with the back of his fingers. 'Admit it. He doesn't make you feel like I did. Like I still do.'

196

The arrogance of him! 'I have no feelings for you at all,' she retorted. 'Of course I love Timothy …'

'No, you don't.' His hand was entwined around her neck and somehow he was kissing her and she was kissing him back. Hot, passionate kisses that made her whole body shudder. He moaned and pulled her closer and she leant into him, pressing her body against his, her lips eagerly responding to his kiss, opening of their own accord to allow his tongue access.

'See, you still love me. Like I love you. I'm sorry, Cassie, for hurting you like that. I should never have walked out on you. I've regretted it every single day since.'

He loved her.

She pulled back from him, her eyes searching his face in disbelief, but she could see that he was telling the truth, recognised the emotion in his eyes.

He loved her.

And she loved him. What the hell was she going to do?

'How can you say that to me now?' Her voice was shaking. She sank down onto the low wall around the fountain, not trusting her legs to hold her. 'You know I'm getting married to Timothy in two weeks' time. What are you trying to do?'

He sat down beside her, took her hand in his. 'Trying to stop you making the mistake of your life. Admit it, Cassie. You don't love Timothy. If you marry him you'll regret it. He'll never make you feel like I do. He'll never love you like I do.'

She had to get away from him before she threw herself in his arms and told him she loved him, too. Before she gave him chance to destroy her life and hurt her all over again. He was just playing with her, she was sure of it. He wanted her because she was marrying someone else.

'You had your chance,' she yelled at him. 'You dumped me. I've moved on and I'm not going to let you wreck my life again.' She couldn't meet his gaze; let him see how her heart was breaking. 'Stay away from me. I don't ever want to see you again.'

Twenty-seven

Jared sat back down on the low wall around the fountain, gathering his thoughts. Cassie was still in love with him, he could see it in her eyes, feel it in her kiss. And he was definitely still in love with her. He'd been trying to fight it ever since the day she'd walked into his office with Sylvia Campbell. What should he do? She was getting married in two weeks, should he stay away from her? Let her have a chance of happiness? After all, he'd already messed up her life once.

He didn't know whether she loved Timothy the twat, or was marrying him because she thought he was a safe bet, but he would stake his career on it that she wasn't *in love* with Timothy. If she was, she'd never respond to him like she did.

He must have been mad to let her go.

He had to win her back, convince her that he'd never let her down again. He realised now how important she was to him: seeing her again, holding her, kissing her, had proved to him that he'd never got over her. That she was the only woman he'd ever loved. Would ever love. He had to talk to her and find out if she was willing to give their love another chance. If he didn't, he'd regret it for the rest of his life. He couldn't let her go again.

What about his trip? He was due to leave in a month's time. A few days after taking Cassie and Timothy's honeymoon pictures.

He got up and walked around, his hands thrust deep in his pockets, his mind in a cotton wool fuzz. He'd loved Cassie before and walked away from her because he wanted more out of life. The need to travel, to photograph far-flung environments was deep in his blood. He knew he couldn't live without it. Not even for Cassie.

'So there you are!' Savannah's voice was dripping with anger. 'Thank you for humiliating me like that in front of everyone.'

He sighed and turned around to face her. Hands on her hips, eyes flashing, she looked like she wanted to hit him. He didn't discount the possibility. Savannah was very highly strung.

'I'm sorry. I didn't mean that to happen and I know it wasn't fair on you.' He levelled his gaze at her. 'But you were flirting with every man on the dance floor when you were dancing. And we aren't a couple, are we?'

That seemed to anger her even more. 'No, we aren't, but when we're together I expect you to have the decency not to cosy up to other women. You were practically snogging her.' He saw her hand go back but before he could react it had slapped his cheek. Hard. 'You are *so* dumped. And when your little friend's fiancé hears about your antics she will be, too. I hope you're both very happy together.'

She spun around and flounced back to the château.

So she intended to tell Timothy. And yes, she was capable of it. Savannah wasn't the kind of woman to put up with being humiliated in public. He had to find Cassie and warn her.

He went back inside and saw Cassie walking through the open doors into the hall.

He quickened his step to catch up with her. She was stepping into the lift. He raced over but the doors closed before he got there. He glanced at the number – second floor – headed for the stairs, and raced up them two at a time. With a bit of luck her room wouldn't be right by the lift and he'd catch her before she disappeared inside. Slightly out of breath he reached the top of the stairs just in time to see Cassie walking into a room on the right. Great, at least he knew what room she was in. What should he do now?

Think. Don't rush in. He stood for a moment, collecting both his breath and his thoughts. What if Cassie refused to let him in? Told him that she never wanted to see him or talk to him again?

He had to warn her: knowing Savannah, she was already asking questions, trying to find out who Cassie was. With Savannah's connections it would be easy for her to find out who Cassie was marrying, and to contact Timothy. He couldn't let Cassie go back to face that. It wouldn't be fair. After all, it was all his fault. He'd asked her to dance, followed her outside, and instigated the kiss.

She'd returned it, though. With passion. He now knew, without any doubt, that she still had feelings for him.

He flexed back his shoulders and strode purposefully towards the door of Cassie's room. Taking a deep breath, he knocked on the door.

Silence.

He knocked again. Louder.

The door opened slightly. It was the dark-haired woman who'd been sitting next to Cassie at the table, and the one she was dancing with when he'd grabbed her and whirled her around the dance floor. Damn. Cassie must have popped in to talk to her.

For a moment, Jared was stumped, his usual confidence deserting him.

'Yes?' The woman raised an eyebrow questioningly.

Jared coughed. 'Sorry, I must have the wrong room. I was looking for Cassie.'

'Jared?' It was unmistakably Cassie.

The other woman opened the door wider as Cassie walked over to them. 'What are you doing here?' she asked, her eyes wary.

'I need to talk to you,' he told her. 'About the wedding photos.' It was the first thing that came into his head.

'Wedding photos?' She glanced at her watch. 'At this time of night?'

'Yes, I'm leaving first thing in the morning and a couple of things have come up that I need to discuss with you. It won't take long.'

201

He saw her hesitate, felt rather than saw the other woman's curiosity.

'Are you two working together on the wedding articles?' she asked. 'I thought you were with that model?'

'I'm covering both assignments,' Jared replied quickly. 'Do you mind, Cassie? We could talk about it in front of your friend if you prefer?'

He saw the panic flit across her face, like a doe caught in the headlights of an approaching car. 'No, it's fine. Perhaps we can have that drink and chat a bit later, Leah?' she asked. 'This won't take long.'

'Sure. Give me a knock when you've finished. I won't be hitting the sack until midnight,' Leah told her.

'What do you think you're doing?' Cassie hissed as soon as the door was safely shut behind them and they were out in the corridor. 'Leah is suspicious enough after that dance. It's a good job I haven't told her that you're the photographer for my wedding.'

She turned and unlocked the door to the next room. 'I'm not even sure I should be letting you in after that performance.'

He knew she would. She wouldn't want to risk anyone overhearing what they were saying. Especially her new journalist friend.

'You'd better make it quick.' Cassie pushed open the door and stepped inside. Jared followed her.

'Now what do you want to talk about?' she demanded. 'I'm sure it's not really about the wedding photos.'

He closed the door and leant against it, his hands in his pockets. 'Yes, it is,' he said firmly. His eyes met hers. 'You see, I can't photograph your wedding for you. I'm sorry.'

Her eyes widened. 'You can't pull out at this late date just because of a little kiss.'

'If Savannah has her way there won't *be* a wedding. She's furious and threatening to find out who your fiancé is and tell him about us. That's why I'm here. I wanted to warn you.'

He saw the emotions flitting across her face. Disbelief, panic, then anger. 'This is all your fault,' she retorted. 'Why did you have to dance with me? Kiss me like that? You've ruined

202

everything. Again. What is it with you, Jared? You didn't want me, so why are you trying to ruin my relationship with Timothy?'

'I'm not. It was just a dance for old time's sake. I didn't mean to kiss you. Besides, you didn't exactly push me away, did you?'

'So you're pulling out of photographing the wedding because your jealous girlfriend has forbidden you to have anything to do with me?'

'Wrong.'

'What?'

His eyes held hers. 'She is no longer my girlfriend, we were never a couple – and no one forbids me to do anything.'

'I don't understand ...'

He reached out and took her hands. 'The reason I'm pulling out is because I love you. And I think you love me too.' He leant forward and kissed her on the forehead. 'Don't marry Timothy just because he's a safe option.'

Her gaze locked with his and he saw her swallow, and lick her lips. He wanted to wrap his arms around her, kiss her again, carry her over to that luxurious bed, undress her, and make love to her. Slowly. Thoroughly. But he'd done enough damage. He stepped back. 'You're making a big mistake marrying Timothy. He's not right for you. You won't be happy with him. You and me, we're meant to be together.'

'Really?' He saw the flash of anger in her eyes. 'Is that why you ditched me and went off to chase your dream? The same dream you're chasing now? Remind me, when exactly are you going to the Arctic?'

'Next month.'

'So you expect me to ditch Timothy, walk away from our wedding, our future together, so I can spend a whole month with you before you swan off again? Yep, sounds like a fantastic idea. Not.'

He paused. She was right. He was being selfish. Timothy could give her the security and commitment she wanted. While he, all he could offer he was love.

'I love you,' he said softly, his eyes holding hers. 'Do you love me?'

Twenty-eight

Emotion swirled through her. Jared loved her. His words brought a whole mass of memories to her mind, of longings to her body. She ached to reach out and touch him, to lose herself in his touch, his kiss. To be his again, as she used to be. But it was madness and she knew it. Yes, she loved him, there was no denying it. But she had no intention of letting him know; of giving into the desire running through her body, because Jared had a passion bigger than her, a passion he'd left her for once and would leave her for again, and there was no way she was going back to that dark place she'd been when he had walked out on her before. Somehow she found the strength to hold it together, tilt back her chin, and face him full-on.

'You and I were over a long time ago, Jared. I agree that there still seems to be some sort of attraction between us. I guess that's only to be expected; we were each other's first love, we were together for years. It's no wonder our hormones kick in when we see each other.' She deliberately avoided making eye contact with him. 'I love Timothy and I've no intention of cancelling our marriage. If you don't want to photograph our wedding then I'll find someone else.'

'Look me in the face and tell me you don't love me.' His voice was quiet, edged with urgency, the deep brown pool of his eyes fixed on hers.

She met his gaze and swallowed as she saw a flicker of pain in his eyes, and something else, something deep, and yearning. He wasn't serious, was he? He didn't really still love her? No, of course he didn't. He just fancied her, like she fancied him, and he didn't like it that she was marrying someone else. Like she said – hormones.

She tried to form the words. She managed to finally move her lips but no words would come out.

'Tell me that you don't love me and I'll go away. I'll never bother you again.'

Say it. Just four simple words. I don't love you. Say it.

He took a step forward so that the toes of his shoes were touching the toes of her sandals. His face was just centimetres away. His body was so close she could almost touch it and it took all her willpower not to reach out and caress his face, his lips.

'I love Timothy and I'm going to marry him,' she said resolutely. 'He's a wonderful man, kind, thoughtful, trustworthy. He loves me and he'll never let me down.'

'Like I did.' The words were so soft she could barely hear them.

'This isn't about you. I got over you a long time ago.'

'Do you and Timothy talk for hours like we did? Do you discuss your dreams, your opinions, talk about every subject under the sun? Do you laugh about silly things? Finish each other's sentences?' He reached out and gently traced her cheek with his finger. She instinctively shivered at both his touch and the heat in his eyes. 'Do you tremble when he touches you? Do your lips part waiting for him to claim them like they are doing now?' His finger traced over her lips which were, God help her, apart. 'You do want me to kiss you, don't you, Cassie?'

Her whole body was screaming for his kiss, his touch, but she wasn't going to let him do that. He couldn't just march back into her life and destroy it then march back out again. She stepped back while she still had the willpower not to step forward into his arms.

'We had something once, Jared, but you destroyed it. You smashed us apart so you could follow your dream. I'm not going to let you do the same to me and Timothy.' She threw her head back, forced the strength into her voice. 'We're over. Now get out of my room before I call security.'

He held up his hands, palm outwards. 'Fine, if you're sure that's what you want. But I mean it, Cassie. I love you and I think you love me. If you do, then what you're doing to Timothy is worse than what I did to you. At least I was honest with you, I didn't string you along. If you marry him when you still love me it will always be between you. Every time he kisses you you'll be thinking of me.'

She licked her lips. The arrogance of him. 'Don't flatter yourself. I haven't thought of you all these years and I'm not going to start now.' *Liar.*

'I know you, Cassie. Like you know me. I know you love me and I understand why you don't want to trust me. I'm different now. If you give me another chance I'll never let you down again.' He swallowed. 'Look, I'm checking out first thing in the morning. If you love me and want to be with me then meet me at the reception desk at eight a.m. If you don't I'll know you're still going ahead with the wedding. I'll call Daniel and tell him I've had to pull out of photographing your wedding for professional reasons. And I'll try to talk Savannah around so that she doesn't tell Timothy.'

Cassie reached out to steady her hand on the wall as he closed the door behind him. OK, threatening to call security was a bit over the top but if he'd have remained there a moment longer she wouldn't have had the strength to resist him. She stumbled over to the bed and sank down on it, groaning as she held her head in her hands. What was she going to do? Jared was right, she did still love him.

She sat there for ages, deep in thought, remembering how much in love she and Jared had been. How happy she'd felt. Then she thought of Timothy. It was true, he didn't make her heart race Jared did but he was a good, kind man and she loved him. OK, maybe she wasn't 'in love' with him she had to admit that, but being 'in love' was overrated. She cared for him a great deal and knew he cared for her too. Mutual respect and consideration was a good basis, probably a better basis for a happy marriage than heady lust and young love, which always faded in the end. There was no going back. She and Jared were over; had been over a long time ago. All she could do now was move forward.

She glanced at the clock. 10.30 p.m.. She always phoned Timothy at 11.00 in the evening so she could say goodnight. She quickly undressed, removed her make-up, and showered. Then climbed into bed and dialled Timothy's number.

He answered on the third ring. 'Cassandra, I was just about to phone you. How's it going?'

She told him a little about the château but could tell by his tone that he wasn't really interested, although he did try to feign interest.

'I'm sorry, sweetheart, but I can't meet you at the airport tomorrow. I'll be in a meeting,' he said. 'You don't mind getting at a taxi, do you?'

'No, of course not.' She tried to hide the disappointment in her voice. Just for once she would have like Timothy to put her first, to show her that he missed her enough to cancel his meeting, come and meet her and swoop her up in his arms. She wasn't being fair; his job was important. Timothy was too committed to let people down. Besides, being impulsive wasn't his style.

She had to tell him about Jared before Savannah did. She formed the words in her head 'You'll never guess what, darling, our photographer is here too, on a photo shoot with his model girlfriend. I forgot to mention to you that we went out together years ago, so we had a dance for old time's sake but his girlfriend got a bit jealous' but before she could say them, Timothy told her he had to go.

'Sorry, I've got lots of notes to read through. Have a safe trip home and I'll see you tomorrow.'

'OK. Goodnight. Love you,' she whispered into the phone.

'Love you too. Goodnight.' And he was gone. No 'I miss you', no sweet endearments and declarations of undying love, of course not. Timothy wasn't a very demonstrative person.

She held the phone in her hand, tears welling in her eyes. Jared was right. There was no chemistry between her and Timothy. If she hadn't met Jared again she could have ignored that and happily married him, accepted that their union, while pleasant, wouldn't be one full of passion. She could have accepted 'caring' instead of 'loving'. Not now, not after feeling the giddy butterflies of love again, the aching desire to be caressed and kissed. She couldn't commit herself to a loveless marriage. It would destroy her.

She had no intention of going back to Jared. It wouldn't work. Once their mutual desire wore off they'd be back to square one – at least he would be, because she didn't believe she would ever stop loving him. And there lay the dilemma, because it wasn't fair to Timothy to marry him when she still had feelings for Jared. She had no choice.

She had to call off the wedding.

Twenty-nine

Cassie had a restless night's sleep. Finally waking at six thirty, she made herself a cup of coffee and sat in bed nursing it while watching the hands move slowly around the clock. Seven o'clock, half seven, ten to eight, five to eight. Eight o'clock. Was Jared waiting in reception hoping she would come down and tell him she'd changed her mind, that she loved him and was calling off the wedding? How long would he wait?

She glanced over at the door, half expecting him to knock. To her surprise, she saw a piece of paper had been slipped underneath it.

She got out of bed and padded barefoot across the floor. Picking up the note – a page torn from a reporter-style notebook then folded in half – she saw her name written on the outside of the top fold. In Jared's handwriting.

Her heart was tap dancing in her chest as she carried the note to the bed, perched herself on the end of it, and took a deep breath before unfolding it.

Dear Cassie,

I love you. I always have and always will. No, I can't promise to give up my dream for you because that will destroy me. I can promise to always love you though, to always come back to you. I understand if that isn't enough but please don't settle for anything less than love.

I'm begging you not to marry Timothy if you aren't sure that you love him. You deserve to be loved, adored, cherished all the days of your life. I don't think you'll have that with Timothy and it will eventually destroy you.

I'll be waiting for you in reception until 8.30 a.m., hoping you come to join me; hoping that you love me and want to share your life with me because I want to share my life with you.

Yours for eternity,
Jared

P.S. I've managed to persuade Savannah not to tell Timothy about our dance. And if you decide that you want to go ahead and marry Timothy I'll tell Daniel that I'm quitting, so hopefully he or Imogen will photograph your wedding. I'm sorry to let you down but it will be too difficult for us both if I do it.

Tears sprung into her eyes as she read it. He sounded so sincere. Was he?

She paced around the room, reading the letter over and over again. In her heart she wanted to run down to reception, fling herself into Jared's arms, tell him that she loved him and wanted to spend the rest of her life with him.

Which would be a stupid thing to do, for both of them.

She was sure that seeing her again had stirred up old memories and Jared thought he still loved her, but he didn't. You can't turn love on and off like that. He'd walked out of her life, left her distraught, and had made no attempt to contact her during the past seven years, whereas a day hadn't gone by when she hadn't thought of him. If he had truly loved her he wouldn't have been able to stay away so long. He'd have got in touch with her when he returned from one of his trips. But he hadn't. And once he was in the Arctic he'd forget about her all over again. It would be out of sight, out of mind. She glanced at the clock and saw it was just past eight. Was he downstairs waiting for her? Would he come up and knock on the door, refuse to take no for an answer? She shook her head. No, Jared wouldn't beg. He'd accept her decision. She just hoped she was making the right one.

She was so deep in thought that it took a couple of minutes for her to realise that her phone was ringing. She fished it out of her bag just as it stopped, and glanced at the screen. Timothy. She frowned. It wasn't like Timothy to call this early in the morning. Surely Savannah hadn't tracked him down already? Jared said he'd talked her out of it. She took a deep breath and hit reply. 'Hi, Timothy ...'

'Cassandra.' She flinched at the undertone of anger in his voice. So Savannah had told him. She braced herself but his next words stunned her. 'Is it true what Amanda has just told me? Did you write this outrageous and deeply personal "Almost a Bride" column in your newspaper?'

Oh shit! This was worse than Savannah telling Timothy about her dance with Jared.

Her mind was racing, trying to remember what was in this week's column. What had she said about Jared? She'd had to mention him, of course, Owen always insisted she did, that's what the public wanted to hear, but she didn't think she'd said much, she hadn't had an appointment with him that week. Then she remembered that Owen had made her rewrite it, she'd added a fictional meeting with Jared –Blake – and said she was glad to going away so she could have a bit of breathing space, clear her mind. Stop thinking about Blake and wondering what her wedding to him would have been like. No wonder Timothy was upset. He was probably wondering if it was true, that she was in France trying to stop thinking about her ex who also happened to be her wedding photographer. What would he think if he knew Jared was there, too?

'Well. Did you?'

She so didn't want to do this over the phone. She'd wanted to talk to him face to face, explain the situation.

She took a deep breath. 'Yes, I did, but it's just journalism, Timothy. You know what my job is like. I have to write things that attract the reader; make them want to read more.' She gulped. 'Owen said the paper is struggling and we needed to add a bit more reader interest to the column. It was all his idea.'

'You're saying he made you write this stuff?'

'I'm a journalist, Timothy, it's my job ...'

'So the photographer isn't an old flame of yours?'

Damn. She had better be as honest as she could. 'Well, we did go out a long time ago, yes. I didn't mention it to you because ...'

'I think it's perfectly clear why you didn't mention it to me, Cassandra. We'll discuss this further when you get home.'

'Timothy, let me explain.'

It was too late, he'd cut her off. A sure sign that he was annoyed. Make that furious, judging by his tone.

Now what did she do?

If only she could talk to Sam, but she'd be on her way to work.

Well, that was it. There would definitely be no wedding now. Last night she'd been thinking of calling it off, now she knew she had to. If Timothy didn't do it first.

They were finished. Even if Timothy forgave her for writing the column and not telling him about Jared, there was no way she could marry him knowing she loved someone else.

She sat there for a moment as the enormity of what was happening hit her. She would have to find somewhere to live. She couldn't stay in Timothy's flat now. It was her own fault. She'd known all along that deep down that she hadn't loved Timothy. She liked him, respected him, thought she could have a happy life with him. But she didn't love him.

She was pretty sure he didn't love her either. He wanted to marry her because he thought it was time he settled down and thought she would make a suitable wife. Why the hell hadn't she seen that before? She guessed she should be grateful to Jared for opening her eyes to the fact that she was about to have a sham wedding. Now she had to try and disentangle herself from this mess as painlessly as she could.

She had to pull herself together and get through the rest of the day. There was one more venue to visit, then they were being driven to the airport to go home. So she had all day to sort out in her head what she was going to say to Timothy.

214

'Miss Tyler, there's a message for you,' the receptionist said as Cassie checked out. She picked up a white envelope and handed it to her.

'Thank you.' She recognised Jared's writing on the envelope and slipped it into her handbag. She'd read it later. She couldn't face dealing with it now. She needed to act professional and give her work her full attention – she didn't want to lose her job as well as everything else.

'Are you OK? You look a bit pale,' Leah asked.

'I didn't sleep very well,' Cassie told her. 'Too much wine last night.' She fixed a bright smile on her face and picked up her bag. 'It's probably a good job we're going home today. I could get used to this fine living.'

'Me too,' Leah said with a grin. She lowered her voice. 'That photographer guy ... is everything OK with you both?'

'Sure. He's someone I knew a long time ago.' She shrugged. 'He asked me to have a dance for old time's sake and his girlfriend got jealous. It's all fine now. He came to apologise for embarrassing me when she caused a scene.'

Cassie didn't get chance to read Jared's letter until the flight home. Leah was booked on a seat further back this time, and Cassie was sitting next to an elderly couple who spent the flight doing a crossword together. The letter had been on her mind all day. Part of her didn't want to read it but she knew she wouldn't rest until she did, so she took the envelope out of her handbag and turned it over. She slid her finger through the top corner, ripped it open and took out the slip of paper, once again ripped from a spiral-bound notebook. Her heart pounded as she read it slowly.

Darling Cassie,

I wondered if the reason you didn't turn up this morning was because you didn't know whether to trust me. Do you doubt if I am genuine, that I really do love you? I want to reassure you again that I do. I love you. I've always loved you. I can't turn the clock back to the day I walked out on you and put it right. I wish I could. But maybe that wouldn't be a good thing. We've both grown since then, matured, become our own person. Maybe we needed that time. But now I've seen you again I can't walk away without telling you how much you mean to me and how much I want to be with you. If I truly felt that you'd be happy with Timothy then I wouldn't try and come between you. But I don't think you will be. Timothy's too uptight, too stuffy, too formal for you and I feel he's stifling you, too. When you're with him it's like the carefree Cassie, the one who laughs over little things, jokes, plays around, enjoys life, has gone. I don't want him to crush you like that but I know it's not my decision.

If you really love Timothy then go ahead and marry him, because all I want is for you to be happy. But if you are only marrying him because you want security, because you think he's a safe bet, then please don't. Whether you love me or not – and I think you do – don't settle for marrying for anything less than love. You deserve more than that.

I'm here if you decide you want me, any time. If I haven't heard from you by 19th July, the day I leave for the Arctic, I won't contact you again.

Whatever decision you make, be happy.

Love you for eternity,
    Jared.

Underneath his signature he'd drawn a heart with LYL inside – Love you loads – just like he'd always done when he wrote to her.

She folded the letter back into the envelope and slid it into her bag as tears were pricking her eyes.

Love you loads. They'd always said that to each other. 'I love you loads too,' she whispered. If only it was a simple as that. How she longed to go back to being that young girl who thought love was enough to get you through everything. She knew now it wasn't. Jared hadn't changed. He wouldn't want to be tied down with her now any more than he did all those years ago. And she couldn't stand for her heart to be broken again. He was right though, she was marrying Timothy for security and that was wrong. It was a good thing, really, that Timothy had read her columns. Now he would be the one to call off the wedding and she wouldn't feel so cruel.

She was dreading facing him. He sounded furious and the last thing she wanted was a scene. She would arrive home by mid-afternoon, and Timothy would still be in his meeting, so she could pack a few things and leave a note saying how sorry she was. It sounded cowardly but if she was honest with herself, Timothy intimidated her when he was angry. He had never threatened her or hurt her but she'd always been afraid of crossing him – he could be so cold and verbally brutal. She needed to arrange somewhere to spend a couple of nights while she sorted herself out. Perhaps Sam could come to the rescue. Failing that, she'd check into a B&B.

As soon as she got off the plane she switched on her phone and messaged Sam. 'Text me as soon as you can please. Crisis!'

Sam phoned just as Cassie's luggage swirled around the conveyor belt.

'OK, spill,' were the first words that came out of her mouth when Cassie answered the call.

'Hang on while I get my bag.' Cassie grabbed the red suitcase, pulled it off the belt, then wheeled it over to a quiet corner, quickly explaining to Sam about Timothy's phone call. 'I'll have to move out of the flat now so was wondering if I could stay with you and Paul for a couple of nights, just until I sort out somewhere to live,' she said.

'You can't be serious? Surely Timothy won't dump you and call off the wedding just because of that column?' Sam sounded incredulous. 'OK, you should have told him about Jared, and he probably won't like your nickname for his mother but it's just journalism, isn't it? Surely he understands that.' She paused. 'How come he read your column anyway?'

'Amanda showed it to him. We mentioned that the newspaper was running a wedding column when we went bridesmaid dress shopping, remember? She must have read it and guessed it was me. Not difficult, really.'

'Even so, calling off the wedding and finishing with you is a bit drastic. I'm sure you can talk him round. Take home a bottle of wine and slip on your sexiest undies.'

'Even if Timothy doesn't call off the wedding, I will.'

'*What*?'

Cassie quickly explained about Jared being in France and what had gone on between them.

'OMG, Jared was in France! And he said he still loves you! What are you going to do? Are you calling off the wedding so you can marry him?'

'No, of course not.' 'But I can't marry Timothy now. Look, I'll explain it later. I just want to know if I can doss down on your sofa for a couple of nights until I find somewhere to live. I can't possibly stay with Timothy any longer.'

'Of course you can. Paul's away until the weekend at a conference up in Newcastle so it won't be a problem.'

'Thank you, Sam. I really appreciate it.' Cassie ended the call, slipped the phone into her pocket, and glanced at her watch. She had three hours before Timothy got home, time enough to throw some essentials into her other suitcase. She could ask Timothy to send the rest later. She bit her lip as tears flooded her eyes. What a mess. If only Sylvia had booked a different photographer, none of this would have happened.

Then what? She would marry Timothy and they would live happy ever after? No, it would never have worked out; meeting Jared again had shown her that. How she wished they had never met again. It had taken her years to fix her broken heart before, now she felt like she'd never be able to put it back together again.

Thirty

She hesitated for a moment before putting her key in the lock and pushing open the front door. Even though she knew Timothy wouldn't be home, she felt nervous walking into the flat. This had been her home for the past few months and now she had to leave it; start all over again. Tears pricked her eyes and she blinked them away. She was doing the right thing, she knew she was, and although she would miss Timothy she had to admit that it wouldn't break her heart not to see him again.

Not like Jared.

She wheeled her suitcase into the lounge, then gasped when she saw Timothy sitting on the sofa. He was holding a glass of what looked like whisky in his hand and several copies of the newspaper were laid out on the table in front of him, all open on her column. She could tell by the set of his jaw, the cold steel of his grey eyes as they rested on her, his granite expression, that he was furious. Her stomach lurched.

'Timothy. I thought you'd be at work,' she stammered.

'You really expect me to go to work as if nothing has happened?' His iceberg tones sent a shiver down her spine. 'Do you think I have no feelings at all?'

'I'm sorry,' she whispered. 'It's just journalism, Timothy. You know what my job's like. I told you, Owen ordered me to write the column. Sales are down, we needed something to bring in the readers or the paper will fold and everyone will be out of work.'

'Owen ordered you to write about our private life? To refer to my mother in such a demeaning way?' He put the glass down and rose to his feet. 'Monster-in-law indeed! After everything she's done for you.' He stood up and took a step forward. Cassie nervously took a step back, her heart thud-thudding. 'Do you realise what this has done to my mother? She's distraught. Amanda is with her now, trying to comfort her.'

His mother. Is that all he cared about after everything she'd written? She'd expected Jared to be the first thing he'd rage about.

'I'm sorry. I didn't mean to hurt her. Of course I don't really think of her as a monster-in-law. I'm not talking about us in that column. It's fictitious. Owen told me to write about a bride preparing for a wedding, so yes, I took a few things we did, such as shopping for the wedding dress, and I built on them, exaggerated them to create a humorous column. That's what journalists do. It's my job, Timothy. It's not true.'

'Our friends don't know that. My mother's friends don't know that. How could you show us up in such a public way? How could you be so cruel?' He was towering over her now, deep furrows of anger etched across his forehead.

She licked her lips and swallowed the lump of fear constricting her throat. 'I had no choice, Owen calls the shots. Anyway, no one will know it's me. I wrote it under a different name.'

'Amanda realised it was you. As did Mother. So will all our friends and neighbours. We're getting married in two weeks, for goodness' sake. How could anyone who knew us not recognise it's you!' He was shouting now and she flinched. He looked so … menacing.

To her relief, Timothy turned away and paced agitatedly around the room.

She didn't know what to do. When was he going to mention Jared? At the moment he seemed more concerned about what she'd written about his mother.

'This photographer, J.M.' He almost spat the words out. 'Why didn't you tell me you used to go out with him?'

'Because it was years ago. We were nothing more than kids.' She swallowed. 'You always said the past didn't matter, that you didn't think we needed to share details about previous relationships.'

'It would have been nice to know from your lips that our wedding photographer was a former lover of yours, rather than from the newspaper. You've humiliated me, Cassandra. I don't like being humiliated.'

'I'm sorry ...' She wished he'd sit down; he was making her feel nervous.

As if reading her thoughts he strode over to the sofa and sat down, perching on the edge of the cushion, like he would stand back up again any minute. He reached out for his glass of whisky and gulped it down.

'Don't you realise that everyone will think this dilemma about whether you should marry me or run off with the photographer is true, too? You've made a fool out of me, Cassandra.'

'It's not me and you! It's Paige and Ian. It's a newspaper column, not a diary,' she retorted. Her head was thudding and she really wanted to get out of there. Why didn't he dump her and get it over with?

'This has to stop when we get married, Cassandra. I'm not having our personal life being turned into fodder for your newspaper column.'

WHAAT? He still wanted them to get married? She hadn't expected that. She gaped at him, stunned.

'I want you to quit your job. I earn enough to support both of us, so there is no financial need for you to work. You can perhaps do voluntary work like Mother, if looking after my needs doesn't sufficiently fill your days. Mother will advise you but you'll have to do some serious grovelling before she'll forgive you, I can tell you that.'

He was deadly serious, Cassie thought incredulously. He really believed that he had the right to order her to give up her job, to grovel to her mother. Who the hell did he think he was?

'I'm not marrying you, Timothy. I'm sorry, I can't. The wedding is off.' She tried to keep her voice steady. He looked so angry; she didn't want to inflame the situation. She just wanted to pack her things and get out of the flat as quickly as she could.

Timothy slammed his glass down on the table and sprung to his feet, his face red. 'What do you mean? You can't call off the wedding. Everything's booked. I refuse to let you humiliate me in such a way.'

'I'm sorry, I don't mean to hurt you or humiliate you, but I can't marry you. I don't love you, Timothy, and I don't think you love me either. Do you?'

'Love!' He scoffed. 'We're not a pair of silly teenagers. We care for each other, respect each other. We make a good team.' He glowered at her. 'Are you doing this because I've dared to complain about your articles? Do you expect me not to be angry at them? Any man would react the same way.'

'It's nothing to do with that. I was going to call off the wedding anyway.' Her words spilled out. 'Meeting Jared again made me realise that you and I don't love each other. Not in the way I want to be loved, and to love back. And care, respect, it's not enough for me. I want to be loved, cherished. I want to feel like I'm important.'

'You sound like a character in a slushy romance novel,' he scoffed. A frown crossed his forehead and his eyes bulged. 'You're not still in love with this Jared, are you?'

She avoided his gaze, not daring to answer. She had never seen Timothy like this before.

'Oh, for goodness' sake, you're acting like a lovesick teenager.' He threw back his head and laughed scornfully. 'Have your fling with your precious photographer if you want. There's no need to cancel our wedding because of a silly infatuation.'

She stared at him in disbelief. Was he really saying that he didn't care if she had an affair with Jared? That he still wanted to marry her? 'You want me to have an affair ...?' she stuttered.

'I haven't asked you to be faithful, have I? An affair or two doesn't matter, providing we're both discreet. Marriage is more than that. It's a commitment to each other, a promise to remain together, to build a home, raise our children. To keep the family unit intact no matter what.'

Providing we're both discreet. 'You weren't intending to be faithful to me? You were planning on having an affair?' she whispered.

'Don't be so dramatic, Cassandra. These things happen. We're adults.'

'Are you seeing someone now?' she demanded. She saw his cheek twitch. 'You are, aren't you?'

He looked at her wordlessly.

'Tell me the truth!' She screamed out the words. How dare he have a go at her over at her article when he was cheating on her? Was it someone at work? A client? She could barely take this in.

'It's nothing serious, it doesn't alter our relationship. Felicity and I go back a long way. Andrew knows about us, he doesn't mind.'

Felicity. His business partner. Bile rose in her throat and for a panicky moment she thought she was going to be sick. She clutched her stomach and took a deep breath. All this time she'd been living with Timothy, planning their wedding, he and Felicity had been sleeping together.

'You're having an affair with Felicity and you expect me to marry you?' She was shaking as she reached out and put her hand on the table for support. 'Are you for real?'

'Do stop overreacting, Cassandra. I'm sure we can be adult about this. I admit that I'm annoyed and very disappointed with your behaviour and the things you've written in this column, but we can work through it.' He was in control of himself again now, playing the part of the calm, reasonable lawyer. 'There is absolutely no need to cancel the wedding; everything is organised. As for Felicity, she isn't a threat to you. She and Andrew will never divorce and neither will we. You'll be secure for life because I promise you, Campbells never divorce.'

Nausea swept over her again. 'I'm not going to marry you, Timothy. Not ever.'

'You're making a rash decision in the heat of the moment. Think about it for a day or two, I'm sure you'll change your mind.' He pointed at the newspapers on the table. 'I'm willing to forgive and forget, and you can see your precious photographer if you want. But I insist you quit your job when we get married. That is unconditional.'

His arrogance, his conceit, his cool assumption that he was such a good catch she couldn't possibly want to walk away from him made her want to scream, throw things, wipe the smug smile off his face. She closed her eyes briefly, fighting down the anger. She didn't want a scene. She just wanted to get her things and go. She never wanted to see Timothy again.

Calmer now, she looked him straight in the face. 'Listen to me, Timothy. I am not marrying you. When I marry it will be because I love someone and they love me. I certainly won't be marrying someone who is having an affair and wants me to do the same. Now, if you excuse me, I'll pack a few things. I'll collect everything else later once I've got myself settled.'

She held her head high as she walked past him into the bedroom. How could she have been so blind as to see what he was like? To think he was decent and honourable? Hurt and angry, she pulled some clothes out of her wardrobe and shoved them into her large red case, the one that matched the smaller one she'd left in the hall.

'You can't do this. Everything's booked. What will everyone think?' Timothy demanded. He stood in the doorway, blocking her exit. 'You're being hysterical. Just calm down and think about it for a while.'

'I don't care what anyone thinks.' She zipped the case shut and wheeled it to the door, standing in front of him. 'And I don't need to think about it.' She took a deep breath. 'Will you please get out of my way?'

They held eye contact for what seemed an eternity. She saw the muscles in his jaw twitch and his eyes narrow. She hardly dared to breath, never mind move. Finally he stepped aside. She let out her breath in relief. 'Very well, have your hissy fit but we both know you'll be back.'

She marched towards the door, pulling her case behind her. She waited until she had opened the door and walked into the hall before she turned and said 'No, I won't.'

Thirty-one

Now what should she do, Cassie thought as she put her cases in the car. She felt too shaken up to drive but didn't want to stay here when Timothy could come out of the flat any minute and see her. She got in, locked the doors, and sat for a few minutes composing herself, then phoned Sam. She was still at work so Cassie left a message telling her all about Timothy's affair, and how the wedding was definitely off. Then she set off. Sam and Paul lived in the town, overlooking the river, so she decided to park the car and go for a walk to clear her head. Sam wouldn't be home until about 5.30p.m. so she had a bit of time to kill.

Cassie walked along the river bank, her mind in turmoil. How had it come to this? She sat down on a bench and watched the ducks swimming in the water. They looked so peaceful, as if they didn't have a care in the world. She envied them and their simple, uncomplicated lives. Overnight, her life had been smashed once again and she had no idea which direction to turn. Tears filled her eyes and this time she let them flow, allowed them to roll silently down her cheeks as she gazed unseeingly at the river, her head full of her memories and shattered dreams.

'Are you all right, lass?'

She gazed at the old man standing in front of her. A little Jack Russell was pulling at the lead he was holding, eager to run free.

'Yes, thanks,' she mumbled, pulling a tissue out of her pocket and dabbing at her eyes.

'Whatever it is, lass, you'll get over it. We always do,' the man told her. 'Either that or we learn to live with it.' He patted her arm. 'I feel for your sorrow and hope it doesn't last long.'

'Thank you.' Her voice came out in almost a whisper. The man meant well, but she wished he would go and leave her alone with her thoughts. As if sensing her need he touched his cap in a gesture of farewell, then set off along the path, the little dog pulling at the lead and yapping as she raced ahead of him.

Time passed unnoticed as she sat deep in thought. She realised now that her feelings for Timothy came nowhere near the depth of love she had felt for Jared. *Still* felt for him. She should never have settled for second best by agreeing to marry Timothy. She should have waited until she met someone she loved as deeply as she had Jared.

Maybe that's exactly what she didn't want to do, she acknowledged. Perhaps subconsciously she didn't want to risk being destroyed again, so had played it safe. It wasn't a deliberate choice. When she'd started dating Timothy she had no idea it would lead to their marriage. She'd agreed to move in with him when he asked because she enjoyed being with him and felt safe with him; marrying him had never entered her mind. If she was honest with herself, she had only accepted his proposal because it had been so public; she felt that she couldn't humiliate him by refusing. Then Sylvia pushed them to book Hollington Castle and that was it, the wedding ball was rolling and there was nothing Cassie could do to stop it.

The fact that she wasn't heartbroken at Timothy's betrayal proved that she didn't love him. She was hurt and angry, yes, but not devastated like she'd been with Jared. Her whole world hadn't fallen apart.

She should be glad that she'd met Jared again, actually, otherwise she'd have sleep-walked into an unhappy marriage and wouldn't have found out about Timothy's affair with Felicity until it was too late. They would never have been happy and with his insistence that the Campbells never divorced, Timothy would have made it difficult for her to get out of the marriage – especially if they'd had children. She shivered, wrapping her hands around her upper arms. She'd had a lucky escape.

A yap and sloppy wet lick on her right hand brought her back to the present. Startled, she looked down to see the little Jack Russell wagging his tail eagerly at her. He nudged her hand again and licked it, obviously wanting her to make a fuss of him.

'Hello, boy.' She stroked his head gently. 'Had a nice walk, have you?'

'Still here, lass?' The kindly man asked. 'Feeling any better?'

She nodded. 'Yes, I am, thank you.' She tickled the little dog under his chin then glanced at her watch. Goodness, it was almost five. Sam would be home soon. She stood up, swinging the strap of her handbag over her shoulder. 'I'd better be going.'

'Bye, lass. And remember, it'll all work out. This time next year whatever's upset you will be nothing but a bad memory.'

The man was right. She would get over this. She nodded and turned back along the river bank. As she reached the car park she saw Sam's car pull in. Sam gave her a cheery wave and parked in her allocated space. Cassie walked over to her.

'Have you been here long?' Sam asked as she got out.

'A while, I've been for a walk along the river bank.'

'Are you OK, hun? The sleaze. I never thought he was good enough for you.' Sam gave her a big hug.

'I'm fine. Well, I'm not but I will be. I guess I've had a lucky escape.' Her voice sounded shaky to her own ears.

'You definitely have.' Sam gave her shoulders a comforting squeeze then pressed the remote key to lock the car. 'Come on, let's get you inside. Have you got anything with you?'

'A couple of cases. I didn't want to spend too long packing, I wanted to get out of there before it blew up. I've never seen Timothy so angry. I'll collect my other stuff later when I've sorted out a flat.'

'Timothy was angry!' Sam spluttered. 'He's been cheating on you with Felicity and *he's* angry?' She shook her head. 'That man is unbelievable.'

'He's angry about the stuff that I put in my column and because I've cancelled the wedding.' Why did her voice sound so strange? Flat and emotionless, when inside she wanted to scream. To rage. To roar.

As soon as they got in, Sam opened a bottle of wine and poured them a glass each. 'Here, drink this then you can tell me all about it.'

It took another glass of wine before Cassie started talking. She told her about Jared being in France, how he'd said he still loved her, how she'd realised she loved him too so had decided she was going to call off the wedding ...'

'You and Jared are getting back together?' Sam squealed.

Cassie shook her head. 'No, of course not. It would never work.'

'But you said he loved you and you loved him ...'

'He doesn't really love me, seeing each other again stirred up old feelings in him. But it's made me realise that I've never felt about Timothy like I did – still do – for Jared. It wasn't fair to marry him when I didn't love him. So I told him I was calling off the wedding.' She chewed her lip. 'That's when I found out about Felicity.' She told her how furious Timothy had been about her cancelling the wedding, how he'd said he didn't mind her having an affair providing she was discreet, like he was. Sam listened in wide-eyed silence. When Cassie finally finished, Sam reached out and touched her hand.

'Oh, Cass, how awful. You must be gutted. I'm so sorry.'

'I am,' Cassie acknowledged. She necked the rest of the wine in her glass. 'Any chance of a refill?'

'Sure, give me a sec.' Sam disappeared into the kitchen with the empty glasses.

Cassie looked around the flat. It was a small, one-bedroom with a lounge diner. She would either have to bunk in with Sam or sleep on the sofa while Paul was away. It was really kind of Sam to put her up, but she knew she couldn't stay her long. She had to sort something out.

What a mess. Tears filled her eyes and started to silently roll down her cheeks.

'I was wondering when you were going to cry,' Sam said, passing her a tissue and putting the two glasses of wine on the coffee table. She put her arms around Cassie's shoulder and hugged her. 'It'll be OK,' she murmured. 'Everything will be OK.'

She remembered the old man's words about how this time next year it would all be a bad memory. 'I just don't know where to go from here,' she stuttered. 'How do I put my life back together?'

'You'll do it. I'll help you find a flat and you still have your job.'

'You don't understand.' Cassie wiped her tears and took a big gulp. 'It's Jared. I still love him.'

'Then why you don't go back to him?'

'What, and let him break my heart all over again? He's still the same, obsessed with his photography. It'll never work.' Cassie dabbed furiously at the tears flowing down her cheeks.

'Look, maybe you could just take it slowly, see how you both get on.'

'No!' The shout startled her. 'I can't risk it. He doesn't love me. He thinks he does now he's seen me again, but he hasn't given a thought to me all these years. He's just nostalgic about our past. As soon as he's away he'll forget about me again, and I can't do it, Sam. I can't let him destroy me again. I might not be able to put myself together another time.' As she said the words sobs wracked her body. Sam squeezed her shoulders and let her cry it out.

Thirty-two

'The Campbell wedding's off,' Daniel announced, walking into Jared's office without even knocking on the door.

Jared looked up from the photo he'd been editing of Savannah's photoshoot in France. 'Really? How do you know?'

'The fiancée, she's just phoned to cancel the photographs. What a bloody nuisance. That would have been a good earner – good publicity too.' He plonked himself down on the chair opposite Jared.

Cassie had called the wedding off. Was it because of him? If so, why hadn't she contacted him?

'Bit of a shock, isn't it?' Daniel remarked. 'Sylvia won't take it too kindly. She won't like her precious son being dumped.'

Jared was still trying to digest the news. At least it let him off the hook. He'd been trying to think of a way to tell Imogen and Daniel that he was backing out of photographing the wedding ever since he returned from France two days ago.

'Jared.' Daniel snapped his fingers in front of his eyes to attract his attention. 'You look a bit stunned. Bit of a bummer, isn't it? We've lost a tidy sum there. We'll bill them a kill fee, of course, but it won't be as much as we would have got. Will that scupper your trip? If you can postpone it for a couple of weeks we can get you more work.'

'I might have to.' He was too stunned to take it in. He was pretty sure Cassie had cancelled the wedding because of him. It was the only thing that made sense. When she hadn't met him in reception that morning he'd resolved to walk out of her life and leave her to find what happiness she could. Now he didn't know what to think.

'Can I check my finances and let you know?' he asked Daniel, willing him to go and leave him in peace so he could think.

'Sure.' Daniel stood up. 'Course, it could just be pre-wedding nerves. You never know, the wedding might be back on by the end of the week. I'll give it a few days before I send them a cancellation bill.'

Jared couldn't stop thinking about Cassie all day. What had happened? Where was she living? He wanted to contact her but wasn't sure whether to, and besides, he only had her work email address. No, this had to be her call. He'd laid his cards on the table, it was up to her to make the next move.

Sam had offered to phone in sick the next day, so she could keep her company, but Cassie had talked her out of it. She needed time alone to get her head straight. She couldn't face going into work yet, so had phoned Owen and briefly told him what had happened. He insisted she took a few days off, told her he'd cancel her column this week, and asked her to write up a bit about the wedding venues in France instead. She thanked him, gratefully.

On autopilot she cancelled the photographs, the flowers, the cake, and the dresses. Sylvia would have to cancel the entertainment, venue, and other things she'd organised. She didn't feel strong enough to cope with the numerous questions her mother would ask, so she inboxed her on Facebook instead. She explained that she'd cancelled the wedding and promised to call and explain when she felt a bit stronger, ending by asking her mum to let the rest of the family know. She sent a similar message to her father, then to Emma, asking her to cancel the horse and carriage. That done, she set about finding a home. She couldn't stay on Sam's sofa forever, Paul would be back tomorrow. She scoured the paper for a flat she could call a home for a while, circled a few possibilities, and phoned the letting agents to book appointments to see them.

Jared must know she'd cancelled the wedding. Did he think it was because of him? Would he contact her thinking she had decided he wanted him after all? She doubted it. He'd asked her to meet him at reception, to go with him, and she hadn't turned up. Then he'd sent her a letter asking him to give him another chance. It was her call now. If she didn't contact him, he'd probably walk away from her like he did before and get on with his life.

The fact that she hadn't had a phone call from Sylvia suggested that Timothy hadn't told her yet. He obviously believed that Cassie would 'come to her senses' and realise what a good catch he was. Well, he'd have a long wait. Hell would freeze over before she married him.

It was two days before Timothy contacted her. At first he switched on the charm and told her how common wedding nerves were and that they could work through it. When she told him calmly that she had no intention of marrying him and conducting an 'open marriage', that she didn't love him, he turned cold and nasty, telling her she would regret humiliating him like this.

Cassie shivered as she ended the call. His tone had been threatening, sinister almost. How could she have thought he was considerate, reliable, a safe bet to marry? It just goes to show what a terrible judge of character she was.

An hour later, Amanda phoned and tried to talk her around to no avail. Then it was Sylvia's turn. Angry and scornful, she told Cassie exactly what she thought of her for humiliating Timothy like this and how grateful she should be that a man like Timothy was prepared to make her his wife, especially after writing that awful column.

'Your precious son is having an affair with his business partner,' Cassie informed her. 'That's why I called off the wedding. And seeing as you think I'm not worthy to be his wife you should be pleased that I'm not marrying him.' Then she cut off the call.

Amanda and Sylvia both tried to ring again several times throughout the day but she ignored their calls and the texts that followed, telling her that they would be sending her a bill for all the money they'd paid out so far and if she didn't pay up they'd be taking her to court. She was pretty sure it was a bluff. Sylvia wouldn't want everyone to know that her son had been dumped or that he was having an affair with Felicity.

Cancelling the wedding was the least of her problems. She had to find somewhere to live, sort out her life. Her mother had sent her a message straight back inviting her to come and stay in Cyprus. 'Give yourself time to heal and sort your head out, dear,' she had said, but she didn't want to do that. She wasn't going to run away.

By the end of the week she'd found a small studio flat, and managed to wangle it so that she could move in on the weekend. Sam and Paul helped her. Timothy had sent the rest of her things in a taxi, with a curt note telling her to give her flat keys to the taxi driver and informing her that he never wanted to see her again. That was fine by her. She settled in the flat over the weekend and returned to work on Monday.

She'd tried not to think of Jared, tried not to cry or to keep checking the calendar to see how many days were left before he went away again. Nothing, however, escaped Sam's eager eyes.

'You're pining over Jared, aren't you?' Sam said when she popped round on Monday evening to see how Sam's first day back at work had gone. 'For goodness' sake, why don't you go and tell him you love him?'

'You know why. Because it wouldn't work. He'll be wanting to go off again – he *is* going off again – and will resent me for tying him down, then I'll have to go through the heartbreak all over again.'

'Look, no one has a guarantee for happy-ever-after, but it's madness not be with someone you're crazy over and who is obviously crazy over you just in case it doesn't work out. You compromise; make it work if you love each other.'

Sam had a point. Paul was often away on business with his job and they were both happy together – but then, Paul was away a couple of days at a time, not months. And he'd never chosen his job over her, not like Jared had.

Jared must know by now that she had cancelled the wedding, but he hadn't attempted to contact her. He had her work email address. No, he obviously didn't care enough. Still, at least it had made her see Timothy's true colours and she was grateful for that.

'It's over, Sam. It was over seven years ago. Seeing each other again just stirred up old feelings, that's all.'

As the days passed with no word from Cassie, Jared had to face the fact that she didn't want him. He heard from Imogen that the reason she'd called off the wedding was because she'd discovered Timothy was having an affair with his business partner. He remembered the woman who'd accompanied Timothy to the party, and Margot's words, 'There'll be three in that marriage'. It seemed his affair was pretty common knowledge.

So it had nothing to do with her feelings for him. He'd made a fool of himself by telling her he loved her and begging her to give him another chance. She might have finished with Timothy the twat, but she didn't want him either. It was time to let go and move on.

Habit and curiosity made him buy the newspaper on Saturday and check out her column. He wasn't really surprised to see that the 'Almost a Bride' column had been replaced by a two-page supplement about getting married in France. There were pictures and information about the château he and Cassie had stayed in, as well as other venues that she had probably visited on her press trip. He closed his eyes, remembering the feel of Cassie in his arms as they danced, the sweet smell of her perfume, her head resting on his shoulder, the softness of her lips when they kissed.

Get over it, she doesn't want you. He threw the paper back down on the desk and stood up. Well, he didn't want her either. They'd had their chance for love and blown it. There was no going back. It was time he got away from here.

When he got home that night, he found a letter telling him the grant he'd applied for from the Animals in the Wild fund had been approved. There was no need to postpone his trip now. In fact, he could go earlier and stay for three months instead of six weeks. Just what he needed to get Cassie out of his head.

Thirty-three

'Cassie, I know this is going to be hard for you, but we need to do a final "Almost a Bride" column to wrap it all up.' Owen told her. 'And I'm going to need it by tomorrow.' He looked at her concerned. 'Would you like me to write it?'

She shook her head. 'No, I'll do it. Is there anything in particular you want me to write?'

'It's up to you, but the readers seem to want Paige to go off with Blake. They haven't warmed to Ian at all.' He shrugged. 'This column has been really popular. I hope sales don't drop when we stop running it.'

Maybe that column had been more true to life than she'd realised, Cassie thought. The readers had seen through Ian before she did. 'I don't think I can handle writing that, but I think Paige should call off the wedding. Maybe warn the readers to think carefully before they get married, and to remind them that they don't have to go ahead with it, even if everything's booked. Is that OK?'

Owen looked thoughtful for a moment. 'Fine by me, but end it with hope.'

End it with hope. Cassie thought over Owen's words as she drafted out the article. Suddenly she knew what to write. This was her chance to tell her story, knowing that Timothy, his mother, his sister, and probably Jared would be reading it.

Almost a Bride

Little did I know when I started writing this column how prophetic the title would be. I've called off the wedding, so 'almost a bride' describes me exactly. All these weeks I've been trying to conform to what Ian and monster-in-law want me to be, feeling guilty for still having feelings for Blake, and now I find out that Ian's having an affair. With his business partner, would you believe? And he expects me to still marry him. He actually said that it would be an 'adult' relationship and I could have an affair too, providing I was discreet. Can you believe it? No thank you, and I told him so in no uncertain terms.

I can't say I'm heartbroken. I knew deep down that he wasn't the one for me but the wedding preparations were all under way, and I didn't feel I could pull out and let everyone down. It's hard to say you've changed your mind when the invitations have been sent out. So I guess finding out about Ian's affair was a get-out for me, because there's no way I'm putting up with that.

I'm OK. Well, I will be once I've got my life back on track. Meeting Blake again has shown me that I didn't love Ian, and reminded me what real love is like. I won't settle for second best again. I'm worth more than that. And going to France to research wedding venues for this column has shown me what I enjoy writing most. Travel writing. So that's what I'm going to do. I guess I should thank Blake and Ian for opening my eyes to what I really want to do with my life.

There, that's told them all. She hoped Owen liked it – and that he got the hint at the end.

He did. 'That's perfect,' he said. 'I think the readers would have liked you to go off in the sunset with Blake, but it's better this way. It's a strong, hopeful ending.' He peered closely at her. 'Is that bit about wanting to do travel writing true?'

240

'Yes, it is,' she admitted. 'I really enjoyed visiting the different places in France. I met another writer there, he travels around quite a lot – Europe mainly, not the Middle East or anywhere far-flung. I fancy doing that.' She hesitated, then took the plunge. 'He said if I ever wanted work on a travel magazine he could point me in the right direction. Obviously I don't want to leave you in the lurch but …'

'It's what you want to do,' Owen finished for her. He stroked his chin thoughtfully. 'Look, I don't want to lose you. You and your column are responsible for turning this paper around. And that spread on the wedding venues in France was good. So why don't we have a go at running a travel spread once a month? See how it pans out? It might interest our readers and it'll give you a bit of experience at travel writing if you do decide to up and leave us.'

'Really?' She could have hugged him.

'Sure. I'm always willing to try new things and I don't want to get in the way of anyone's dream. Just give me a bit of notice to replace you. OK?'

'Of course.' She could feel her grin spread from ear to ear. 'Thanks, Owen.'

Jared smiled as he read Cassie's column. So she was telling any of Timothy's friends that read it exactly what went on, and letting them know that she hadn't run off with the photographer. She was moving on with her life, and he had to as well. What they had was over.

How he wished it wasn't. He knew he would never love anyone like he loved Cassie, but he had to respect that she didn't feel the same way. He had more pride than to beg her to be with him.

He shoved the newspaper in his case and resumed his packing. He was leaving in the morning. It would be a long journey, but he was looking forward to it. Maybe it was a good thing Cassie hadn't returned his love because he would have been torn whether to go or not. Now he had nothing to stay for. His heart ached for her but he'd get over it.

Thirty-four

True to his word, Owen started to run a monthly holiday feature. For the first article he sent Cassie on a press trip to Venice. He'd arranged it through a travel agency, and once again she went with a group of other journalists. She found it fascinating. The organisers not only showed them around Venice itself, where they went on a water taxi along the Grand Canal under the Rialto Bridge, visited St Mark's Square and other famous landmarks, but also took them to some of the neighbouring islands in the lagoon. Cassie found the fishermen's and lace maker's island of Burano the most fascinating, with its bright, multi-coloured houses and little canals.

Jared still lurked in the back of her mind. She ached for him, longed to share the sights she saw with him. Maybe I was a bit hasty sending him packing, she thought. Maybe I should have given our love another chance.

It was too late now. She'd had no communication from Jared since she'd left him waiting at the reception desk in France. He'd accepted her decision and gone to the Arctic. She guessed he was busy filming polar bears and not giving her a second thought.

You turned him down, she reminded herself.

Even so, he could have tried harder to win her back.

And then what? Cancelled his trip? Missed out on his dream? And what about her? Would she have missed out on the

243

opportunity to come to Venice, to write travel articles, to realise what she wanted to do with her life?

She gazed around at the women sitting outside the doors of their cottages making lace. This was their life, probably the only life they had ever known or would know. Was it the life they wanted? Had their dreams been stifled because they'd fallen in love? If she had admitted to Jared how much she loved him, she would be stifling his life and hers. She'd made the right decision.

If only her heart would accept that and not keep aching for him.

You can't come to Venice without going on a gondola, the guide insisted when they returned to the mainland. So they all piled into a few and sailed up the Grand Canal. As they passed several couples cuddled up together, Cassie imagined herself sitting in the back of a gondola snuggled up to Jared, resting his head on her shoulder, feeling the warmth of his body leaning against hers.

She had to stop thinking about him and accept that they were over.

Thirty-five

All Jared could think about on the flight home was seeing Cassie again. The time in the Arctic had proved to him how much he loved her. Damn, he'd do anything to get her back. He had to show her that, make her believe it. Daniel and Imogen had offered him a permanent position in the company; if he accepted it he'd be based in the UK and be earning a good salary, so could provide a home for them both. Maybe they could settle down and have kids.

He glanced at his watch. 2.30 a.m. He'd been travelling all night and was tired and jet-lagged. He'd grab a few hours' sleep, have a shower and change, then go and see her before he lost his nerve. He had no idea where she lived but he knew where she worked. If she wasn't at work that day perhaps he could persuade someone to give him her address or leave her a note. He had to try.

'There's someone waiting to see you,' Maisy the receptionist said as soon as Cassie walked in. 'He's been here for over an hour. He's just gone the loo.'

'Really?' she asked, surprised. 'Do you know what he wants?'

'To ask you to join him for dinner,' said a familiar voice behind her.

Jared! She spun around in disbelief. What was he doing here? She wanted to run into his arms, hug him, kiss him, but she couldn't move. All she could do was stare at him.

'Well, will you?' he asked softly.

'I ...' she stammered.

Maisy coughed as the doors opened and a man stepped in, reminding Cassie they were in the public reception area.

Why had he turned up like this just when she was getting over him? 'Look, I can't do this here,' she hissed. 'I need to get up to the office, I'll lose my job if I'm late.' Not strictly true, but she didn't trust herself with Jared. It would be so easy to fall into his arms.

'Then meet me for a drink later so we can talk,' he pleaded. 'You owe me that. You owe it to both of us.'

Cassie hesitated. She wanted to, more than he would ever know, but she didn't trust herself.

'Would you like to me to phone up and say you've arrived but got delayed by a member of the public?' Maisy suggested. 'The Courtesy Room is free. I can make sure you aren't disturbed.'

It wouldn't hurt to hear him out, would it? Cassie nodded. 'Thank you.' She turned to Jared. 'You have exactly five minutes.' She led the way into the Courtesy Room on the left.

'I love you, Cassie,' Jared blurted out as soon as she shut the door behind them. 'Please give me a chance to make it up to you. To show you I'm not the same person I was. I won't let you down again.' He stepped closer, so close she could feel his breath on her cheek. 'You love me too, I know you do. I can see it in your eyes.'

She tried to deny it but his face was getting closer and closer and she couldn't tear her eyes away from his, couldn't resist the love and passion she could see in the dark pools. Or deny the love she felt for him.

He wrapped his arm around her neck, gently pulled her to him and their lips met, softly caressing at first, then exploring deeper and deeper until it felt that they were one and the same, their bodies melting into each other, and she knew that he did love her and that she loved him. They belonged together. Always had. Always will.

'I'm so sorry for being so selfish all those years ago,' he said, pulling away from her and gently pulling her down onto the sofa behind them. 'I wish I could go back and put it right, but I can't.' He lifted her hand to his lips and kissed it softly. 'I'm sorry I hurt you. Truly I am. Do you think you could find it in your heart to forgive me and give me another chance?'

Of course she could. The past didn't matter, they had been so young. Too young. If he'd given up his career and they'd got married then it might not have worked out. Jared might have resented her, wished he'd followed his dream. Their love would have been destroyed beyond repair and that would have been a tragedy.

'I won't go away again,' Jared murmured, slipping both hands around her waist and pulling her closer. 'Isobel and Daniel have offered me a permanent position in the company.'

He was actually planning on giving up travelling, on being a celebrity photographer so they could be together.

'Have you accepted the offer?' she asked, nuzzling into his neck.

'Not yet. They want my answer by Friday.'

So if she turned him down he wouldn't accept it; he'd carry on being a wildlife photographer. She could hardly believe he'd give up his dream for her. It was what she wanted seven years ago, but not any longer. Now she realised that you shouldn't give up your dream for anyone. That it didn't have to be one or the other. If you loved someone, you'd compromise and make things work somehow.

'Then tell them thank you but no thank you,' she said, kissing him on the tip of his nose.

She saw the flash of pain in his eyes. 'You mean ...' He pulled away. 'It's too late for us, isn't it? I should never have assumed we could start afresh. It was too long ago ...'

She wound her arms around his neck. 'It's not too late at all. I love you and I want us to be together. But you don't have to sacrifice anything. All I need to know is that you'll come back to me.'

His face lit up as he bent down to kiss her. 'Oh, Cassie.'

They were so engrossed in their embrace, in their love for each other that they didn't hear the door open. It was Cassie who heard the cough first. She pulled herself away from Jared and turned to see Owen standing in the doorway.

'I take it this is the photographer,' he said.

'Yes.' She hoped her face wasn't as red as it felt. 'Jared and I, we're ...'

He nodded. 'Yes, I can see that you've made up. Nice one.'

'Sorry, I'll be up in just a minute. Did you need me for something?'

'Oh, I was just going to remind you that I need your piece on Venice for two this afternoon. But I can see you're busy.' He held out his hand to Jared. 'Pleased to meet you, mate. You saved my paper.' He looked at Cassie. 'Five minutes.' Then he was gone.

'So will you meet me after work for a drink?' Jared asked. 'We can talk about things properly.'

She nodded. 'I finish at five. Where shall we meet?'

'Pass me your phone and I'll give you my number.'

Cassie took her mobile out of her bag and handed it to him. Jared keyed in some numbers and handed it back to her. She immediately rang it so he had her number too.

'I tell you what, let's make it a proper date and have dinner,' Jared suggested. 'How about The Oriental, at 8 p.m.?'

She smiled. He remembered that she liked Chinese food. Timothy had always preferred Italian so they always went to Italian restaurants.

'Sounds lovely. I'll catch a cab there.'

Thirty-six

Jared arrived at the restaurant early. He'd pre-booked the table, a secluded booth where they could talk uninterrupted, but waited for Cassie at the bar. She arrived a few minutes later, looking enchanting in a rainbow silk dress with a tiny silver belt, the skirt slashed up into points that started above her knee and finished at mid-calf, revealing a tantalising flash of legs as she walked. She wore her hair loose and matched the dress with silver sandals and a silver clutch bag. Her face looked alive, her eyes shining. She exuded happiness.

She looked how he felt. He could hardly believe that they'd found each other again, that he had a second chance of happiness. This time he would treasure their love, nourish it, make sure she knew that she meant everything to him.

He saw her look around, then her eyes lit up as they rested on him, and she walked over to the bar, smiling broadly.

'You look gorgeous.' He stood up, wrapped his arms around her, and kissed her on the cheek – although he would have preferred to kiss her on the lips for a long, long time then take her to bed. *Take it easy, slow down.*

'What would you like to drink?' he asked.

'Rosé, please.'

'Would you like a drink at the bar or to go straight to our table?' he asked.

'Let's go to the table. I'm starving.'

He smiled again, reached out for her hand, and felt her fingers wrap around his. 'Me too.'

They walked together, hand in hand, then he pulled out her chair for her, kissed her on the cheek, and sat down on the other side of the table. He reached out and took her hand, and covered it in feather-light kisses that made her shiver with anticipation.

'I love you, Cassie,' he murmured.

'I love you too,' she replied softly.

It was like old times, but better. They talked and laughed all evening, finishing each other's sentences, sharing anecdotes, and all the time he wanted to lean over the table and kiss her, caress her, make love to her. Did she want that too? There was only one way to find out.

'Fancy coming back to my place for a nightcap?' he asked softly. He held his breath as he waited for her reply. Was he rushing things?

It seemed an eternity before she nodded. 'That sounds lovely.'

'Coffee or more wine?' Jared asked as they stepped into his apartment.

Cassie looked around. It was very light and spacious, tastefully furnished with black and smoked glass units, a black leather sofa and armchair, and laminated floor. Very masculine. Jared's camera and a bulging folder lay on the smoked glass coffee table. 'Nice,' she nodded.

'I've got it on a six months' lease,' he told her. 'I always rent furnished as I'm never at a place long enough to choose my own furniture, and it would be too much hassle to keep selling it or putting it into storage.'

She nodded. 'No strings, no roots.'

'That's how it used to be. That'll change now.' His eyes met hers and she swallowed at the love they held. 'What would you like to drink? More wine, something stronger, or coffee?'

'Coffee please. Milky with one sugar.'

'I remember.'

Cassie slipped off her sandals and sat down on the sofa, curling her legs under her. It felt so good to be back with Jared again, as if she'd come home. They'd always slotted together with no awkwardness. Like two sides of the one coin, her mum used to say. And it still felt like that, despite the years in between.

He carefully carried the coffees over and she grabbed two place mats from the rack of six on the cabinet, placing them in front of them both as he put the mugs on the table.

'Thanks, no point making myself extra cleaning up.' He sat down on the sofa next to her, just fractions away. So close that she could hear him breathing, that if she moved her leg slightly it would touch his. Suddenly she felt awkward and unsure but then his arm snaked around her shoulder and pulled her to him and she was lost in the sweetness of his kiss.

'I can't believe I'm here with you, that you've given me a second chance,' he murmured when they both came up for air. 'I'm so sorry how I treated you all those years ago. I was selfish, stupid ...'

She put her hand over his lips to silence them. 'No, you were young. You had a dream and you were right to go for it.' His eyes widened in surprise as she continued, 'I was hurt, yes. Heartbroken,' she admitted ruefully, 'but I can see now that what you did was right for both of us. 'Look at what you've achieved. You're an incredibly talented photographer. If we'd have remained together, got married, had a family, you would have had to settle for a mundane job just to bring money in. You'd never have had chance to develop that talent, to do what you really wanted to do.'

He gently removed her hand from his mouth and kissed it. Then kissed the tip of her nose. 'I hurt you so terribly, I regret that.' Then he frowned. 'You said it was the best thing for both of us.'

She nodded. 'It was, I can see that now. We were too young to settle down. I've had a good life despite my broken heart.' She gave him a mock-grimace. 'I enjoy my job on the paper. And I love writing the travel columns. I've discovered what I really like doing and I sort of understand why you couldn't give up your dream for me. You shouldn't give up your dream for anyone. That's why I don't want you to take this partnership with Imogen and Daniel – unless it's what you really want.'

'You mean you're OK with me going away for weeks on end to work on my next project?' He looked confused.

'I'm not saying I won't miss you. Or that I wouldn't prefer you to stay,' she admitted. 'But it's what you are, Jared. It's part of why I love you and I don't want you to lose yourself, your dreams, and aspirations because you're with me.'

She saw his face soften, his eyes darken with desire. 'You're amazing,' he said. Then his lips found hers, kissing her deeper, urgently. She responded with the same flaming passion, her arms winding around his neck. She wasn't sure whether he was pushing her or she was pulling him down but she was lying down on the sofa with Jared on top of her, trailing hot kisses down her neck, her throat, her shoulders, his fingers slipping down the straps of her top. She reached a hand and stilled him for a moment. He looked up questioningly.

'Besides,' she said. 'I might be away myself sometimes writing my travel articles. So it could be you home alone. How do you feel about that?'

His eyes met hers, soft, tender, full of love. 'Wherever we are, we'll have our love to sustain us.' He leant up on his elbow, his expression suddenly serious, and tenderly traced the outline of her lips. 'I promise you I'll always keep in touch with you, that even if I'm not with you you'll always know how much I love you. And that I'll always come back to you. Always.'

She gulped, the sincerity and love in his voice bringing a lump to her throat. 'I promise the same.'

His gaze held hers and she could feel the love shining out from it. 'Then that's all that matters.'

He groaned as she pulled him down to her. 'Oh, Cassie, I'm never going to let you go again. I'm going to show you just how much you mean to me.'

'Now that,' she said, slipping her hands under his T-shirt and running them over his smooth, lithe body, 'sounds a very good idea.'

Rosie Orr

Something Blue

Anna has a grown-up son, an ex-husband somewhere in Australia, and a feckless married lover. Sporting new scarlet underwear, and not much else, she is horrified to open her door one afternoon not to lover Jack but to son Sam and his girlfriend. They have come to announce their engagement – and to tell her that their wedding is only weeks away!

Anna is soon in the throes of preparations for a traditional Irish wedding: keeping at bay the Versace-wearing mother of the bride, dealing with the return of her ex-husband, and wondering whether Jack will ever have the gumption to leave his wife. And then the big day arrives, bringing hotel cats, destroyed crème brûlée and a surprisingly attractive photographer…

Kate Field

The Magic of Ramblings

A warm-hearted debut for fans of Kate Morton: with love and friendship it's never too late to find a happy ending.

Running away can be the answer if you run to the right place…

When Cassie accepts a job as companion to an old lady in a remote Lancashire village, she hopes for a quiet life where she can forget herself, her past and most especially men. The last thing she wants is to be drawn into saving a community that seems determined to take her to its heart – and to resuscitate hers…

Frances has lived a reclusive life at Ramblings, a Victorian Gothic mansion, for over thirty years and now Barney is hiding away there, forging a new life after his medical career ended in scandal. He doesn't trust the mysterious woman who comes to live with his rich aunt, especially when she starts to steal Frances' affection – and maybe his own too…

Jo Bartlett

Somebody Else's Boy

Will Nancy and Jack be allowed to embrace the future, or will their histories forever bind them to the past?

Drama teacher Nancy O'Brien puts her ambitions on hold to support her family, and returns to her idyllic seaside home town, St Nicholas Bay. Jack has his own reasons for heading to the Bay; a young widower desperate to come to terms with his loss, he hopes setting up home there with baby son, Toby, might just enable him to survive the future.

As Nancy and Jack become closer, not everyone is thrilled, in particular Toby's grandmother, who can't bear to see her late daughter 'replaced'. When Spencer – the only man Nancy's ever really loved – reappears, her living arrangements with Jack seem set for disaster.

Kristen Bailey

Souper Mum

Monday morning can't get any worse for harassed mum-of-four Jools
Campbell when, after a frantic school run, she's cornered in the
supermarket by pompous celebrity chef Tommy McCoy, who starts
criticising the contents of her trolley. Apparently the fact that she
doesn't make her own bread or buy organic is tantamount to child
abuse. In a hurry and short of patience, she berates McCoy for judging
her when she hasn't the time or the money to feed her family in line
with his elitist ideals.

Unbeknownst to Jools, her rant has been filmed and immediately goes
viral on YouTube, making her a reluctant celebrity overnight. With
McCoy determined to discredit her by delving into her personal life,
Jools decides it's time to fight her corner in the name of all the fraught
mums out there who are fed up with being made to feel bad by food
snobs like him. Armed with some fish fingers and her limited cooking
repertoire, Jools must negotiate the unfamiliar world of celebrity while
staying true to her instincts as a mum.

Jenny Kane

Another Glass of Champagne

Fortysomething Amy is shocked and delighted to discover she's expecting a baby – not to mention terrified! Amy wants best friend Jack to be godfather, but he hasn't been heard from in months.

When Jack finally reappears, he's full of good intentions – but his new business plan could spell disaster for the beloved Pickwicks Coffee Shop, and ruin a number of old friendships... Meanwhile his love life is as complicated as ever – and yet when he swears off men for good, Jack meets someone who makes him rethink his priorities...but is it too late for a fresh start?

Author Kit has problems of her own: just when her career has started to take off, she finds herself unable to write – and there's a deadline looming, plus two headstrong kids to see through their difficult teenage years...will she be able to cope?

A follow-up to the runaway success *Another Cup of Coffee*.

For more information about **Karen King**

and other **Accent Press** titles

please visit

www.accentpress.co.uk

Year	Venue	Attendance	Gate Receipts	Cattle	Sheep	Pigs	Horses	Trade Stands
1949	Louth	30,677	7,238	183	83	305	378	183
1950	Stamford	23,709	5,448	287	94	420	424	237
1951	Grimsby	32,488	7,135	224	97	406	327	206
1952	Grantham	15,931	3,984	325	87	423	481	211
1953	Brigg	23,809	5,842	236	81	363	355	248
1954	Boston	26,915	6,797	323	72	388	325	288
1955	Lincoln	39,870	6,148	382	89	346	333	253
1956	Sleaford	43,361	7,046	418	87	424	382	267
1957	Brocklesby Park	41,971	7,118	351	69	417	305	200
1958	Burtoft	38,556	8,696	471	77	487	310	246
1959	Lincoln, at the	47,036	10,450	472	68	413	440	269
1960	Society's own	43,879	9,251	436	86	365	424	282
1961	Showground	45,594	10,147	361	94	345	479	264
1962		46,355	9,566	365	59	324	514	267
1963		45,597	9,595	337	75	319	487	269
1964		46,594	10,799	320	74	280	483	279
1965		51,133	10,434	258	81	158	451	280
1966		44,948	12,267	273	77	242	406	273
1967		46,932	12,497	270	75	239	617	269
1968		49,823	13,294	204	71	215	624	263
1969		49,193	12,504	162	95	258	297	279
1970		52,256	13,853	189	106	229	591	290
1971		54,994	14,555	244	117	221	601	283
1972		58,237	15,459	213	140	190	711	300
1973		59,501	20,001	245	82	92	653	327
1974		63,108	23,418	204	87	—	811	331
1975		69,786	37,618	216	78	—	752	345
1976		73,079	44,584	201	72	112	805	387
1977		69,302	55,655	236	89	114	747	396
1978		80,904	64,909	173	110	153	837	460
1979		82,132	64.323	252	122	113	805	466
1980		80,288	79,839	255	118	107	738	523
1981		80,466	100,708	256	123	133	833	523
1982		58,429	59,439	231	172	238	825	527

BIBLIOGRAPHY

General view of the Agriculture of the County of Lincoln — Drawn up for the consideration of the Board of Agriculture and Internal Improvement. Thomas Stone, London. 1794, and later editions.

Lincolnshire Chronicle.

Lincoln Rutland & Stamford Mercury.

Encyclopaedia Britannica.

Institute of Agricultural History and Museum of English Rural Life. University of Reading.

Social England, Volume VI, Section II, Agriculture, W. E. Bear. Cassell, London.

Victorian Lincoln, Sir Francis Hill, C.B.E., L.L.M., Litt.D., F.S.A. Cambridge University Press, 1974.

Directories of Lincolnshire.

The Royal Show, Lincoln. Harrison and J. W. Ruddock & Sons, Lincoln. 1907.

A History of Lincoln. Drury & Sons, Lincoln. 1816.

Letters, Annual Reports, Lists of prizes and premiums, Minute Books, and Catalogues of the second and the present Lincolnshire Agricultural Society, and the North and South Lincolnshire Agricultural Societies.

Lincolnshire Life 1970 (article by Mr D. Clark, former secretary of the Society).

The Shire Horse. Keith Chivers. Futura Publications Ltd. London. 1978.

The Lincolnshire Farmer. (article in 1963 by W. E. R. Hallgarth).

Lincolnshire. E. Mansel Sympson, M.A., M.D., F.S.A. Cambridge University Press 1914.

Lincolnshire Archives.

Lincoln Public Library.

Lincolnshire Museums.

Notes from the Society.

Acknowledgements

With thanks to farming and Ministry relatives and friends on various occasions over the last half century.

The paragraph on the Lincolnshire Buff poultry is based on information from Riseholme College of Agriculture; "Our Poultry", "The Book of Poultry"; and "Domestic Poultry", all of the eighteenth century.